THE VISITOR

Jay Trott

ISBN-10: 1512237515
ISBN-13: 978-1512237511

TRUE
NORTH

Special acknowledgements to Beth Trott, Linda Trott and Lynne Gomez for kindly reading the manuscript and making excellent suggestions for improvement.

AWAKENING

JOSH WASN'T REALLY SURE WHY he was there. Or rather, it seemed he was there because of the girl. He just didn't remember coming there. He was waiting in the dark for the restaurant to close and for her to walk to her car. It was snowing, a light, dream-falling snow—and wasn't it strange? He did not feel cold. He did not feel much of anything at all.

Then he saw her. She was pretty in an unaffected way, with bags and paraphernalia dangling from her arms. He smiled; it was like she was always planning for a party. She walked toward her Subaru beyond the aura of the parking lot lights, reached into her pocket, pulled out her keys—and promptly dropped them in the fluffy snow.

The keys fell into four inches of windswept powder and disappeared from view. She was flustered; he could tell she did not know where they were as she bent over in the shadows and felt around clumsily, her arms full of stuff. They had disappeared into the snow and it was dark.

Suddenly he was by her side. He wasn't sure how, exactly, but this was the way things had been for him lately. He plucked them from the snow and handed them to her. He handed her the keys and his hand touched hers—she was not wearing gloves and neither was he—but he did not feel a thing. He thought he might feel something—a spark—love—was that why he was there?—but he felt nothing.

She was clearly surprised. He looked at her and she looked at him and they stood there for a few moments looking at each other, frozen in time. Would she turn on him, a stranger in a deserted country parking lot at night? For a moment he thought she

1

would—but she didn't. Something in her did not want to turn. She was trusting by nature. She wanted to trust him.

He saw this in her and felt a rush of—love? He did not know exactly what it was. At this point Josh was going on feelings and emotions and nothing more. The filters were completely off and what was left was something like a bare wire. He saw her as a fellow traveler and he saw an open heart. It was almost as if he could read her mind. Strange, he had never been interested in reading people before.

He realized she was not like him or the people he normally associated with. She was not "city." That was why she was not afraid of dark parking lots or strange men. She did not reach for the pepper spray, if she had any, which he doubted. She wanted to trust people. She wanted him to be a nice man who helped her in a moment of need and picked her keys out of the snow.

The thing was—was he a nice man? He wanted to be. He did not know what he was.

Her trust was all the more surprising because he knew he was not conventional. In fact he was a bit of a fright. While he was waiting for her he had caught a glimpse of himself in the shiny windows of a Land Rover and was startled by his appearance. He saw a gaunt young man gazing back at him with pale skin and large eyes. For a moment he didn't recognize himself.

Josh was a good-looking fellow with wavy black hair and one very distinctive trait—but more about that later. His coat was open in spite of the cold and he looked, well, febrile; although he also did not look that way because his lips were blue from the December cold. He seemed deserted in his own self. He did not look like someone a country girl would want to know.

How could he not recognize himself? It was just like everything else lately—his memories were jumbled and vague. He honestly did not know how he came to be standing in a parking lot in a snowstorm waiting for this girl. And yet he was very clearly waiting for her. Somehow he knew she would be coming out of the restaurant. It was the whole reason he was standing there in the cold.

But why couldn't he remember anything more? What was it? Amnesia? Josh laughed at himself. He remembered the article from *The Lancet*—apparently there was no such thing as amnesia. There were no known medical reports of someone receiving a blow to the head and walking around for weeks or months with no idea of who he was until something happened to jar his memory. It only seemed to happen in the movies.

He came crashing back into the moment and realized he had just laughed out loud. She looked a little surprised but still did not seem frightened. Once again he experienced this warm feeling for her, whatever it was. It made him a little dizzy.

"Thanks!" she said, looking puzzled. "Where did you come from? I didn't see you."

"I don't know," he said truthfully. "It just looked like you could use some help."

"I feel like such an idiot. A little snow always sends me into a spiral. I know, it's Vermont. But I'm dreading it."

"You don't like the snow?"

"I love it—when I'm in my cozy log cabin. But I hate driving in it. Had an accident, completely lost control of the car and spun around several times. Ever since then I've been terrified."

Accident! Josh stood there riveted to the snowy pavement for a moment at the sound of that horrible word. There was a jolt. He saw himself in a car and he was sliding and he hit something and then he was in a hospital. He remembered thinking this is what it feels like to be on the other side.

She was looking at him, puzzled, because he had not replied. He wasn't being rude, not intentionally anyway. He was struggling to bring himself back to the moment from this terrible memory.

"Perfectly understandable," he blurted at last. "I was in a rather bad one myself. I think."

"You think?" she said with a merry laugh. "You don't know?"

"Seems like there are a lot of things I don't know lately. But listen, why don't you let me follow you home?"

"No—that's way too much to ask. You don't even know me."

"I don't know. I sort of feel like I do."

She looked puzzled again. "Well, anyway, don't worry about me. I'll be fine."

He had gone too far, been too forward. Only it was not forwardness at all. The only thing he wanted was for her to get home safely in her little car. He knew it seemed strange for a complete stranger to make such an offer; he could not remember having done anything so gauche in the past. But a lot of things were different now. He had never cared about anything the way he cared about this girl and her safety in the cold but beautiful snow.

And yet why did he care about her? He had absolutely no idea. He could not remember meeting her. He did not know anything about her. All he knew was that he was connected to her in some way. Was he a stalker? He sensed this was not the first time he had stood in that parking lot at night waiting for her to come out of the restaurant. The truth was he did not know what he was.

"I'm sure you will," he replied. "You have a good, sturdy car there. If I had a wife or a daughter, this is just the kind of car I would want them to have."

She did a sort of double take, and it occurred to him how strange such warm words must seem coming from a stranger. They were the overflow of a tenderness that sneaked up on him and surprised him.

"Anyway, thanks again," she said as she slid into the car. "And button up that coat. You look cold."

He closed the door for her. Gallantry was not necessarily his thing, but he wanted to do it. Then he began wiping the snow off the windshield with his bare hands. She rolled down her window.

"Thanks, but you don't have to do that."

"You can't see where you're going."

"I have wipers. Anyway, thanks again."

She rolled up her window and drove off towards the road.

He was left standing there alone, very much alone in the Vermont mountains without a car in the lot and none on the road. A thought occurred to him—why not follow her anyway? He wanted to follow her, but he could not find his car. He stumbled around the empty lot in the snow. It should have been easy to find. What was he driving?

SLEIGHRIDE

J ILL'S RIDE HOME WAS TERRIFYING. This was how it had been for her ever since the accident. The little Subaru was sure-footed, but she was in a dance in her mind, all jangles and nerves. Even the slightest turn was imposing and threatened to overthrow her.

She crawled home in second gear. At one point a pick-up truck with a plow came up behind her, out on the state highway. He was clearly unhappy with her extreme caution, but there was nothing she could do. She felt paralyzed, and his impatience made it worse. He flashed his high beams a couple of times and finally passed her. Then she felt foolish. Vermont girls are not supposed to be afraid of a little snow.

The drive home took three times as long as usual. She was mad at herself for being afraid of the snow and mad at herself for not being able to help it. How long would it be before she got over this irrational fear? Would she ever get over it? She thought about her father and the bold way he drove in the snow, not foolishly but with confidence. She used to be like that. Would she ever be confident again?

The lights in the cabin were on and woodstove smoke was floating up from the chimney, but if she was looking for comfort after her treacherous drive she was likely to be disappointed. Brian was passed out in front of the TV, a half-empty beer bottle on the table beside him. Peter had gone to bed—he had hockey practice at five in the morning, although it would probably be cancelled. She went to his room and kissed him and spruced up his blankets. She missed him.

She wandered back out into the great room but had no desire to greet Brian or sit with him by the warm stove. Would he sympathize with the terror she had just experienced? No, he would probably laugh at her. He might have sympathized once but not now. Besides, she hated the smell of alcohol on him. Why did he have to drink so much? He was not a good companion when he drank.

She went into the kitchen and ate a little of the dinner she had brought home from the restaurant—turkey and mashed potatoes, comfort food. She didn't bother putting it into the microwave to warm it up. Then she made herself a cup of green tea with plenty of honey and stood there sipping it with the sounds of some inane TV show filling up the background.

She decided to go upstairs. She did not go up there very often—not anymore. She used to go up all the time. It was her studio. But it had been a long time since she had put on her smock and stood in front of a canvas with a paint brush in her hands. She did not turn on the loft lights. She ascended the last few stairs and glanced over at her paintings, her other children, hulking along the back wall, the outlines of their artwork faintly visible in the shadows.

She turned the old rocker around and sat down to gaze at the snow through the gable picture windows. Why was she sitting by herself in the loft looking out at the snow? She knew why. It wasn't just the snow. It was because of that guy in the parking lot.

There was a time in her life when she could not wait for it to snow. Nothing was more exciting to her than the flurry in October or the borderline November storm, or the real thing when winter finally came, the snow with all its mesmerizing beauty. There was no winter pleasure she loved more with her painterly eye than the falling snow. But it was not excitement she had felt as she walked to her car in the first major snowstorm of the season. It was terror at the thought of driving home.

And there were other terrors in her life as well. There were the debts that never seemed to get any smaller. There was Brian's growing indifference towards her. There was Peter and her anxieties for him, a sweet child but undersized and maybe too sweet for the real world. Was that why he insisted on playing hockey? To show how tough he was? She didn't care if he was tough. She liked the fact that he was different from other boys, not so kinetic, not so mean. But she worried about him.

Most of all there was the painting. It was her joy, but she had given it up. She could not take the rejection anymore, pouring her soul into a painting only to have some snooty gallery dealer tell her it was "not their thing." She could not take the trauma of exposing her work to the ruthless art market. It would be one thing if she had support from Brian, but he did not support her. He did not seem happy when she spent so much time painting and said nothing at all to her when she stopped.

Right now she was thinking about something else, however, sitting there in her rocking chair in the dark. There was a little elevation in her spirits for the first time in months—because of the gallant stranger in the parking lot. Her feelings were all mixed up. On one hand he struck her as a bit of a poseur. His coat was unbuttoned in the bitter cold like the teenagers at the bus stop. His get-up was prep-school Goth.

The most ridiculous thing about him, however, was the lock of white hair right in the center of his forehead. His hair was all black except for a single white lock. Not even blond, pure white! She almost laughed when she saw it. She was laughing to herself now. It was bad enough when girls did that sort of thing, but men?

On the other hand, he had come to her rescue. She was upset about the storm and fumbling around in the snow and he had come and found her keys. True, she was a little unnerved by his sudden appearance. She did not remember seeing him as she walked to the car. But strangely enough she was not frightened. He appeared so suddenly that she didn't have time to be.

The whole encounter was delightfully odd. There was the strange laugh that came out of nowhere. What was that all about? There was the offer to follow her home. It could be taken two ways, of course, but she chose not to think about the other way. To her it was pure gallantry, like wiping the snow off her windshield with his bare hands.

And then there was the comment about her car. She shook her head in amazement. It wasn't a pick-up line. It was far too awkward. The warmth and solicitude indicated by the words seemed perfectly genuine. But who says things like that to complete strangers? It was like something you would say to your sister or someone you really loved. It was particularly strange coming from him. He did not look the part.

She smiled at the scene as she played it over in her head. It was very vivid, as if preserved on film. She didn't usually remember things quite so clearly. She told herself it was because he was so strange. It was not common to meet someone like him in their small mountain town. In fact she never had, and she had lived there her whole life.

But was that the only reason why the memory was so alive—and why she wanted to cherish it? Jill blushed as other thoughts came to mind. He was definitely intriguing. He was cultivated. She could hear it in the way he talked, the way he chose his words. He had expressed concern for her safety. Brian was not concerned and had not been for years. All he cared about was his band, as far as she could tell. He never paid any attention to her anymore.

The warmth of this exotic stranger made her feel special, singled out. It gave her secret pleasure. She felt guilty about the fact that she was sitting there thinking about him with Brian snoring downstairs and Peter asleep in his bed. But she could not help it. She could not deny a certain lightness in her being. Like the snow, dancing about in the eves.

She refused the offer to follow her home, but the truth is she wanted him to. She was terrified of the slippery roads—but this was not the only reason. Part of her wanted him to be a disinterested Sir Galahad, but another part of her, it seemed, had very different feelings. She wanted Sir Galahad to follow her home because she wanted to feel a connection to him. She wanted him to be interested in her.

And yet this was a foolish fantasy. "Home" was no romantic getaway. "Home" was Brian passed out on the couch and their son Peter asleep in his bed. "Home" was a house that hadn't been cleaned in weeks because she couldn't do everything and furniture that was worn and a refrigerator full of half-used take-out food, some of which was long past its expiration date.

Still, the encounter in the parking lot had broken into her mundane life. The colors were dark and uncertain but perhaps more interesting for that very reason. In any case she couldn't stop thinking about the handsome young stranger as she sat up there in her loft with the snow gently falling.

Would she ever see him again?

DISCOVERY

THE NEXT TIME JOSH SAW JILL the ten-inch snowfall had been plowed and the state roads were glistening black in the pale December sun. He found himself sitting in a booth in the restaurant watching her wait on the other customers.

Now in the morning light he saw her clearly. She was a little taller than average, maybe five-eight, and she had unmanageable chestnut hair, a mane, or at least it looked unmanageable to him, wild and diffuse. She was pretty, with incisive eyes and cheerful features, no make-up, not someone who would stop you dead in your tracks if you saw her on the street; someone whose attractiveness would grow on you—if you had taste.

She did her double-take again when she saw him, apparently an adorable twitch.

"Hello!" she said, seeming flustered.

"Hello! Get home okay the other night?"

"Oh, no problem. Four wheel drive. Although the roads weren't plowed."

"No, probably too early for them. Glad to see you made it, though."

"Well, thanks again. For cleaning off the car—and all."

"I didn't want to see you driving around with your windshield covered."

There was the solicitude again. It made Jill feel singled out. "I hate to admit this, but I didn't have a scraper. I meant to get one, but—you know—first snow—"

"I bet you have one now," he said with a smile.

9

"Yes I do. Went to the drugstore first thing the next morning and bought the deluxe model."

There was an awkward pause as he tried to think of something else to say. Then he said the worst thing possible. "So you're a waitress."

"I guess so," she said, looking confused again. "Actually I'm a starving artist."

"Really! What, a painter?" The strange thing was he already knew the answer. He was tingling as he said it.

"I guess so. I do paint. Whether or not you would consider me a 'painter' is another question."

"Well, the only way I can know that is if you let me see them."

"See what?"

"Your paintings."

"Now why would you want to do that?"

"I love paintings."

"Come on."

"No—really. I'm serious. I studied art history in college. I've been to some of the greatest museums in the world. The Louvre, Uffizi, Brit Museum."

This was not just talk. It was coming back to him, piece by piece. He loved Botticelli. The name popped into his head and displaced the fog with blue sky. He loved Rembrandt and Raphael and Velasquez. He could see their paintings now, as he talked to her, just as he had seen them in person. He loved the Impressionists. He loved Chagall.

But she didn't look like she believed him. "Okay—so then who's your favorite painter?"

"I have a lot of favorites. I did go through a major Monet phase at one time. Water lilies."

"Like the room at the Met?"

"Even better, l'Orangerie. I used to stand there and wonder what was running through his head when he painted all those. And the room—mesmerizing."

"So I guess maybe you do know about paintings. But I'm still not sure why you want to see mine."

"What if I told you I have a feeling about you."

"What kind of feeling?"

"You know—an intuition. I'm thinking you're probably a lot better than you're letting on."

"I don't know about that. Are you some kind of collector?"

"No," he said with a smile. "I'm not going to be doing any collecting today."

"So you literally just want to see them."

"Yes. Does that seem so strange?"

"It does seem kind of strange, to be honest. Also there's a little problem. They're all at my house."

"Why is that a problem? I could follow you over after work."

"You really want to do that?"

"I do."

He fixed her with that dark gaze. She blinked and looked away.

"I guess it would be all right. The thing is I don't get off until ten."

"That's fine with me. In the meantime why don't you bring me some coffee?"

"Okay. How about something to eat? The oatmeal is delicious."

"Oatmeal it is, then. Thanks."

Josh ordered coffee because he was cold, but when it came he didn't feel like drinking it. Instead he became enthralled by the steam wafting through rays of sunlight in slow motion. It was beautiful. Then Jill brought the oatmeal, and it was the same thing all over again. For the first time in his life he was struck by the smell and the texture of oatmeal. It seemed so wholesome; he was fascinated by its wholesomeness. But he had no desire to eat. This worried him. Where was his appetite?

"You didn't touch a thing," Jill said reprovingly when she brought the check.

"Guess I'm not in the mood," he said, pulling himself back to her. "See you at ten?"

"I don't know. It still seems kind of silly."

"Come on. Indulge me."

She hesitated. "Okay—see you then."

Jill brought his dishes to the kitchen; when she returned she was surprised to see he was gone. Now she had no way to take back her foolish offer. She was not sure if she wanted this stranger coming to her house. Actually she did not know what she wanted. She was excited to see him again. She could not pretend otherwise. She had been thinking about him ever since the night in the parking lot; in fact just that morning.

It was a big surprise when he showed up in the restaurant. Was he interested in her? Was he there because he wanted to see her again after their first fleeting encounter? It was possible. One thing seemed certain—he was not there for breakfast. He paid for his food but had not eaten a thing. The dishes were in the same place where she remembered putting them. Did he buy breakfast just to see her? Was that the reason for the large tip? Or was she just flattering herself?

Those glowering eyes—all the personal comments—"I have a feeling about you." Who says things like that to a complete stranger? He knew nothing about her or her art. He did not have the slightest idea of whether she was any good. So what was it all about? Was it a line? It certainly sounded like a line. She wasn't sure whether she wanted it to be. She was intrigued by him. He was good looking, in a waifish way. And yet he was so strange! He was Greenwich Village, and Jill was a small-town girl.

He did know something about paintings, however. That part, at least, was not a line. She knew the museums he mentioned; remembered them from school. It was an odd coincidence that this man who showed up out of the blue to pull her keys out of the snow was also an art lover. Or was it a coincidence? Had he heard about her paintings somehow? No, this seemed ridiculous. How could he know?

He was right, though—she did want him to look at them. She couldn't help herself. Since college she had experienced nothing but rejection. She had gone into a shell and was hiding from the world, in fact had stopped painting altogether. And now someone who seemed to know what he was talking about was interested in her paintings. It was hard to resist this interest, even though it didn't make any sense.

But *why* was he interested? She could not get past this question. Also he was a little strange. She was not exactly afraid of him, but she was not exactly comfortable either. And now she had allowed him to talk her into coming to her house! How stupid. What made her think she could trust him? His concern could be just a show. He could be a clever con artist, or worse.

Jill was upset with herself. She should not have been inviting men to her house, strange or otherwise, no matter how intriguing they might be or whether they were interested in her painting. Her relationship with Brian was not great and had been deteriorating for years—but it was not right to invite another man to Brian's house. She knew better. What was she doing?

Besides, what if he hated the paintings? He came across as someone who thought of himself as a sophisticate. She doubted that he would like the sort of thing she did. She'd heard it all from the galleries. Her work wasn't "edgy" enough. She could picture him reacting the same way. In fact he kind of reminded her of some of the gallery slugs. He was not like her, with his Goth persona and white lock of hair. He would not like the things she liked. Was she setting herself up to fail?

The rest of the morning was jittery. She kept looking out the windows, hoping to catch a glimpse of him and convince herself that he was not as odd as he seemed and she was not completely out of her mind to let him follow her home. But there was no sign of him. Then it was ten. She was done, but she took her time getting out of the restaurant, half-hoping he would be gone when she did.

Unfortunately this was not the case. She jumped when she spotted him sitting in a large gold Mercedes not far from the Subaru. In her mind there were eyes in every window as she gave him an embarrassed little wave without exactly looking at him. It was too late to try to call it off. She did not want to be seen talking to him, especially after they had done so much talking in the restaurant.

Then she had another harrowing thought. What if people saw them drive off together? Fortunately Josh was discreet. He waited until she was out of the lot before starting his car and caught up with her on the state highway. She headed for the mountains and snow-covered roads with him not far behind, sliding all over the place with his antique rear-wheel drive car.

Finally they reached a clearing in the woods and the tidy log cabin sitting up with a view. Jill shook her head as she looked at the gleaming image of the oversized Mercedes in her rear-view mirror. It was conspicuous, to say the least. Then she checked to make sure Brian wasn't home. She could not imagine how she would explain the exotic stranger.

She pulled up to the front door and the Mercedes pulled up behind her. At that moment she realized she did not even know her visitor's name.

"Well, this is it," she said.

"Wow—quite the view," he said, looking out at the mountains.

"Sometimes it's the only thing keeping me sane," she replied—and then glanced at him in surprise. "By the way, my name is Jill."

"I'm Josh," he said with a little smile.

"Well—come on in."

"Are you sure it's okay?"

"I guess so. Brian's at work."

"Who's Brian?"

"That's my—um—significant other, I guess you'd call him."

"So you're not married?"

"No, you know how that is—me a so-called artist and him a musician. Somehow we never seemed to get around to it." This was her usual excuse when people asked.

"Too conventional, probably."

"No, that's not it. I always wanted to get married. But Brian—well, he's kind of hoping the band will take off. So the marriage thing keeps getting pushed back."

"Do you think it's going to take off?"

She shrugged. "I certainly hope so, for his sake. It's been fourteen years. They're not getting any younger." She stopped and waved at herself.

"What?"

"I guess I'm not getting any younger either."

Jill pushed the door open and led him into the kitchen. She warmed up some coffee as they made small talk about the beauty of the Green Mountains and winter and its pleasures. Then she handed him a cup and pointed him in the direction of the loft.

Josh did not know quite what to expect as he walked up the circular staircase. He was a bit of a snob when it came to paintings. What if he didn't like what he saw? What was he going to say? It was not his style to be gracious and consoling—but he did not want to hurt Jill.

And why was that, exactly? Was he in love with her? He did not know what he was. He did not know why he was drawn to her—if he was drawn—or how he felt about being alone with her. All he knew was that she was a painter and he felt a strong desire to see her paintings. It made no sense because he knew nothing about her—but there had to be some reason why he was there. He couldn't think of any other.

He felt awkward. It was not his style to go chasing after local artists. But then he reached the top of the stairs and looked around at the paintings on easels or mounted on the back wall—and immediately went into some kind of zone. It was like the mountain air, clear and pure, only it was in his head. The more he realized what he was looking at, the more his amazement grew.

It wasn't just that the paintings were good in the sense of being well-made. They were very good in that sense, in the way few painters can achieve, so that the viewer's natural resistance is overcome and he is drawn directly into the painting. But it was so much more than that. They were expressive. All artists try to be expressive, but few really succeed. They were also highly distinctive. This was a new kind of painting, with none of the usual tics of Modernism—and yet no antique mustiness either.

He stood there for a moment trying to get his bearings. It was not what he was expecting to find in a log cabin in the Vermont woods. He walked to the nearest canvas to take a closer look. A girl was pruning a rose bush and an interesting man was sitting behind her on the stone steps of a large house, a powerful-looking man but also a wreck of himself, full of the sadness of the world.

Josh looked down and saw the word "Cosette" hand-written on a piece of paper. He looked at the painting again and blinked. It was a work of genius. It was perhaps not a mature painting. There were some things he thought she might have done differently, but these were trivial reservations. The two principals were astonishing. You were drawn irresistibly into their faces as if they were real people. It was like Rembrandt; not the actual style but the passion and the depth. And the garden! Beautiful.

He glanced surreptitiously at Jill. What was he looking at? Could this unpretentious waitress really be the source of such a painting, so unlike anything he had ever seen before? Was it even possible? He looked at the painting again and shook his head.

"What?" Jill said.

"I don't know. Incredible."

"Incredible? Is that good or bad?"

"Good. It's an amazing painting. Masterpiece."

"Okay—now you're teasing me."

"I'm not teasing you. Why would you say that?"

"Because I don't believe you."

"Believe me. I never flatter people about their paintings. Never."

"You really like it? You think it's good?"

"It's amazing. You have the whole history of art in this painting, but it's also completely new."

"Not sure I'm following you. Although I guess I do tend to soak up things."

"That's even better. You do it unconsciously. Other painters couldn't do it if they tried."

He stood there silently gazing. Jill was dying to ask him again if he really did like it. She was hungry for reassurance after so many years of neglect but did not want to seem needy; so she bit her lip.

Josh took one last look and moved on to the next canvas. He saw a thin middle-aged man seated at a table, writing on rough paper, all browns and grays. She was doing something entirely different here. The colors and composition brought him to the sorrow in the man's face like a funnel. He stared at it with his mouth open. So much emotion, yet so subtle and understated in every way.

"Bonhoeffer in prison," Jill said.

"What?"

"German pastor. Plotted against Hitler and managed to get himself killed."

A waitress in Vermont who paints pictures about German pastors killed by the Nazis! It certainly wasn't what he was expecting. He thought he was going to see flowers and gardens. From looking at her he just assumed her muse was nature. Apparently there was a lot going on in that unruly head of hers.

"Very expressive. The use of color to the mood and the way everything pulls in one direction. Did you use a model? It's a remarkable face."

She nodded. "I used photographs, but my uncle also posed for me a couple of times, to help me get the perspective right. He's usually hung over in the morning, so it was perfect."

"Accidental angst. Those lines in his face—your uncle really looks like that?"

"No, I put those in myself. Map of suffering, I guess. Actually I kind of had those old cowboy photographs in mind. He wasn't wind-beaten, but he was weather beaten. If you know what I mean."

"I'm jealous. I want those lines for myself."

"Trust me—you don't want them."

"So tell me, how did you get to be so good at doing faces?"

"I don't know. I guess it's just that I love faces. They humanize a painting. They're real. They can tell a story all by themselves. I'm babbling."

"No, you're not."

"Believe it or not, I have thought about this. Maybe it's better just to say I love faces in paintings and leave it at that."

"But it's not just faces per se. Some faces are shallow faces. There's so much depth here, in both of these paintings. Although maybe not so much with Cosette."

"No—I don't see her that way. She's supposed to be innocent. But I do choose my subjects carefully, if that's what you mean. I assume Shakespeare chose King Lear carefully. I look at a lot of paintings and my first reaction is—why did they paint that? Why go to all that trouble?"

"You are a humanist. You are interested in the human story. That's what you want to paint."

"I do like to tell stories. I'm a little stubborn that way, because people keep telling me it's not the right way to do things. But I don't really care. I like to have a lot going on in a painting. I'm kind of bored by static canvases, to tell you the truth."

"If you can paint like this, you have a right to be stubborn."

Josh moved on to the next painting, and then the next. They were all so good, they all showed talent, some a little raw but others executed at such a high level that it was disorienting. At one point he wondered if he was dreaming. His unreal world seemed even less real. He let his hand brush against Jill's ever so slightly just to reassure himself she was real. She seemed solid enough; he could feel the touch. Can you feel a touch in a dream?

Next he came to a painting that stopped him cold, a large canvas with a dramatic scene. This one was fully mature, and it was astonishing.

"That's...from the Bible," she said, jumping in and sounding a little embarrassed.

"I know. I can see that. What's it about?"

"Well—the name's right there."

Josh looked down. *The Blind Man*. What's he doing?"

"He's putting mud on his eyes."

"Oh! Right. I vaguely remember something about that from Sunday School."

Jill laughed.

"What?" he said.

"Somehow I can't quite picture you in Sunday School."

"My mother made me go. But what exactly is going on again?"

"The blind man goes and washes the mud away, and then he can see."

"A miracle—if you believe in that sort of thing."

"Actually I do. But for me it's about much more than that. Like the miracle of sight itself. Maybe you have to be a painter to understand."

"Try me."

"Okay, first the whole idea of 20/20 vision. We have this thing we think of as perfect vision. Perfectly brilliant and clear. And everybody takes it for granted, as if were just this ordinary thing. But *why* do we have 20/20 vision? Have you ever thought about that? I'm not just talking about the pleasure it gives, or the clarity, but the very idea of it, the very existence of it when there are so many other possibilities."

"Hmm. This is a little over my head."

"Sorry—you think about things like that when you paint. And then there's the whole idea of having your eyes opened in so many ways. That's really what I was thinking about when I made this painting. But you probably don't believe in that, either."

"I don't even know what you mean," he confessed.

"Well, for instance you're probably the kind of person who would say this guy is better off being blind. Right? After all, he was born that way. He's begging, he's making a living, he's pitied, he's comfortable in his misery. Leave him alone. Why change?"

"Okay, I'll bite. Why change?"

"For this," she said, gesturing to the view of the mountains from the gable windows.

Josh didn't know quite what to say to that. "So I take it you're religious."

Jill turned a little red. "Okay—here we go. That's why I can't do this anymore."

"I was just making an observation."

"And what does that observation have to do with anything? I can't make real art if I'm religious?"

"I didn't say that."

"No, but you were thinking it. I know—I get it. You're not supposed to make 'religious' paintings these days. Funny, the MFA is full of them, but now it's supposed to be a mortal sin. You could walk into a gallery with the *Pieta* in your hands and some smug twerp with wire-rimmed glasses would smirk and tell you it's 'not their thing.' It doesn't matter how good the painting is. It doesn't matter if it's heartfelt and moving or well-composed or well-executed. It's a 'religious' painting. And Lord knows, we can't have any of those."

"Okay, I'll admit it," Josh said, withering under this blast. "I do know what you're talking about. You would definitely have a hard time getting a gallery to take this painting, no matter how brilliant it is—and it is brilliant. I'll just put that out there right now so there's no misunderstanding. But let me also say that's not the *only* reason you're likely to have a hard time."

"Oh, here we go."

"No, hear me out. This is important. You are doing something new. It's not new like Cubism was new or Abstract Expressionism was new, but it's too new and advanced for the typical gallery. They think in genres. They think in terms of what they know they can sell. You don't fit in any genre. I'll bet you don't even think about genres when you start a painting. Am I right?"

"You are right."

"So when you walk into a gallery with something like this you scare people. You're transgressive in a new way, and you don't even know it."

"Yes, I'm transgressive because I tell stories and sometimes I even make 'religious' paintings. I'm surprised they haven't put me in jail yet."

"I'm not saying it isn't ridiculous. I'm just pointing it out to you. Van Gogh had trouble getting people to take any interest in his paintings, and your work is just as transgressive as his, in its own way. It's just as threatening to the prevailing order. Besides, let's face it—it's hard to recognize great art, hard to overcome the natural resistance and inertia; hard for great artists to be salesmen, which is what commercial artists are all about. History is littered with great artists who struggled in their own time."

"But what does any of this have to do with me?"

"It has everything to do with you," he said looking at her seriously. "You have to stay faithful to your muse and have confidence that your audience will eventually find you."

"I don't know. I don't really feel too confident right now. In fact that's why I stopped painting."

"You did what! You can't stop painting."

"Why not?"

"You have to make more of these! I can't believe you would even think about stopping."

"I can't take it anymore. You don't understand how hard it is. You have to give yourself completely to a painting like this in order for it to be any good. You can't just be part-in; you have to be all-in. But then people ignore you and act like you're not even there, and you just lose all confidence."

Josh looked at *The Blind Man* again. "Okay—to be perfectly honest, I might have been one of those people you're talking about. I know what you mean because I might have been dismissive of a painting like this myself in the past."

"But not now?"

"No. I don't feel that now."

"What changed?"

"You," he said without looking at her. "Also I seem to be at an interesting point in my life. I don't feel the old snark coming on when I look at this painting. Now all I see now is the artistry and the emotion."

Josh was being completely serious. Something had changed, and it seemed to have something to do with Jill. He had not been in the habit of giving out compliments in the past, least of all to contemporary artists. He tended to assume that nothing that was contemporary could be any good, but now he felt the folly of this idea. He wanted to say these things to her. There was something about Jill specifically that made him want to say them. He told himself it was because of the quality of the artwork.

Not that there was any doubt about her talent. Jill was just what he implied—a great painter. In fact he wondered as he stood there looking at *The Blind Man* if she was one of the greatest painters he had ever seen, and at such an early age. True, the painting would not ingratiate her to the secretariat. They would call it 'reactionary' or use some other dismissive term to deflect its genius and keep her in her place. But it was amazing. The attitudes and expressions of the bystanders. The symphony of color.

"Did you have a model for *him*?" Josh said, pointing to the man with mud on his fingers.

"No, that was pretty much out of my head," Jill replied, calming down a bit.

"It's different. I'm used to seeing a pretty face and long blond hair."

She laughed. "As you can see, I'm not into pretty. I don't really do pretty in any of my paintings. 'He had no beauty or majesty to attract us to him.' That's the kind of thing I'm into."

"Beauty is shallow," Josh suggested.

"Not the beauty of nature. I have no problem with that, as you can see. I'm talking about human beauty. I just have no interest in it, as a painter. I'm more interested in beautiful qualities, if I can find them. That's where the story is."

"What kind of qualities did you have in mind?"

"Oh—love, joy, peace, patience, kindness, gentleness. That kind of thing."

"I see."

"Do you really?" she said with a little laugh.

"No, I do. I may be like your blind man, but I'm perfectly capable of appreciating those qualities."

Josh gave the painting one last lingering look and moved on to the next one, which was set off by itself in a far corner of the loft. At first he did not understand what he was seeing—he was still lost in the *Blind Man* and the discussion.

"What's this?" he said.

"Another 'religious' painting, I'm afraid."

"I don't recognize the story."

"It's Judas."

"Judas! Good. Someone I can relate to." But as he focused on the painting something strange started happening to him. "What's all that red stuff on the ground?"

"You mean the blood? I thought it was pretty obvious. This is the version where he falls down and bursts open. Spilled his guts, as it were."

Josh wanted to make a clever reply but couldn't. Suddenly he felt dizzy, weak, as if every last ounce of energy had been drained out of him. He stumbled to the railing overlooking the great room

21

and grasped it with both hands. He had to fight the temptation to throw himself over the side.

"Are you all right?" Jill said.

"I have to go."

"What is it?"

"I don't know. I feel funny."

"I'm not surprised. A guy who goes around in the middle of winter with his coat unbuttoned."

"I don't know—I have to go." Josh hurried down the stairs and to the door with Jill behind him.

"I'm sorry you don't feel well," she said, feeling a little dazed herself.

"I just need to get home." The words startled him as they came out of his mouth. He realized he had no idea where "home" was.

Josh half ran to his car and drove away. Jill watched the Mercedes pull out of the driveway and wind down the mountain road. She did not know what to make of such strange behavior. Was he really feeling ill? It seemed a little odd for it to come on so suddenly. One moment he was very chatty—full of friendly advice and even warmth—and then he was completely changed. His pale face looked even paler.

It seemed to come over him when he was looking at Judas. Did something in the painting upset him? He mentioned the blood. She knew some people were sensitive to the sight of blood—her father was like that. But not to this degree. Not enough to make him act like he had a split personality.

She did not know what to think. On one hand, she was sorry he left. It was the first positive, objective feedback she had received to her paintings in a long time, the first time someone who was not a professor or a family member had indicated that they might be worthy of her own aspirations. She did not know if she could trust herself to believe him. He seemed to be going overboard with some of the things he said. But she was not immune to praise. She was gladdened by his kind remarks.

Jill had had her share of criticism from the local art market. She could not remember ever having anything but criticism. No one had looked at her paintings and said anything to encourage her. Some had even made rather cutting remarks, especially about the Biblical paintings. She was too sensitive, she knew it. She knew these negative reactions had sent her into a shell. They were the real reason she had stopped painting. They deprived her of her forward motion.

It was hard to drink in Josh's praise the way she wanted to. She was like someone in a desert who suddenly comes across cool water and cannot drink it deeply. She looked out at the winterscape after he was gone and it was as bright and fresh as it could be. It was energy to her now, all the beauty she beheld. Her dreams and her hopes were not nothing. She could paint something that an astute critic could admire.

There was a lot to think about in the discussion and some of the things he said. First of all there were his comments about *Cosette* and *Bonhoeffer*. Jill worked so hard on those paintings. It was nice to have someone look at them and see some of the things she had put into them. His admiration was obvious, and this both pleased and amazed her. It is one thing to look at your own painting and feel it has value; it is quite another to have your feelings affirmed by someone else.

There was his willingness to try to see things from her point of view. He admitted he might have had the same resistance to religious paintings in the past that was such a thorn in her side. But he also said he had changed his mind. Ironically, *The Blind Man* had caused him to see things a little differently. This wasn't her intention, but she was amused and gratified by the result.

And then there was the other thing he said. She approached this very carefully. She set it off in her mind until last, saving the best, perhaps, but not knowing if it was the best or something else entirely. He said "you" when she asked him what had caused him to change. What did he mean by this "you"? Was he referring to her painting? Was it the painting itself that converted him, as his words seemed to indicate? Or was he referring to a possible interest in her?

Jill had very mixed feelings about this question. She tried to convince herself she wanted it to be about the painting. The prohibition on paintings like *The Blind Man* was one of her pet peeves. There seemed to be a presumption in certain circles that religion was not to be taken seriously. But Jill had eyes. She could see the paintings they had hanging in their galleries, and she could see how trite they were. These were the paintings that were deemed worthy of being taken seriously? It was maddening.

She was tired of the fatuous prejudice against faith. God forbid that you should make any attempt to use art to express the things that you loved and were meaningful to you! Now if you hated faith and you hated religion—then you could be a real artist. There was an entire cottage industry of religion-hatred masquerading as fine art. In that case the bar was set suspiciously low.

Jill wanted Josh to be a convert. She wanted his "you" to refer to her painting and his willingness to see things in a new way. She was willing to convert the world one person at a time, and Josh's comment was rewarding because he seemed like a hard case. It was easy to believe him when he said he had been dismissive of religious paintings. It was written all over him and the way he dressed and talked and acted. If there was hope with him, there was hope with anyone.

Then again, did the "you" mean something else entirely? Was he saying he was willing to think about taking religious art seriously because of her and not specifically because of her painting? That his feelings about her were the cause of the change? In short, was it his way of communicating a partiality for her? The implication seemed to be there. She felt it when he said it.

If this is what the "you" meant, then Jill was not sure how she felt about it. Part of her wanted him to feel just such a partiality. She recognized this and was torn between wanting to embrace it and feeling ashamed. Jill was starving for attention in more ways than one at that point in her life. It was not just indifference to her art that was bruising her and taking away her positive energy. It was Brian's indifference and the strange and random home life they had settled into in recent years.

Josh seemed to have shown interest in her even before he knew about her paintings. But did she want him to be interested in that way? She was not sure. She thought about Brian and Peter and felt guilty. She thought about Josh's strange behavior and felt turned off. Still, there was the "you." She could not deny that it thrilled her when he said it.

IDENTITY

J OSH WASN'T REALLY SICK. He didn't know what he was. Literally. He had to get out of there because he was afraid…of himself. He hurried down the snowy road very much aware that she was probably still standing in the open doorway watching him. This may have been the reason why he ran away. She trusted him—and he did not know if he was worthy of her trust.

What he did know was that something was very wrong with him. Very wrong. It started with this dream-existence he was living where the only time he was conscious of himself was when he was with Jill; where he seemed to show up where Jill was in various times and places and there was nothing in between, no interstitials, complete void or darkness.

And then there was the accident. He remembered it now. A terrible, violent crash. Was he—dead? Was that the reason for the strange gaps in his life? Why he would simply seem to show up somewhere with no idea of how he got there? Why everything seemed so unreal, including Jill and her paintings?

Was he living in some sort of after-death dreamworld? Was anything that he was experiencing real? No—Jill certainly seemed real. He touched her; she seemed real. The cold seemed real. The sunshine and the snow seemed real. The oatmeal seemed real. He remembered looking at it, almost falling into it in his mind. His senses filled up with its solidity even now.

Could it be a concussion? He remembered his uncle telling him about a football concussion he had in prep school and how he "woke up" at the dinner table at a friend's house that night with no memory of how he got there. He could certainly have a concussion from the kind of accident he was in. It could explain many of his symptoms, including the feeling of dissociation that he had to struggle to overcome.

But then there was the painting in Jill's loft. Something happened to him when he saw that painting. He had feelings he did not want to have, horrible feelings apparently connected with the blood. He did not run away because he was sick in his body. He ran away because he was sick in his soul. He looked at Jill and suddenly did not trust himself to be alone with her. He had terrible thoughts. Why did he have to have such thoughts! He did not want them. He ran away.

The last thing he wanted to do was to hurt Jill. She was the color in his life, the only color. He wanted to love her and show her a great love. And in some strange sense he did love her and had from the moment he talked with her in the snow in the parking lot. It was not like any love he had ever felt before. It was definitely not the usual insanity between a man and a woman. There was no thunderbolt, no obsession.

If anything—if he had to describe it—it was more like a feeling of warmth and assurance. Sexual love is a conflagration but the feeling he had when he was with Jill was more like peace in a meadow. It had a quality of joy and made him happy in a way that he had never been happy before. It was the reason for his gentle banter with her. He was not generally given to gentle banter or gentleness of any kind. He also was not given to being supportive. He was no cheerleader.

This was not the case when he was with Jill, however. He wanted to be gentle with her. He wanted to be her cheerleader. Now partly this was because of those astounding paintings of hers. He felt like he had discovered a great artist. Nothing could be more wonderful or more gratifying for someone who loved art as much as he did. Jill could not stop painting because Jill was his discovery. No, it was more than that. She could not stop painting because the world could not afford to be deprived of her art.

Josh knew something was different about him because of his openness to Jill. It was hard for him to be open to new artists. He had fallen in love with *The Blind Man*—his antagonism toward such paintings had melted away. On the other hand, he may have been uniquely qualified to see the value of her art. He had no sympathy for the rear guard that used to be the avant-garde and was clinging to the past while it degenerated into self-parody.

Jill offered the possibility of something new. He did not know if she was the new thing that was coming—the new age, the new identity—but she was the new thing that was already here. Her paintings were not the negation that was Modernism and yet they were not in any sense old-fashioned. They were not even a synthesis of the two; they were an entirely new thesis. It was funny to talk with her because she did not seem to be aware of it. She was not consciously trying to frame a new aesthetic. He could not imagine her concocting a manifesto. She seemed to be simply following her muse.

She was, apparently, a natural genius. And this was just what terrified him. These dark thoughts he had, the ones that suddenly came over him while he was standing there looking at that terrible-wonderful painting—they scared him to death. He had discovered a rare painter, if his senses were to be trusted. She was laboring in obscurity in the Vermont woods—not even realizing who she was or the value of what she was doing—and he had discovered her. And was he now going to destroy his own discovery? Was that why he was there—to destroy the very thing that made him happy?

Why? Because he could not accept happiness? Those terrible thoughts—how he hated them! How he hated his own flesh and bones for having them! For a moment he wanted to throw himself over the railing of her loft and smash his head on the hardwood floor—that's how upset he was with himself. Instead he ran away. He hardly said a word to her. He did not attempt to explain himself. What was there to explain? That he was flooded with dark thoughts? That he was fearful for her safety—because of him?

He could not imagine what she was thinking about such strange behavior. Part of him wanted her to think the worst. He did not want her inviting him to her house. He did not trust himself. Terrible thoughts came into his head when he saw the blood in the painting; violent thoughts connected with the crash. He did not want them but could not help having them. He felt like a black hole, not at all the kind supporter he was trying so hard to be. A darkness overtook him. He could not pretend otherwise.

He saw what the painting was about. Identity shattered, happiness shattered, annihilation. That was the thing about him and Jill. He understood her perfectly. It was not hate that he saw in the painting. It was the same thing he saw in all her paintings: love. This was what made her paintings so unique. They were filled with love. This love was not in any sense sentimental or cloying; Jill said herself that she "didn't do pretty." And yet it was palpable in every canvas, even Judas.

Josh closed his eyes and saw the blood again, oozing from the earth. He did not know the echo Jill had in mind, but something about the blood caused a great disturbance in his soul. It caused him to think dark thoughts and made him feel like he had no control over himself. But how could blood in a painting send him spinning out of control? He had seen plenty of depictions of blood in paintings before. He had seen his fair share of blood-soaked movies and video games. What was so different about Judas?

As soon as he was out of sight of the cabin he pulled off the road into a little plow turnout and sat there trembling in the cold. He was afraid to drive because he did not feel like he was in control of the car on the snowy mountain road and because there was something else making him afraid to drive. He did not know what it was. Then it came back to him. The accident.

A terrible accident and he was in it. Bits and flashes of scenes came bursting into his mind without coherence. He saw himself talking with a nurse in a bright office somewhere with the dark winter night pressing on the windows. He seemed to be in a hurry. The nurse had a lot of questions and then she had a strange face and he had to get out of there.

Then he was in the car. It seemed like the same car he was sitting in right now, a gold Mercedes. He was driving and it was dark and it was night and snowing. He went right through a stop sign because he was in a hurry, he was impatient, and then he was going faster in spite of the snow and he did not feel in complete control of the car but he didn't care, he didn't slow down at all, it was fun, being a little out of control on the snow.

Then the thrill razored into terror as he realized he was going too fast. There was a hard bang that was like all of his teeth being knocked out of his head at once. *Bang!* A blinding flash of light. Then nothing.

There had been an accident. A terrible accident, and he was in it, strangely in the same car he was in right now, or so it seemed; although he could not be sure this was not a dream. But was this the reason for his panicked reaction to the blood and the violence he felt? Was it his own blood spilled out all over the car on a dark country road on a dark winter night?

Again he wondered—could he be dead? He did not believe in ghosts—but was that what he was? What would it be like to exist in the shadow land between life and death, if there were such a place? Would it be any different from the unreality he was experiencing now?

Then he had an even more terrible thought, connected with the blood. Was he some sort of vampire? He laughed out loud but then he stopped laughing. It was outlandish, it was ridiculous—but what was the deal with the blood? Why was he suddenly afraid of being with Jill—so afraid that he felt he had to run away?

Josh did not believe in vampires, of course. Ancient cultures ritualized the drinking of blood, which they thought had the power to give life. Stoker threw sex into the mix by making his vampire prey upon beautiful young women. In the prim Victorian era it was sensational to have the mysterious Count suck poor Lucy's blood.

The modern remix? Dracula for girls. It was not invasion literature anymore—no, something very different from xenophobia was in play. Modern vampires were hot. They had the Manfred thing going for them. They were not so much bloodthirsty monsters as stylish Bad Boys. The girls seemed to like that sort of thing. Maybe they thought they could change them, like Jane and Rochester. But that was fantasy as far as Josh was concerned. Bad boys were just bad, or at least the ones he had known.

So no, obviously he couldn't be a vampire, as if such creatures actually existed. He'd read *Interview* in the postmodern way, not as if he gave any actual credence to the notion of the Undead. And yet what was going on with him? Why did everything seem so unreal— his disordered sense of space and time? Why did he have this strange reaction to the sight of blood in Jill's loft, not of revulsion but of something like…appetite?

This last thought caused another painful idea to jerk his mind. Was he was one of the bad boys? Suddenly he felt more low and depressed than he ever had in his life. He did not want to be a bad boy. That was not the way he saw himself. He never wanted to see himself that way. Bay boys were cruel, soulless. They did not care about anyone but themselves. They were the very opposite of what he wanted to be.

Josh saw himself as one of the good guys. He was respectful of authority. He loved nature and was sentimental about Christmas. His parents had taken him to church when he was growing up. All right, so he hadn't been in a while—but he sort of liked church. He appreciated things like goodness and kindness and respect. He agreed with the Ten Commandments. He was loyal to family and friends and generous with his money.

But something had changed. He did not know what. All he could think about at that moment were the bad-boy things he had done in his life—and unfortunately there were many. He never thought of himself as a bully, but there was that poor boy they taunted in Jefferson Elementary, the one with the strange tics. Sure, they all taunted him—girls as well as boys—but did that make it right? Josh could picture himself joining in and he was thoroughly ashamed. The bitterness of his own cruelty and lack of compassion washed over him and darkened him to the very core of his being.

He thought of himself as the faithful knight who wants to be devoted to a soul-mate—this was how he saw himself in his own mind ever since he'd read the Arthurian romances as a child—but what about the girl whose heart he broke while they were sophomores in high school? Why did he break her heart? He didn't realize how much he was breaking it, but it was broken nonetheless. He could still hear her crying. It was another spot of darkness on his being.

There were other things, too; dark marks like Cain. But by far the worst of all was the still-fresh memory of the accident. He now realized with horror that he was not alone that night. There was someone else in the car with him. It was Carol, and he was sure she did not survive the crash. He did not know how he knew this but he did. He had killed Carol, killed her just as surely as if he had put a bullet in her head.

Carol was a nice person. She thought he was the one. He knew she did. He did not happen to feel the same way. It was not that he didn't like her or was not attracted to her. He just wasn't in love with her. But he was willing to let her think he was. There was no one else in his life, and Carol was an acceptable companion. After all, she was on the pill. No harm, no foul. It was the way things were these days.

Josh let her think what she wanted to think. He did not lead her on. In fact he tended to be quite cool and aloof with Carol. In a sense, his treatment of her was a clear reflection of his feelings; but she interpreted it as something else entirely—woundedness?—he did not know what. Then he realized—it was because she saw him as a bad boy. His seeming badness stirred something in her that she herself did not understand and made her tender when she should have been tough.

So Carol was in the car with him that night. Now he could see it vividly in his mind. He was sliding around in the snow and acting like a jackass. He knew he was scaring her but he didn't care because he thought he was in control. The car was fishtailing wildly and he was laughing and whooping it up. Why wouldn't she laugh with him? It irritated him that she wasn't laughing. He was going to get her to loosen up. He went a little faster.

Then he remembered something else—they were not wearing seat belts. This was a particularly damning detail. He never wore one himself when he could avoid it, not since he'd had his own car. He liked the feeling of freedom, rebellion, but what difference did it make if he killed himself with his idiocy? The point was that Carol was inclined to follow his lead. She did not want him to think she was afraid or did not trust his driving. She did not want him to think she was uncool.

This was what tortured him as he sat in a snowy turnout on a lonely country road. He had deliberately influenced her not to wear her seat belt. He didn't tell her not to wear it. He didn't have to. She was in love with him and would do whatever he did. She could not resist him because she loved him, and he used this power over her to make her do what he wanted. He was glad when he saw she didn't put it on because it would spoil the fun.

All of this came back to him now as he remembered the terrible moment when he realized they were going to crash. Everything seemed fine—and then all of a sudden it wasn't. He had no control at all over the car. He hit the brakes hard but it felt like they were accelerating. They were sliding toward the massive concrete slab guarding the driveway to the town garage. It seemed like an eternity between. The concrete mass kept coming, coming, coming. They hit it dead-on.

The last thing he remembered was putting out his hand to stop her from flying into the windshield. He had no thought of himself, but it was too late. The Mercedes was a restored classic. It had no airbags. Josh and Carol were headed directly for a solid concrete wall with no seat belts and nothing between them and the windshield. Were they going to die? There was impact and the flash of light. Then everything went black. No, he had not actually seen Carol dead but he knew she was. He knew this sweet girl had not survived the crash and he was the cause. He wailed out loud. He had fulfilled her vision of him. He was one of the bad boys. There was no crazy wife in the attic to blame for his erratic behavior. He had toyed recklessly with her life and destroyed it. He had destroyed her soul, and now his own soul was also lost.

If he was not "undead," then what was he? He could not have survived such a violent crash. He was almost sure of it. But that was not the only thing. His life was a series of scenes with no connecting tissues. At first this scared him, but now it made him mad, it made him rage. He had moments of lucidity, like his encounter with Jill in the parking lot or her loft, but there did not seem to be anything connecting them. It wasn't physically possible to appear here and there; he must have traveled to the parking lot—but that was just it. He had no memory of it. None at all.

There was the thing with food. He had no desire for it. He hadn't eaten anything in the restaurant, even with good wholesome food sitting there staring him right in the face. He couldn't even remember the last time he had eaten. How can someone live without eating? You can't—unless you are not exactly human. Unless you are something that does not have to eat...or worse, feeds on something horrible.

Even Jill had an air of unreality to her, now that he thought about it. Did he just dream all those incredible paintings? Because that's exactly what they were—incredible. He never expected to find someone like her laboring in obscurity in a sleepy little village. But no, Jill was real. Somehow he knew she was. The experience of seeing her paintings was too vivid to doubt. Could he have made them up in his own mind, like you do in a dream? No, he did not know the story with the blind man and had never heard of the German pastor. How could he have made such things up?

So Jill, at least, was real. But this brought him back to his apparent obsession. What was it really about? Why was he hanging around waiting for her in an empty parking lot in the snow? He *was* waiting for her—right? He was pretty sure he was. The very fact that he was in a position to "rescue" her was damning. He had no other reason to be there. He had never been there before, that he could remember. It had to be about her.

But why? Was it possible he had seen her someplace before and fallen in love? This was the happier interpretation, although still creepy. The other possibility was too horrible to contemplate—that she was his victim. He remembered his conflicted reaction to the blood in the painting. Did it remind him that he had an appetite for destruction? Just like the appetite that destroyed poor Carol?

The last thing he wanted to do was to hurt Jill. He—loved Jill. Being with her was like light or color. It illuminated his whole being. Besides, how could he do harm to such an incredible talent? Or was he just fooling himself again? Was it really love that drew him to Jill or was it something else? He looked down at his hands. Something was wrong with them. They did not have the pink flush that hands should have. It was almost as if they were not his hands. He moved them. The sight of these monsters moving under his will was jarring.

So was that it, then? Was he a vampire, or something like it? Was this what he had become as a punishment for his sins, for what he had done to Carol, for wasting his life and his moment? Was it his terrible punishment to be reincarnated in a ghoulish form and turned into a bloodthirsty killer? To go around destroying young women whom he did not want to destroy?

He tapped the dashboard with his finger. Plunk, plunk! It was solid enough. It was not an illusion. He slapped it. He could feel the impact with his hand. His body certainly seemed real. Could he have a solid body and also be "undead"? No, it seemed to him that he must be confused somehow. He had been in a nasty accident. It was a bad concussion. Maybe that's why things seemed to keep fading in and out and he found himself in places without knowing how he got there.

The alternative was unthinkable.

STIRRINGS

J ILL WAS ALL IN A LATHER after Josh left. She had so many emotions she didn't know what to do with them—so she did nothing and just let them take her, overpower her. She lay down on the couch and let them ravish her in the morning sun.

Who was this strange man? She didn't know everyone in their small mountain village, of course, but she knew most, having been a waitress for several years in the only restaurant in town and a regular at church. She knew she had never seen Josh before. She would have remembered if she had. He was someone you would remember.

There were a lot of country folk in town, Yankees who could be seen in their plain clothes and their plain cars and owned farms or worked in the town garage or post office or whatever; and there were the local aristocracy still carrying on, who had lived there for generations and had some money and showed at least some interest in the arts; and there were retirees who had come to the Green Mountains looking for a certain lifestyle and were from Boston or New York. The old Hippies, people called them.

But there were not any like Josh. He exuded culture and sophistication in the very way he carried himself, like the art professors she had known in school. And then there was that strange lock of hair. When she first saw him in the light, at the restaurant, she almost laughed. Did he have any idea how affected it looked?

Then she caught herself staring at it while he was looking at her paintings. The more she did, the more she became convinced that it was natural. It was actual white-gray hair with all the usual tints and mixed in with the black in a way that could not have been done by dyeing. This realization changed the way she thought about him. If the white lock had created a barrier before, now it had almost the opposite effect. It fascinated her. His exoticness was not fake but real. And she had been too quick to judge.

She had seen him three times now and did not know what to make of these encounters. The first night in the parking lot was particularly strange. There was no reason for him to be there. Neither the restaurant nor any of the neighboring stores were open. Did he just happen to be walking by and see her looking for her keys? It was possible. People do like to walk in the snow. He himself had expressed an appreciation for the beauty of snow, which she shared.

But then he showed up again! In the restaurant! Was he there to see her? She could not be sure, but it seemed suspicious. She was shocked when she first saw him but the shock didn't last long. After that she was glad, so glad that she blundered into letting him come to her house to see her paintings.

How did that happen, exactly? She did not know. The request took her completely by surprise. She was impressed by what he said about his background. She knew the museums he mentioned, most of them anyway, and if he really had traveled to see them—well, that was something. You don't see too many young men with a travelogue like that, not in her part of Vermont anyway. Then too he had been kind to her in the parking lot. So when he invited himself she just opened her mouth and said yes.

Then he was there in her house. Yes, it had actually happened. She didn't dream it. How did she feel about this unexpected turn of events in her uneventful life? She was a little ashamed to realize that she felt happy. Nothing happened between them, which made her even happier. She did not want to be unfaithful to Brian; but just the fact that this fascinating stranger had been there alone with her in her loft was like sunshine. She wasn't necessarily proud of feeling this way, but there it was.

All these thoughts went through her head before she allowed herself to indulge in the very great pleasure of his reaction to the paintings. Understand, it had been a long time since Jill had the luxury of being appreciated. Her mother was supportive, but her father was a practical man and had been quietly hostile to the idea of her becoming a painter. By far the best time of her life was college, where she was treated like a star. Her professors loved her and were not bashful about saying so. Maybe it was because they'd had to suffer through so much bad painting and so many mediocre students in their careers.

After college, however, the praise had been sparse. This lack of positive response from the world was deflating to someone with Jill's passion and drive. She had always been on fire to paint, ever since she discovered that she *could* paint, that it came easily to her; not just the drawing, which few people can do naturally, but the coloring and paint-mixing and all of it. She could paint all night and all day. The only time she was really happy was when she was painting. She would go into the canvas and get lost in there for hours. She would hum to herself. She heard herself humming and knew she was happy.

Jill felt her paintings were good—she could not have kept going otherwise—but of course she knew this was just her own opinion. She did not want to live in an echo chamber of self-absorption, as she had seen so many others do. She wanted some objective corroboration. She was already too hard on herself. It was easy for her to see the flaws in her work. She was also humble. She could not stand people in the art world who were full of themselves. She was determined not to go around touting herself as an "artist" until the world agreed—and not even then, because that was not what it was all about for her.

One reason she needed encouragement was she was on a new path. Her paintings did not look like any other paintings. They were unique to her vision, which she guarded ferociously. She refused to indulge in clichés just to get a picture in a gallery. She hated the whole gallery scene anyway. It was condescending and cold and phony, as far as she was concerned. These were not people who loved art the way she loved it. In her mind they didn't even know what art was. And the paintings they featured? There was talent in some of them, but they were not what she considered first-rate. They were not anything she would have brought home and hung in her own house.

They pretended to be different, but Jill was genuinely different, and this difference isolated her. For example, she wanted her pictures to tell stories. This was her natural impulse in painting. She loved the challenge and the dynamism. She wanted to frame an incident with the meaning it had for her and bring this meaning directly home to the viewer. She felt a great love and wanted to put this love in the faces she painted. She wanted to move people with her paintings, start a revolution. She longed for the restoration of something that had been lost in the falling leaves.

But story-telling was not fashionable anymore. In fact it was prohibited. People talked about the liberation that modern artists obtained when they rejected representation, but to Jill it was just another form of slavery. The modern age was no more liberated than any other. It was just as formulaic, just as rigid in its own way—more so, because it left no room for dissent. You had to create the same thing that everyone else was creating or they would not let you into the club. You had to toe the line.

Jill was painting wonderful paintings and nobody wanted them and nobody seemed to realize how wonderful they were. This was her purgatory. She would bring paintings to galleries that had her lifeblood in them, paintings she had poured out her soul to create, and they were treated as if they were nothing. It wasn't so much that people said mean things about them as they seemed to dismiss them. They looked at them in their world-weary way but were not engaged by them. They said "very nice" or "you have quite a talent" but they didn't really mean it. She knew these were just things they had learned to say over the years to keep people like her placated.

No one would give her a show or had any interest in redeeming her from the pit of obscurity. There was no reaction to her work from the outside world; in part, she realized, because it was all stowed away in her loft. She saw this weakness in herself. She knew her reticence—her modesty—was hurting her and holding her back. But this was not something she could change or even wanted to change. She was not into self-promotion. She had a very low tolerance for people who were.

After a while she started to get discouraged. She lost the confidence she needed to walk up to a blank canvas and offer herself as a sacrifice. Brian wasn't much help. Oh, he was supportive in a vague way, but he had no way of knowing how good she was. They had been together for fourteen years and she had given up on him ever being able to appreciate her work. In fact it seemed to be getting in the way of their relationship. There were times when there was no food in the house. There were times when the laundry was not done or an important date at Peter's school was missed.

Brian blamed these things on her painting. No, he did not come right out and say so, but she could see it in his looks. To be honest, she felt he could have taken a more active role in house-keeping and taking care of Peter. But he always had a good excuse. After all, he was the one with the regular job; he was the one working nine, ten hours a day, and at night he was rehearsing with the band that was going to make them rich and famous someday. Every night, it seemed.

A word about the band. Jill wanted to believe in them. She thought they were not just good but very good. They had met at UVM and gravitated to each other and really seemed to have something. Brian was an excellent songwriter and singer and a talented keyboard player. They had a very gifted guitarist, Leo, or as everyone called him, "the Lion." The drummer and bassist were also very good. They would often rehearse in the barn in the summer and she would sit there on the porch looking at the mountains and listening to them and dream right along with them. She thought they were that good.

There's not much difference between a starving artist and a starving band, however. There were lots of good bands out there and not enough record labels to go around, especially since the music market had collapsed. Just getting through to a decision-maker was almost impossible. And Brian was no better at self-promotion than Jill. He might have been worse. He was all about the music, which is what he loved, and seemed to have a blind faith that the business thing would work out for itself in the end.

Over the years Jill gave more and more of herself to just keeping things going. She gave up her art to pay the bills. That's what she was doing at the restaurant. At thirty-three, she was disillusioned and tired. She was worn out with dreaming for Brian and never having those dreams come true. She was worn out with seeing her pictures in the loft and not seeing them hanging in a gallery; with the fact that they were not being seen and seemed to have no chance to go anywhere but her loft.

That was why she stopped painting. It seemed futile, pointless. There was too much to do, with work and housework and taking care of Peter. Painting was a full-time thing in itself. She could not just go up to the loft on a schedule and brush on a few strokes. That wasn't how she worked. When she was painting she was completely absorbed by the painting. Otherwise she could not do her best work. Otherwise it was just workmanship and nothing else, no inspiration, no ecstasy. She was not interested in that. She would rather not do it at all.

She stopped painting one day when it seemed to her there were better things to do. Then she lost interest in it. The smell of paint that she used to love so much just began to seem smelly to her. She went up to the studio and cleaned up her merry mess and put everything away. She told herself this was so she would be organized and ready when she started again, but she knew it wasn't true. She wanted everything to be neat because she was done. She was tying up the loose ends of her life.

But now she felt something stirring again. Of course she knew why. It was because of Josh and his reaction to the paintings. "You have to keep on painting." She played the mental tape of him saying these words over and over again. His abrupt departure was a bit of a sour note, awkward and strange, but it did not detract from her happiness. Not really. She just lay there in the sun and reveled in the praise that was so freely and so genuinely given.

Eventually she roused herself from this delightful reverie, like someone who is afraid of overindulging in sugar, for fear it will lose its sweetness, and made herself a salad for lunch. She poured some raspberry dressing over it and sat at the kitchen island pushing it around with her fork. Then she realized she wasn't really hungry for salad. She loved salad, but she was hungry for something else. She wanted to paint.

She left the salad on the counter and walked upstairs as if in a trance. It had been so long since she had gone to the loft with the intention to paint. She unpacked her things, her familiar old friends, and put them out neatly, with tender care. She picked a large canvas out of the closet and put it on her favorite easel, the one she always used when the fire came upon her. She mixed her paints for a while, musing, enjoying the thing she had always loved so much, the thing she seemed born to do.

Then she took a deep breath and started to paint. For the first time, she did not think about what she was painting. She did not imagine a specific scene; she just started stroking the canvas lovingly with her brush. She mixed up some lighter colors and made a few more strokes. Only then did it dawn on her that she was painting a portrait. There was an inchoate human shape in there somewhere. Then she saw with some embarrassment who it was. She had fashioned a white curly lock. She was painting Josh.

Jill stood back and looked at it and shook her head. Really? Josh? But it was too late. The painting had already bound itself to her. She had begun to feel the same tenderness toward it that she felt toward all her paintings, her children. She wanted it to be good. No, she wanted it to be great. This urge, which was very much part of her being, soon eclipsed her initial reservations. The painting possessed her.

She worked quickly—much more quickly than she usually did—but the results pleased her. The painting seemed to paint itself. She was not so much the painter as the medium through which it was coming into being. She was so absorbed that she did not even stop when Peter arrived home from school. He barely responded to her cheerful greeting, like a typical teenager, eager to let her know that he didn't need her, but she wasn't offended. She took it as a sign that she could keep right on painting.

December night fell early and she was still painting feverishly. Then she heard Brian coming through the door. To her relief, he had brought pizza. Actually he was in a rare good mood. It was full moon and he was on his way out to yet another band rehearsal. He and Peter ate the pizza while watching an episode of *Heroes*. Jill kept right on painting until she finally went to bed, exhausted. She had a dream about Josh. He was with her in a gallery and they were looking at her paintings. She did not want this dream to end. She did not wake up when Brian came home.

She didn't have to work the next day, so she sent Peter and Brian off with lunch and a kiss and went right back to her painting. She painted literally all day long without stopping. Working at such a frenetic pace, she managed to finish before the school bus arrived at three. Normally it could take her months to finish a painting, with all the preliminary drawings and all the details and revisions and her relentless drive to perfection. But it was not so much perfection that she was driving for this time. She was more interested in getting the painting out of her head and onto the canvas.

When she finished, she stopped and looked at it—and then she was a little shocked at what she had done. It was a very good likeness of Josh. And that was the problem. She had painted a picture of another man, a very passionate picture, dark and glowering. She had never painted Brian in all the years they were together. There were no glowering pictures of him in the gallery that hung in her loft. But now there was one of Josh, the mysterious stranger. It stuck out like a sore thumb.

She could not leave it there. It was still wet, but she took it and put it in the closet where she kept her canvases. It was too raw, too open. What was she thinking? Was she falling in love with the strange man who seemed so interested in her and her art? She put the painting away but could not get it out of her mind. Many times a day she would go to the closet and peek at it. She told herself this was because she wanted to see if it was dry, but it wasn't the real reason. She just wanted to look at the painting.

But was that so strange? Didn't she always enjoy looking at the paintings she made after she was done, her creations? Why did she feel so guilty about this one?

She knew why. Otherwise she wouldn't have put it in the closet.

CHANGES

W HICH MAY BE A GOOD TIME to discuss the very interesting topic of Jill and Brian. Like so many couples of their generation, they were having a hard time making a commitment to marriage. Or rather Brian was. Jill wanted to get married from the first time she met him, but Brian wanted to wait. His excuse was always the same: he wanted to get them in a "better position" for marriage, whatever that meant. Over the years this excuse became flimsier and flimsier to Jill's ears.

Peter came along in their senior year in college. He was a surprise but not a wholly unwelcome one. They felt they were committed to each other even without the wedding rings to show it. Another thing that came along was Spectrum, Brian's band. Basically it was because of the band that their lives were on hold. It became the top priority in Brian's life. It wasn't so much that he was opposed to marriage as he never got around to proposing.

The years went by and began to pile up like winter snow and Brian's big break never seemed to come. There were lots of good things that happened, tantalizing glimpses of success, but the golden ring proved elusive. Brian spent more and more time practicing and traveling with the band and doing tech things, and after a while they seemed to drift apart. Even in bed they drifted apart, way too early for a couple just barely in their thirties.

Jill was getting tired of putting her life on hold. Actually in the last year she had begun to entertain thoughts about making some changes. She still loved Brian, in a way; she cared for him and wished him well. But he had changed. The band had taken a heavy toll on their relationship. Actually at this point it didn't seem like much of a relationship at all. It was not like they spent their evenings together cuddling on the couch. He was hardly ever around for that. She was left with the tasks of taking care of Peter and the house pretty much by herself.

But did she have to take care of him, too? Did she have to do everything just so he could pursue his dream, which was beginning to seem increasingly dubious? It was one thing to clean up after him and do his laundry and take care of all the bills and get the oil and tires changed on his truck while there was still some hope of Spectrum making it. Jill didn't mind giving of herself for someone she loved. After all, he was working hard. He had a full-time job plus he was rehearsing with the band every night.

Over the years this routine began to grind her down, however. She felt for Brian, she understood what the band meant to him, but were they going to spend their entire lives in a holding pattern? Was it always going to be like this—no companionship? Brian's personal habits had become troubling as well. He had fallen into the band lifestyle. It is one thing to drink too much beer when you are twenty-two and come home acting goofy; it's quite another when you are thirty-three and you have a young son in the house.

It wasn't that Brian was abusive when he was drunk, but he was not Brian. She was not afraid of him, but she found herself walking on eggshells around him; and she was tired of walking on eggshells. She thought she understood. He was probably depressed. After all, he had staked his whole life and identity on the band. But she did not drink herself and did not understand why anyone else needed to drink. If anything the drinking was probably getting in the way of success, taking up his energy.

Jill was just as frustrated as he was by the glass ceiling that seemed to have settled over the band. But it seemed like it was partly his fault. He was not doing the things he needed to do. He preferred having a beer with his friends to working on publicity. Also he was too modest. She admired his modesty, but she knew how much harder it was to be noticed when one was not actively raising one's hand. She knew how much competition there was out there to become America's next great band.

She had begun to lose respect for Brian. It seemed like he did not want to grow up. He wanted to be with his band and his beer-drinking buddies and didn't show much interest in spending time with her or Peter. She was lonely and tired and felt like he didn't respect her, but he rebuffed any attempt on her part to make her feelings known or bring up things that he perceived to be negative. At that point they were barely even talking to each other. Jill was full of resentments that she was unable to keep from storing up, and Brian kept insisting that nothing was wrong.

One of those resentments was her feeling that Brian had made her give up her painting. He had never been very supportive. He praised her, but she never felt he took it seriously. He did not understand that painting was at least as important to her as his band was to him and showed no sign of making concessions to her passion. He expected her to take care of him and Peter and the house and also work to help pay the bills so he could have the freedom he needed to devote himself to the band. He told her it was what he had to do if they were ever going to realize their dreams. It took total dedication.

This was what made her give up painting, she told herself. It wasn't exactly true, or at least it wasn't the whole story, but there was some truth in it. She was a total immersion painter. She could not do her best work unless she had long stretches of time where she could just walk into her canvases and live there. She had been able to find the time in the early years, when Peter was a baby. But now she was working more hours and Peter was thirteen and seemed to take more of her time than ever, with soccer and hockey and all the other things kids get themselves into. Brian did not help with any of that. She couldn't even get him to come to the teacher-parent conferences.

Jill resented Brian when she thought about the fact that she didn't go upstairs to paint anymore. She resented him even more when she did go upstairs and saw everything put away. It was like her life had been put away. And what was the gratitude she received for this sacrifice? There wasn't any. Brian still assumed he was going to make it big. He seemed to think she should be thanking him. It was true that he had a job and contributed to the family budget, minus beer money and band expenses. But Jill could not help thinking that she would be better off without him. At least she would only have to take care of herself and Peter.

The thing she missed most, though, was the companionship. She longed for it. They used to have so much fun together. They were best friends when they were younger, but not anymore. Not for a long time. What was the reason for being together if the only time they saw each other was when she handed him a sandwich in the morning and put his dinner on the table at night? Jill wanted someone to hold, and he did not seem willing to take that role. Would he ever be willing? She did not know. He seemed to become more cold and distant as the years went by.

It was holiday season and Jill loved the holidays, but she was feeling down. Thanksgiving was a disaster. They went to Brian's parents' house and listened to his sister argue bitterly with his father about politics all day long. And now Christmas was coming, but Jill did not feel the Christmas spirit. What she felt instead was the burden of having to clean and decorate the house and send cards and buy presents for Peter and all their family and friends with the money they didn't have and without any help from Brian, who of course was busy with the band.

But now so much had changed—because of Josh. Where there had been nothing but gray now there was bright sky again. The most important thing was his support. She had the positive reinforcement she needed. Some artists don't seem to need it. Van Gogh had none; Melville went to his grave thinking he was a failure. Some artists have the kind of drive that enables them to keep going even when they have no applause from the outside world and no assurance that their work has value.

Jill was not like that. She did not need Warhol-like adulation or worldwide fame, but she needed something to make her feel she was not wasting her time. Her natural modesty made her feel the need for some positive reflection from the outside world. She did not have a big ego or an indomitable belief in her own artistry. She felt that what she was doing had value, but she was too much aware of her own vanity to let herself believe it without some confirmation. And this is just what Josh had given her. It was because of him that she was painting again.

Josh had brought light into her life by taking a strong interest in her art. She felt energized. But was this the only reason that she spent so much time thinking about him? Was it just his support that made her feel happy or something else? Something about Josh made her smile. It had been some time since she felt like smiling, and she was grateful for that. He was charming in his own way, almost endearing, from his impractical dress overcoat to the improbable white splash on his forehead. It was cute, how he talked to her, how he tried to be reassuring. He was very considerate in his own way.

He was her rescuer. He picked up her keys in the parking lot and inspired her to start painting again. True, he was not your typical knight errant. He was thin and not very robust. He dressed like the art lover he professed himself to be instead of wearing the plain, sturdy clothes that made sense at that time of year in her part of the world. She was not surprised when he told her he was sick because he looked sick. He was pale and drawn. There was something else about him, too, something she couldn't quite put her finger on. He did not seem comfortable in his own shoes.

She thought about the first time she had seen him, when he picked up her keys and wiped the snow off her windows. In one sense it was endearing, but in another sense it was extremely odd. He had appeared at her side in a flash, almost as if he had been watching her and waiting for an opportunity. This thought made her shiver. She definitely did not like the idea of strangers watching her. But he had done nothing untoward. He had not attempted to take advantage of her in any way. He acted like a perfect gentleman. She took his offer to follow her home in the spirit in which it was offered.

But this was not the only thing that was strange about him. She thought of him sitting there in the restaurant and staring at his coffee as if he were in a trance. He definitely did not fit in with the ruddy country folk who were enjoying their eggs and bacon—but she loved the country folk and felt a little put off by this show of difference, as it seemed to her. Then she brought him a delicious breakfast and he did not touch it. He just sat there staring at it. Why buy a breakfast if you have no intention of eating it? Was it because you did not like the honest country food? If so, Jill was not impressed. If there was one thing she couldn't stand it was snobbery.

Jill had mixed feelings about Josh. But she could not deny she had feelings. A couple of weeks went by and there was no sign of him—and she was surprised at how distressing this was. She found herself glancing around the parking lot, hoping for him to materialize again. Every time she walked out of the restaurant kitchen she checked the booths to see if he was there. She even kept her eyes open in the grocery store, the only other place in town she visited with any regularity.

Then a few days before Christmas she was startled to see Josh at the restaurant, sitting in the same booth as before. She did not hesitate. She went right up to him.

"Hello there! Feeling any better?" she said a little saucily.

"What do you mean?" he replied. He would not look at her. It was strange, as if he didn't know her.

"You seemed a little under the weather the last time I saw you."

"Oh—that. No, I'm fully recovered. I think."

"So what can I get you? A cup of coffee?"

"Coffee's fine. I'm not very hungry."

"Then what are you doing in a restaurant?" she teased.

"To tell you the truth, I don't know. It just looked so inviting in here, so cheerful."

"You mean you didn't come to see me?"

"Maybe I did. That's what scares me."

"Scares you! Why?"

"I can't tell you." He still would not look at her. She did not know what to say. "Listen, maybe I should go. Tell me to go, if you want me to. I won't be offended. I don't belong here anyway."

"Why would I want to do that? I have something to show you."

"Really? What?"

"A new painting. I got kind of inspired after you left."

Now he did look up. "I'm so happy to hear you say that. I really am. I can't even tell you how it makes me feel."

"Well? Do you want to see it?"

"I would love to. Is it here?"

"No, of course not. It's home."

"Oh—then I don't know…"

"Why? It didn't stop you last time."

"I told you, I'm afraid."

"Of what? Brian? He's at work."

"No, not Brian. Something else."

"Just come over. I think you'll like it. There's a little surprise for you."

He could not resist her. The happiness he felt when he was with her was coming back like a wave, in spite of his misgivings. "Should I follow you over after work, like last time?"

"That would be fine. And by the way, you don't have to stay if you don't want to. I know you didn't come in to eat."

She smiled at him and headed for the kitchen. When she looked back he was already gone. She glanced over toward the door but there was no sign of him. He must have been in a hurry. She found herself laughing. It was one of the strangest conversations she'd ever had in her life. He really was odd. And what was all this about being "afraid"? Was it what it sounded like? Was Josh actually a romantic under that cool exterior of his—afraid of losing his heart?

The rest of the morning dragged by. Jill took orders but then realized she wasn't listening and had to take them all over again. She went through her usual routine but the only thing she could think about was her rendezvous with Josh. She could not wait to get out of there and show him the new painting...of him. She laughed to herself. It was going to be so much fun.

Finally she ran out of the restaurant and found him parked by her car, just like before. Once again he waited until she was out of the lot before leaving. She was happy to see his car show up in her rear-view mirror—but then she began having second thoughts. This was now the second time he had come to her house when Brian and Peter were not home.

It was kind of forward. It was sending a message she was not sure she was ready to send. She did not want him to think she was in love with him. Last time he invited himself, but in this case the invitation came from her. It was a significant difference. What if he misunderstood her? His strange talk at the restaurant made her think he might. It sounded like love talk. Did she want it to be love talk?

But then she had another change of heart as she pulled in the driveway. After all, there was nothing she wanted more than to show Josh the painting. She was actually giggling as she unlocked the door. He looked at her quizzically but she couldn't help herself.

They went straight up to the loft. Hardly a word was said, which was a little spooky for Jill. She was too nervous and excited to say anything. Then as she approached the closet another thought came over her. Did she really have the courage to show him the painting? It was, well, hot. There was a rakish quality to him that she had not put in there intentionally. It was a painting that lots of women would probably love in the age of *Fifty Shades of Grey*.

She went to the closet and touched the frames of her canvases with her fingertips as she felt her way to the lonely painting in the back—she did not bother to pull the light string. Soon enough she found it and realized that the paint was still not completely dry. She picked it up carefully and carried it out to the loft. What would he think? Would he like it?

Josh was looking at *Cosette*, or pretending to. She carried the new painting over to the work easel and put it in its rightful place, where it had not been for two weeks.

"Come over," she said, waving with excitement.

He walked in her direction. "That looks like me," he said after a surprised pause.

"It is you," she said, suppressing her laugher.

"You painted a picture of me? Why?"

"Why not? You got me painting again. What do you think?"

He looked at it. "I think it's incredible. I don't mean the likeness. I'm not in a position to judge that. But the perspective, the thick strokes, the richness of the colors."

"I don't know. As I look at it now it seems a little—dark."

"You wanted it to be dark. You see me as dark, and that's why you want to know what I think about it. You want to know if you're right and I am dark."

"Well, I did meet you in the dark, if you remember. But no; I didn't mean you are dark. I mean the painting is dark, the overall tone. Compared to my other paintings."

"That's exactly my point. I make the painting dark."

Jill had talked herself into a trap and decided to change the subject. "So—can I make you something to drink? How about a cup of tea?"

"Can I stay up here and look at the paintings?"

"Of course. I'll let you know when it's ready."

She made her way down the spiral staircase and put a kettle on the stove. Then she put together a plate of some scones and cookies and red grapes. She steeped the tea in a pot and carried everything over to the table in the great room. She called to Josh, who came down reluctantly.

"Do I really look like that?" he said as she poured them each a cup.

"What do you mean?"

"Oh, you know. Kind of pale. Sickly."

"Have you looked in the mirror lately?" she said with a laugh. Josh did not laugh. He was afraid of looking in the mirror.

"I don't know. I guess I haven't been myself."

"You mean you're not always like this?"

"Oh no, not at all. I wish you had seen me last summer. I had quite the tan."

"Maybe you should see a doctor."

"My father is a doctor," Josh said as a new memory came flooding in. So that was why he was reading *The Lancet*. His father had a subscription. "He wanted me to be a doctor too, but I fell in love with art."

"And how did he feel about that?"

"He supported me. He can be kind of overbearing about some things, but he loves art too."

"I wish my father did. He thinks art is a waste of time."

"He has a daughter who paints like Velasquez and Rembrandt. That must mean something to him."

"Not really. And I don't pretend to put myself in the same league with those guys."

"Well, I would. You are a great artist. I think you kind of know it deep down. It's impossible to be as good as you are and have no inkling of it. In any case you should not underestimate yourself."

"I don't think there's any danger of that as long as you're here," she said with a laugh. "But I don't really spend a lot of time thinking about it. When I'm painting, I just want to paint. I put everything else out of my mind."

"That's good. That's the way it should be." He thought for a moment. "By the way, do you happen to know what makes your paintings so different?"

"I'm not exactly sure what you mean."

"It's the love."

"The love?"

"Yes. Your paintings are full of love. You weren't aware of that?"

"Well, I am always looking for something special when I'm thinking about ideas for paintings. Let's just say I tend to throw out anything that goes in the wrong direction."

"You mean in a negative direction."

"Since you put it that way—I do think something has gone missing from painting. I miss it, anyway. And I'm always thinking about how I can put it back in."

He looked out the window and was quiet for a moment. "Mind if I say something that's probably going to sound completely crazy?"

"Help yourself! I like crazy," she said with a smile.

"Something new has been happening to me lately. It's new for me, anyway. It's probably old-hat to someone like you. I'm going to call it 'love,' because I don't know what else to call it. My father would call it a firing of neurons, but that's his thing. It's a sort of warm feeling. I don't really have the words to describe it. I'm almost tempted to call it a rainbow love, since you're a painter. It has colors." He stopped and looked at her. "Is any of this ringing a bell?"

"Not really. Should it?"

"Well, that's what I'm wondering about. Here's the thing. It seems like this feeling is somehow connected with you. Or at least the only time I have it is when I'm with you or looking at your paintings. Actually the only time I feel alive is when I'm with you."

Jill looked at him blankly. "I'm not sure I understand."

"I don't either. That's what's so strange about it. I don't know why I'm here. Meeting you and coming here and seeing the paintings—it's like it is all connected somehow. But I don't know how. Does that make sense? No, of course not. I talk nonsense and ask you if it makes sense."

"I think it kind of makes sense. I'm not sure."

"I want to be here, and yet I'm afraid to be here. I'm kind of terrified of it, to be honest. I've hurt so many people in my life. I'm afraid of hurting you."

"You can't hurt me," she said, laughing off his seriousness. "You're my main cheerleader."

"No, I'm not talking about that." He stopped. "I should go. I've outstayed my welcome."

"You haven't even touched your tea."

"No, I need to go. I'm feeling good right now, sitting here talking to you, better than I've felt in a long time. I don't want to jeopardize anything."

He pulled himself to his feet. She did not attempt to stop him. In the doorway he said goodbye and started to reach out as if he wanted to hug her—and then got a very strange look on his face, almost like panic. He turned and walked down the steps to his car.

She had a lot to think about. She was pleased by his positive reaction to the painting. She wasn't sure where he was trying to go with the "dark" thing, but other than that she was pleased. And she could not help feeling flattered by what he said about her as a painter. She did not let herself believe it, but neither did she dismiss it as nothing. She squirreled it away as motivation.

As for the rest—what could she say? It seemed like he was in love with her. He had a strange way of putting it, but Josh was strange. She sensed something almost like sadness as he talked about his "rainbow love." Was it because she was with someone else, unattainable? If so, she was glad he could not read her mind. She *wanted* him to think that way. She was pretty sure she did.

BLUNDER

J ILL WAS VERY HAPPY, if confused, after this second conversation with Josh. Certainly his reaction to the painting was all she could have hoped for and more. *What* she was hoping for was confirmation that her work had value and she was not completely self-deluded.

She knew her paintings were not amenable to the spirit of the age. The first time she became aware of this was in college. Her professors wanted her to go places where she did not want to go and adopt ideas that seemed used up and useless to her. They shook their heads at the subjects she chose; they warned her to be careful. They thought of themselves as faithful counselors, but to her mind they were Polonius, protecting an illegitimate power. She was not interested in hanging onto the past. She wanted to explore the possibility of something new.

She had been rejected many times by many galleries. They were always category rejections. She was ruled out because she was not like the others. Every time she ran into a steel door she lost confidence in herself. It made it difficult for her to pick up a brush and do the hard work of painting, which was highly demanding, both physically and emotionally. When she quit she told herself she was just taking a break; but the longer she broke the more she drifted away from the great stream of art. It was such hard work, and lately she had begun to wonder if she could even do it anymore.

She would go upstairs and look at her pictures and they seemed pretty good to *her*; but she had no way of knowing. She had no one to tell her they had value or reassure her about the difficult path she was on. Swimming against the tide requires a stout resolve, and lately her strength had been flagging. She lost her momentum. She lost her passion for painting. She looked at what was going on in the art world and felt her resistance melt away. They were too strong. They were filled with fine words and arguments, and she was just a waitress from Vermont.

Until Josh came along, that is. Josh loved her paintings. He thought the new painting of him was "incredible." Jill was not used to hearing such words applied to her art, especially from someone who actually seemed to know what he was talking about. He compared her to two of the greatest painters in history, two painters she respected and loved. She did not trust herself to believe him, but neither was she deaf to his kind words. The flame that had almost died out was rekindling. She felt her strength returning and her enthusiasm.

She remembered when he called her a humanist. The strong men of the art world also liked to call themselves "humanists," but as far as she was concerned their art was anti-human. They were destroyers, not healers. Jill wanted to make art for the purpose of feeding and mending the human soul. This was the humanism of the Renaissance and most of her heroes. For Josh to call her a humanist was a great gift to her. It gave her a new way to think about herself and a new reason to paint.

She was stunned when he said her art was based on love. It was surprising to hear him say something like that. He didn't seem like the type. More importantly, it was a revelation. The moment he said it she knew it was true. It solidified her concept of what she was trying to accomplish as an artist. Whole new possibilities opened themselves up to her—not because she had changed, but because she finally had a clear vision of what she was about.

But this was not the only reason why his visit had been so electric. His description of her paintings as an expression of love led him down other fascinating paths as well. There was the enigmatic disquisition on "rainbow love," a new and higher kind of love, apparently; a love that could not be described in words. And it seemed this rainbow love was somehow connected with her. She did not know how, exactly. He did not come right out and say he loved her. But he wouldn't do that, would he? It wasn't Josh.

The astonishing thing was that he said it at all. He had sat there on the couch talking tenderly about love. It seemed strange when it was happening and it seemed even stranger now. Men just don't do that sort of thing. She could not imagine her father doing it. Certainly not Brian. And Josh, of all people—the art connoisseur with the flamboyant lock of hair. She did not know what to think.

And then there was this: "The only time I feel alive is when I'm with you." To her this was the most romantic—if tragic—thing a man could say to a woman. She had heard men say things like "I couldn't live without you." Brian used to say this to her, a long time ago. But what Josh said was different. It was the statement of someone who had died in his own mind. It suggested wilderness and wasteland and abandonment. It seemed he believed that love can bring back the dead.

What could all this love-talk mean? The obvious interpretation was he had feelings for her. He said she was the reason for the rainbow love; it seemed pretty straightforward. But in another sense it was far from straightforward. The very fact that the meaning seemed obvious made her wonder if it really was obvious. He did not act like an ardent lover while he was sitting there on the couch. He spoke in a tone of quiet reflection—disinterested, thoughtful, clear. He did not look at her or try to move closer. He took the first opportunity to run away.

Which brought her to the other thing. He said he was afraid of hurting her. She smiled when she thought about this. He did not need to be afraid. She was not in love with him—certainly not as much as he seemed to be with her. She was not so much in love that she could get hurt. If anything he was the one who was in danger of getting hurt, if his warm words were any indication of where his heart was. She was glad Josh had come into her life but could not entertain any serious thoughts about him even if she had been so inclined—not now. She looked around the room at Brian's things and Peter's things scattered everywhere. She looked at the photos of them on the wall. Not now. No.

After all, Brian would be coming home in a few hours, her partner of fourteen years, the father of her son, her—friend. She tried to come up with a different word but couldn't. And this made her want to cry. Was that all Brian was to her now? Her friend?

Then again, was he even that? His beer-drinking buddies seemed like better friends in his mind than Jill. He laughed and talked with them. He lived with her and shared her bed, but they didn't really share it, did they? It wasn't like that and hadn't been for a long time. He didn't hold her anymore. He used to hold her every night.

Brian had not paid any attention to her in years. There were times when she would come to the bedroom fresh from a hot shower, fragrant and pink, and remove her bathrobe to finish toweling off—and it was like she wasn't even there. He did not seem to notice. This was painful for Jill. She wanted him to want her that way. She wanted him to think of her as being desirable, even if she was not the fresh-faced girl he had met in college.

She was not unattractive, she thought. She had a pretty face; at least that's what people told her. She had a trim body that she kept fit with a disciplined diet and walks through the woods. Why couldn't he show at least some appreciation? Why did he seem to stiffen up when she tried to embrace him? Was he interested in someone else? Maybe one of these rich women parading around in bikinis that they meet on the job—the ones he and the boys laughed about on Friday nights when they were sharing a cold beer and didn't think she was listening?

Jill did not know why Brian seemed to have stopped loving her. All she knew was he had. It would be different if they were married. In that case the sheer tidal forces of society might have held them together. But what was holding them together now, when Brian never had any time for her and was never home? Other than Peter and a mortgage, what was holding them together? Was she willing to spend her life with someone who did not appear to love her and was unwilling to commit to her? Who forgot her birthday every year? Who had long ago forgotten their anniversary, which was not really an anniversary but just the day of their first date? Who did not do anything special for her on Mother's Day because, after all, that was a scam for married people?

And then along comes this stranger and he has an obvious interest in her—how could she not be flattered? How could she not experience some happiness at his appreciation of her both as an artist and as a woman? Jill did not believe in being unfaithful, but she and Brian were not married. There was no vow of faithfulness. There was an implied vow from the love they once had for each other, but neither one of them said "I love you"

THE VISITOR

anymore. Jill had gone on saying it long after Brian stopped, for years in fact. But she could no longer force the words to come out—because she was not sure if she believed them.

That's why she had been thinking about leaving him. Seriously thinking about it for quite some time. She could not see them going on this way forever. She was tired of being embarrassed when she tried to explain their status at church or Peter's school, tired of seeing the question mark in her parents' eyes and their worry. She wanted to get married, but Brian would not even discuss it. He had framed things long ago by saying it was in her best interest as long as he was pursuing success with the band. This was the story he had carried forward for fourteen years, and she could not break through.

Jill was getting tired of being part of Brian's story. The excuse wore thin, and then she stopped believing it. The truth was he did not want to marry her. That was how it seemed to her. She had been avoiding this painful conclusion for years, but she couldn't put it off forever, not after she turned thirty and began to realize that this was her life; it was really happening and there were no mulligans. She had been fooling herself about him out of her good nature, but at some point you have to stop fooling yourself and take a hard look at your situation and do what's right for you...and Peter.

Would he ever get over his obsession with the band? There was certainly no sign of letting go. He might become frustrated and lose interest over time, if they never broke through, which seemed increasingly likely; but how long would it take? Another ten years? Did she really want to stay in the kind of relationship they had now for ten more years? It would kill her poor father if she did. He had never agreed with her arrangement with Brian in the first place. It might even kill her.

She wanted to have more children but was afraid to. It was hard enough as it was on Peter, coming from a house where the parents were not married. Some of the kids at school made fun of him. She knew they were just picking up signals from their parents, but this did not make it any easier. And to some degree she agreed with them. She agreed that children should have the stability of a mother and a father who were publicly committed to their well-being. Besides, how could she have children without Brian's participation? He had not made love to her in over a year.

Yes, Jill had been thinking for some time that maybe it was time for a new start. She doubted Brian would be hurt very much by a break-up. It seemed to her they had broken up long ago, as far as he was concerned. At least that's what his actions told her. Who knows, maybe he would be relieved. Maybe he wanted to break up but was afraid to tell her, or maybe he was just hanging around because of inertia. In any case he couldn't expect her to wait forever. If he did not want to marry her, then he could not deny her the possibility of finding someone who would.

She had been trying to screw up the courage to talk with him about it. Many were the times when they were in the kitchen alone and Peter was off riding his bike or in the woods and the words were on the tip of her tongue and she *almost* said something. But she could not bring herself to do it. Somehow she could not bring herself to plunge in, not without some provocation from him or some sign he was thinking the same thing or would at least welcome a frank discussion of their situation and their prospects.

There were no provocations, however—none of the usual dust-ups that couples typically experience. That was the spooky thing. Brian did not even seem engaged enough to get mad at her; or at least that's how she interpreted it. Perhaps this was because they weren't really a couple in his mind. Perhaps he felt so removed from her that he did not even want to fight. There was no passion in their relationship of any kind, and this depressed her. She would almost rather brawl. At least it would make her feel alive.

She made up her mind to talk to him in the summer when Peter was off at camp, but the perfect opportunity never seemed to present itself, or she was not aware of it if it did. Then Peter came home again, which made it harder, since he was always hanging around. He was her Jacob, always around the house, happy at home, even interested in what she was doing in the kitchen. She decided to put off the big conversation until school started. But this time she was determined. She felt she had to say something for the sake of her sanity. Unfortunately their schedules were so crazy, and she was so involved with Peter and school and sports, that there never seemed to be time.

And then the holidays were coming. She could not do it then, for Peter's sake if nothing else. Her plan was to get through the holidays and make a good show of it, if she could—but the New Year would bring a new resolution. The bracing cold of January would harden her resolve and help her make a clean break while she still had time, while she was still young enough to start a new life and find someone who would show her some affection.

Then Josh came along. Was it a sign that the time had come to be firm and to act? He admired her. She could not be sure if it was just because of her art or something more—but there was all the talk about love, and there were all the fits and starts in conversation that tongue-tied lovers are known to have. He had sat there on the couch in the sunlight and talked to her with glowing eyes about a "rainbow love." What man talks to a woman about such things unless he has a particular interest in her? After he left she sat with her fresh, sweet cup of tea and let these thoughts wash over her again and again. She smiled as she thought of him and his earnest words. The more she knew him, the more interesting he became.

But then she came back to earth again, because she looked up on the wall and saw a picture of herself and Brian when they were building the log cabin. It was one of the best times in their life together, such an adventure, camping on the mountain while the building went up, so full of excitement and anticipation. And the result was good. They used a kit but Brian was a very talented carpenter and knew how to make the kit better. The photo was of them standing together on the valley side, holding hands and looking up at it. They were so happy and so proud.

The thing was she still loved Brian on some level and in some inscrutable way. He was still the fresh-faced boy to her with the dark, kind eyes and the dimple; the one in the photograph; the one nobody else really knew except her. He was still the one she'd had so much fun with and dreamed so much about. She had placed herself in him and now she could not just unplace herself, as much as she might want to. It was not that easy. She thought of Eve's curse. Was she cursed?

After all, he did not actually mistreat her. He was kind to her in many ways, and he was a good person at the core, she believed he was. He neglected her, but was it partly her fault? Was she unconsciously pushing him away because of his perceived disinterest? Was it a self-fulfilling prophecy, this idea that he had moved on and no longer had any intention of marrying her or spending his life with her?

The clouds rolled in as she sat there in her chair going over and over these conflicting thoughts and feelings. Then a light snow began to fall and it was pure romance, falling on the pines and hardwood trees and in the meadows and in the silent forests. She sat there entranced, not thinking about the laundry to do or the dishes or the supper or even the woodstove to be stoked; not thinking about any of that but relishing her sweet tea and the magical snow.

It was in this blessed reverie that Jill made a serious mistake. She forgot all about the painting she had left on the easel upstairs. Peter came home from school and she roused herself and hugged him and made him a P&J and started doing all the things she had been neglecting—and then she just forgot about the painting, right out in the open; naked, as it were. It went completely out of her mind.

Dusk came early, as it did in December on the east side of the mountain, the world losing its shape and darkness pressing in against the windows at the ungodly hour of four-thirty. Jill was in the kitchen with all the lights on—she liked a lot of lights in winter—making dinner, humming happily to herself, when Brian came home from work. She greeted him with a perfunctory kiss, maybe a little more distracted than usual, and then she lost track of what he was doing. He was always doing his own thing anyway and it never had anything to do with her.

But then Brian did something he did not often do. He went up to the loft. There was an old Fender amp he kept up there in the closet with her art junk, as he called it, that he had bought second-hand when he was in high school. The amp was well-worn, but it had a particular sound he could not get out of any other. He wanted it for the demo they were making of the new song.

At first he did not notice the new painting. He hadn't bothered to turn on the lights—there was still some natural blue light—and to tell the truth he didn't pay that much attention to her paintings anymore. He went straight to the closet and pulled out the amp from its special place just inside the door. He was on his way back to the stairs when he caught sight of the striking pale figure on the easel. It was twilight, which made the paleness of Josh's face stand out in relief, glowing in an eerie way.

He almost dropped the amp. He came closer and began to have some very strange emotions as he realized what he was looking at. Who was this person in his loft? Who was this man and why was she painting him? He thought she was taking a break from painting. That was what she told him. She had put her things away, but now he looked around and saw the same old familiar mess. Apparently something had changed.

Brian turned on the loft lights and felt his blood run cold. The painting was kind of creepy, but that was not what shocked him. It was the guy. He was smoldering. This was the actual word that came to his mind. *Smoldering.* Who was he? Was it someone she met at the restaurant, one of the galleries? Why was she so interested in him—interested enough to go to the trouble to paint his picture?

Now another dreadful thought took hold of him. Was this what she was working on the night he came home with the pizza? Was that why she was too busy to come down and eat with them? Was she upstairs working on this smoldering portrait while he and Peter were sitting down there on the couch, right below her, watching TV? The thought was like mercury pouring into his ears. It set his head on fire.

He carried the amp downstairs and put it down by the front door with more of a thump than he meant to, since normally he treated it very lovingly. He was angry, upset. There was a strange man in his house and he did not like it one bit. He didn't know what to think. He trusted Jill and gave her a lot of freedom, as he saw the space created by his absences, but maybe he had given her too much. Maybe she had taken this gift of freedom and used it to shop for a better deal.

He tried to control these feelings, suppress them. It was just a painting, he told himself. It didn't mean anything. She did paintings all the time. But the more he tried to put it out of his mind, the more it seemed to mock him. He did not go into the kitchen to get his usual beer, although he needed one. Not with Jill there. Instead he knocked around doing pseudo-band things. He fussed with the equipment, rolled up cords, turned knobs superfluously, all with a little extra snap.

He stayed away from Jill until she called them to dinner, stayed away and pouted in silence, and when he finally did make a grand entrance he was dark and brooding and dangerous. Unfortunately Jill did not notice, which made him even angrier. She was ignoring him! Why wouldn't she pay attention? He glowered some more—nothing. She wouldn't even look at him. It was infuriating.

Then a funny thought occurred to Brian. Didn't he pretty much sit there brooding every night? Didn't he always have his face in his food and nothing to say? Maybe she couldn't tell the difference between his present sulky behavior and his usual sulky behavior. He tried to remember how long it had been that way. When exactly had he descended into the funk that made him want to disappear into himself at the dinner table? A few months ago? Years?

However long it was he didn't like it. The thing was he was a little down. It was the band, it was the job; it was everything. But mostly the band. He sensed their moment slipping away. If they were going to make it, wouldn't it have happened by now? All the rising acts on the music scene were younger than they were. There was Adele. How old was she? And how many Grammies already?

He felt the band was good, he felt they were unique and had something to say, but they just didn't seem to be able to get over the hump. And the longer it went on, the more anxious he became. Lately he had taken to blaming it on his job. On one hand he liked his job. He was a good carpenter and they needed the money. But he was working all day and came home exhausted. He didn't have the energy he needed for the band and the rehearsals. Their weekend performances were actually beginning to slip. Instead of moving to a higher level, they seemed to him to be losing ground.

And why did he need to have a job? For this house. That was another reason why he came home brooding. Everything he saw was painful to him because it reminded him of the need to make money. He wasn't even making enough to keep up with the debts. And then he would look at Jill and he would look at Peter and he would feel guilty for having such thoughts and become even more depressed. It just went round and round.

He was mad about the painting but did not know how to vent his anger. He never really got into fights with Jill. For one thing they were not together enough to get in each other's way. But the truth is he was a little afraid of her. He avoided fights with her because he was afraid of her sharp tongue. And then there was the artist thing, which was also kind of intimidating. Actually everybody was afraid of Jill, although she herself did not seem to be aware of this.

He knew it, and in some ways he was proud of it, of her verbal prowess, when they were out in company. But he could not come up to her wisecracks. She always had the best of him, which was part of the reason why he had become so silent around her in recent years. He knew they had been growing apart and he felt bad about that, but it was easy to grow apart from Jill because there was a bit of the Stranger in her. There was something about her that engendered respect and made you keep your distance.

But now he was mad, he was hurt, and he wanted her to pay attention. He wanted to talk to her about this new painting of hers. He had to know what it was about, why she painted it, what it was doing in his house. The opportunity he was waiting for did not come during dinner; besides, Peter was there, so what could he say? He had practice in half an hour, so he went out to the living area and sat down on the couch and looked at the snow flying about in the light from the porch spots, itching for a fight.

Jill started doing dishes and Peter was still in there. He was talking to her about something he learned in civics. He seemed animated. Brian was surprised. Did they always talk like that? Were they ever going to *stop* talking? And then he couldn't wait any longer. He had to go to rehearsal. It was a big night. They were finishing up a demo for a big-time producer in Memphis named Clark Thompson. They managed to get through to this guy from a friend they had made at one of their concerts in Williamstown. It seemed he was interested. Was this their big break?

They were going all-out, just in case. They had a great new song, Graham had written it with him, and they had been working on it for weeks in the studio, getting it just right. They really needed a producer to help them but they couldn't afford it, so they were going to have to do it themselves, which made it harder and slower-going. Sometimes he thought he was going to burst, he was so sick and tired of all the details Graham was insisting on, but it had to be done. When they went in there it just had to be right.

She was still talking to Peter, still doing SOMETHING in the kitchen, and he had to go. He didn't have time for a big blow-up anyway. He went to the rehearsal and they played and they worked some more on the song but his heart wasn't in it. He was thinking about Jill and the painting. The music did not have the soothing effect it usually had. It did not touch him at all, although he was careful to hide all this from his band-mates.

He got home about eleven-thirty and Jill was sitting there watching *Raymond* and laughing. It made him angry to see her laughing, as if she were laughing at him and his wound. He came in and stomped the snow off his boots and slammed the door behind him. This time she looked up.

"Hey!" she said in her usual friendly way.

"Hey yourself," he groused.

"How did it go? Did you finish?"

"Yeah, we finished. I'm certainly not doing any more."

Now she became aware of his tone. She was looking at him quizzically. "Have you been drinking?"

He lost it. "No, I haven't been drinking. Why the hell would you say that?"

"Is something wrong, then? Was there a problem with the song?"

"No, the song's just fine. That's not what the problem is."

"Can you tell me?"

"I don't know. Maybe you should tell me."

"Tell you what? I don't know what you're talking about."

"That painting upstairs. Count Dracula. What the hell is that supposed to be?"

Jill blinked. She thought she had put the painting away. "You got it. It is Count Dracula."

"I thought you didn't like that stuff," he said skeptically.

"Normally I don't. I surprised myself. My first 'dark' painting."

"You sure that's all it is?"

"I don't know what you mean."

"Yes you do. I can see you do."

Jill just looked at him. He knew he had the upper hand—he knew there had to be more to it than she was admitting—but he also knew he had lost. It was the same old thing all over again. He was never able to get the better of her. He said it was Count Dracula and she agreed with him. What was he supposed to do after that? But he was still fuming. Something was not right.

"I'm going to bed," he growled.

Jill did not reply. She was afraid to. She was caught. What could she say? She had painted a passionate picture of another man. And in fact he had been there that very day admiring the painting. She was glad Brian went to bed. He was angry, and he had caught her by surprise. She needed to think about things. She needed to get her mental house in order before she could talk to him about the painting.

But then she began to wish he hadn't gone to bed. She had a few things she wanted to get off her chest as well. He may be angry about the painting, but she was angry about years of neglect. She was angry about the fact that he was never there and she was always taking care of everything. She was angry about his sense of entitlement, the dirty underwear on the bathroom floor, the piles of dishes in the sink, the raised toilet seat, the apparent inability to take off his boots when he came in from the mud and snow.

Jill started to cry, sitting there all by herself on the couch with *Raymond* going in the background and Christmas coming. It started as a little trickle but became stronger and stronger until it was just gushing out, a violent convulsive cry. She cried for at least a half an hour. She only stopped because she was too exhausted to go on, both from the convulsions and from trying to keep it from Peter.

She sat there trying to gather herself, trying to pray but not quite being able to, not knowing what to pray for and feeling ashamed about that, ashamed and conspicuous, trying to think but not being able to think, because she was full of too many emotions. She went upstairs and put the painting back in the closet, giving it one last long look. Poor Josh! Then she went to the bedroom.

Brian was already asleep, his back to her, snoring. She could smell the booze—he didn't tell the truth about that. She climbed in silently beside him and settled into her usual spot at the very edge of the bed. It took her a long time to get to sleep.

TINSEL

T HE PAINTING WENT BACK INTO THE CLOSET. Brian did not say anything about it the next day, or the day after that. Jill looked at him, she watched him. She was expecting him to say something, but he didn't. And this puzzled her.

She was glad he didn't say anything. She didn't really know how to respond if he did. Could she lie again? She did not want to. She hated lying. Actually she was tempted to come right out and tell him about Josh. But it would just complicate things. It was not because of Josh that she wanted to separate from him. That had been going on for a long time before Josh ever arrived in the scene. She did not want it to seem like she was dumping Brian for Josh. She wanted to be clear about her reasons.

Also Jill did not know how she felt about Josh. It was not like she was romantically involved with him. She did not want Brian to get the wrong impression. He was jealous, but did he have any reason to be? Nothing had happened between her and Josh. He was not exactly forward, not exactly physical. Did she want him to be? She wasn't sure. He was so strange in so many ways.

The one thing she did know was she longed to see him again. She longed to have him come and talk to her about her paintings. It was kindling for her artistic fire and healing for old wounds. She also wanted to hear more about "rainbow love." No, not to flirt with him. She wasn't the flirting type. She was intrigued by it and wanted to know what he had in mind, why it seemed so important to him, why he talked about it in a mystical way. It was surprising to hear something like that from him.

She longed to know more about him, where he came from, why he knew the things he knew about art. She thought about the painting and how she had felt when she was painting it, the passion she felt, which had been absent for some time. She blushed. Was she in love? She honestly did not know. One thing she did know was she was not ready to talk about the painting with Brian. If it came up again, she would have to stick with Count Dracula. Actually it did have the look. She went upstairs and peeked at it again when no one was home and laughed to herself. She couldn't wait to tell Josh about his new nickname.

Fortunately Brian did not seem inclined to ask any more difficult questions. Instead he just sulked. He was even terser than usual, more abrupt in his responses and angular in his motions. They were going to be alone together on Christmas Eve. She and Peter were going to church early, and then Peter was going to her parents' house, to be on the scene for the present-opening ritual in the morning, where Jill and Brian would join them for breakfast.

This is what they had always done since Peter was a toddler and the log cabin was being built. But it meant spending the evening alone with Brian. In the past they had enjoyed this little break. It was their romantic getaway. But not anymore. Jill did not want to be with him at all, never mind alone. She was afraid of him asking about the painting. She was afraid of him not asking and sulking instead. They'd already had a terrible Thanksgiving. Did Christmas Eve have to be ruined as well?

Of course Brian was not going to church with them. He used to, but not anymore. He had to finish the demo. It was supposed to be hand-delivered to Clark Thompson on the 28th by Logan, the friend who was helping them make the connection. Logan was flying down the day after Christmas anyway and offered to help. Jill rolled her eyes when Brian made this excuse, but her back was to him and he didn't see it. She was glad he didn't. She did not want him to know she was having reservations about the band.

Still, he couldn't come to church with them on Christmas Eve? Really? It wasn't like he was not a believer. They didn't talk about this anymore, but at one time he seemed to believe and enjoy going with her to church. Could he not take a couple of short hours out of his busy demo life to spend some time with her and his son? To set a good example, if nothing else? Was this really the signal he wanted to send—that the band comes first in everything? That nothing is sacred but fortune and fame?

It made her angry, but she swallowed her anger. Besides, she was still traumatized over being found out with the painting. She was not going to confront Brian over church because she did not want him to bring up the other matter, especially in front of Peter. She still didn't know what she was going to say if he did. If she stuck with the Dracula story, then Peter would probably be interested. She would have to explain it to him. He might even want to see the painting, which was more than she could handle.

So Jill kept her mouth shut as Brian walked out the door with a six-pack of Indian Pale Ale under his arm. She went to church with Peter and sat in her usual pew and said hi to her friends with a fake smile and tried to be touched by the music and readings but could not. The familiar carols were played and she sang along but there was no joy for her that night, not with everything that was going on; not with the prospect of spending the evening alone with Brian after he finished his six-pack of beer.

She heard the great old readings again, the fall of man, the promise, Abraham and Isaac, the prophecy, the annunciation, the birth. The words and images did not stir her as they usually did. She was not able to focus on them. She looked at the readers and tried to listen but her mind kept wandering to the painting of Josh, as if it were hanging there right in front of her. Why? She was playing a dangerous game with a man she hardly knew and a double game with the father of her son.

Christmas Eve was spoiled in the end not by Brian and his insensitivity but by the lack of purity in her own heart. Her parents took Peter after the service. She kissed him tenderly at the door of their SUV. All of a sudden she did not want to let him go. She was overcome with emotion. Tears started to dribble down her cheeks and then she did let him go because she did not want him to see them, not on Christmas Eve. Her mother saw them, however. She gave her a funny look before stepping into the car.

Oh well, Jill could not help herself. She was in a mess and she did not know how to get out of it or where it was going. It was starting to snow again, the light flakes landing on her nose and in her hair, later the beautiful dance of the snow in her headlights, in the high beams she put on so she could see it better. It was just a flurry; there was not enough to cover the road, so she was not afraid. She gave her heart to the falling snow, so pure. It lifted her spirits a little—made her forget—but not enough.

She arrived at her empty, lonely cabin and turned on all the lights and went to the kitchen to make herself a holiday eggnog. She took the carton out of the refrigerator and opened the door to the liquor cabinet and peered in. What did they put in eggnog again? Wasn't it brandy or something? There wasn't any, so she settled on some of Brian's rye and tapped a little nutmeg on top and went into the living room and sat down to look at the tree.

The eggnog made her feel better, warm. The snow was flying about in the spotlight outside, the tree looked beautiful, she felt herself starting to relax and starting to feel something like gladness. She turned on the stereo and found a station playing ancient Christmas music. It sounded nice, it sounded clean, she needed clean for her emotions, she needed to think, so she left it there.

A long time went by, with her sitting there in a dream, she did not know quite how long, but then she heard Brian's old Bronco pulling into the driveway with its characteristic engine rumble, and she just sat there, anesthetized, she did not move. The door opened and he came in and said hello and she said hello back, and still she did not move.

Something had changed. He seemed to be in a good mood.

"Well, aren't you going to ask me?" he said.

"Ask you what?"

"We finished it! The demo. It sounds great. I'm kind of surprised at how it came out."

"Oh, I'm so happy for you," she said with genuine emotion, and she got up to give him a hug and knew right away he had been celebrating.

"Yeah, something just wasn't quite right. We didn't know what it was, but something was missing. Then Lion came up with this idea for a synthesizer riff between the verses and it was perfect. Just made the whole song take off."

"Did you bring a copy? I'd love to hear it."

"No. We still have a couple of little tweaks to do, but it will definitely be ready for Tuesday. It's definitely going on the plane. Hey—do we have anything to drink?"

"I'm having an eggnog. Want one?"

"Oh yeah—it's Christmas," he said a little sheepishly. "Sorry about the church thing, but we really had to get this done. Good thing we worked on it because this could really wind up putting us over the top."

Jill was glad for him, she really was. She wanted him to succeed almost as much as he did, not because of the glitter and the stardom but because she wanted it for him. She wanted him to be happy. She went to the kitchen and made him what she was having, and what the heck, she made another one for herself, too. She was feeling good and she wanted to feel better.

When she came back Brian was making a fire. She hadn't had the energy to make one herself, but she was glad that he was because she wanted one. She wanted it really to be Christmas Eve. She wanted to feel the joy of the season. She handed him his drink and they sat down on the couch together. He sat down first, and when she sat down she did not sit right next to him. They had gotten out of the habit of doing that, and besides, she felt a little— funny. Almost shy.

He surprised her by moving closer. He never did this. He put his arm around her, and she began to get an alarming notion. Did he have something in mind? He was in an ebullient mood. He almost glowed, and he never glowed anymore, or at least not when he was with her. His hand was on her and it was warm and she could feel intention in it.

Jill was surprised. She did not know how she felt. Her first instinct was to pull away. For one thing, she had made up her mind to leave him and did not want to be sending mixed signals. There was no doubt it would complicate things if his warm touch and loving behavior led to the end they suggested. Sleeping with him would make it much harder to say goodbye when one of her main reasons for wanting to say goodbye was not sleeping with him.

On the other hand, she wanted to do something to make up for the painting. She still felt badly about lying to him. She told herself it wouldn't be so terrible, if it was what he wanted. She could let him have his way. It would be her penance. It would be her way of making it up to him and healing the wound she had caused.

He wanted to play with the toy train they had bought for Peter several years ago and which Peter always set up under the tree and surrounded with a little village. He got down on his knees and turned the train on and watched it go round, its little light on and smokestack smoking, and Brian's eyes shone. And she looked at him and was touched by that, his eyes shining. He gestured to her to come down. He wanted to show her something Peter had done with the village—the little sheep and cows he had added without saying anything to them and purchased with his own money.

Jill smiled and laughed with real delight when she saw them. Brian looked at her when she did this with his head kind of cocked as if he hadn't looked at her before—which he hadn't, not this way, not for a year at least, maybe several years—and then he put his warm hand on her again, he put it on her waist and he looked into her eyes. She felt his hand there, but she was not aroused by it. She was waiting to see what would happen and preparing herself to be accommodating.

Accommodating? Yes. First of all, he was drunk. She did not like it when he got drunk. She also didn't like the idea that he apparently had to get drunk to feel any interest in her. When was the last time he had put his hand on her suggestively, the last time he had looked into her eyes with puppy eyes? She couldn't remember. Literally. That's how long ago it was.

The hand was lying there for a moment, but then it became a gentle caress, slowly at first, barely moving, as if testing to see how she would react, but then a caress. He drew her to himself on the soft plush rug and kissed her passionately. He kissed her as if he were thirsty. She tried to return his kisses in kind. She did not feel the same passion, but she tried to seem like she was feeling it, for his sake, not to disappoint him.

He caressed her back and the outside of her thighs, and then he began to caress her breasts with carpenter's hands, hard and calloused from working with wood but like when they are soft for the wood, when they are caressing the wood because something special needs to be done, the grain needs to be regarded, this was how he caressed her breasts through her blouse, there under the lighted Christmas tree with the fire crackling and little train running and the Christmas music playing in the background.

It was not a caress to Jill, however. It was the touch of a man whom she had ceased to love because he no longer loved her, a man who was only interested in her now because he had been drinking and because he was a man. She kissed him while he caressed her but the thought in her mind was, let it be over. Go ahead and do what you want and do it quickly, and let it be over.

He began to undress her.

"Here?" she said.

"Do you mind?" he said with a besotted smile.

"No, I guess not."

He removed her outer clothing. He took his time, romantically kissing her and caressing her for every button unbuttoned and zipper unzipped. He did not know that this elaborate show of foreplay was not stimulating to her. It did not matter in his present state, and she made sure to seem responsive, to seem to be feeling the same enthusiasm. Then he removed her undergarments and kissed her tenderly all over, warmed by the fire. She ran her fingers through his hair and used the opportunity to indulge in facial expressions that were more appropriate for the feelings she had.

He undressed himself hurriedly. She did not help him. More kissing and caressing—he really was trying hard to please her—and then he was on top of her and going through the familiar motions. That's what they were to her—familiar motions. Her eyes were open and she was looking up at the cathedral ceiling and it was as if she were up there floating around somewhere and looking back at them and at him, going through the familiar motions. There was something faintly ridiculous about it.

She bestirred herself and closed her eyes. This would not do. She was not present, but she didn't want him to realize it because she knew it would bruise him. She tried to get into the spirit of things. She tried to take pleasure in his pleasure but nothing seemed to happen, she was jaunty, she was out of tune with the times, she felt the rug on her back and it was making her itch.

But then something odd happened with her eyes closed. Brian became Josh. Her strange elfin friend came to her and it was no longer her drunken consort on top of her but he. At first she tried to resist this thought, tried to shoo it away, but then she began to feel aroused. She began to feel what Brian wanted her to feel but couldn't feel before because—well, because it was Brian.

There was the sound of the little train and there was the crackling of the warm fire and the smell of hickory and there was the soothing effect of the eggnog, a second one now finished, and there was the thought of Josh, and she began to feel aroused. Her heart rate and respiration increased. She was startled to hear herself moaning. Something was happening to her. Something happened to them together, to her and Josh, oh no it was Brian, it was not Josh. She opened her eyes and it was Brian.

She lay very still and he lay on top of her. He evidently did not want to move, but she could not wait to move, or rather for him to move, now that she had returned into herself. She smelled the booze on him and wanted him to move, to get off her, let her get off the hard floor, the scratchy rug, to be himself again, not paying any attention to her or showing her any love; because it was not Brian she had made love to that night. It was Josh.

Brian did roll away at last and went to the kitchen to put some more rye in his glass. It was over and he was not thinking of her now. She went to the bedroom and wiped herself off and put on her flannel pajamas and got into bed. She lay there on her back in the dark thinking about what had happened. Thinking about Josh.

So she was in love with him after all. This proved it. She wasn't sure before, she wasn't sure how she felt about him, but now it seemed obvious. Didn't it? Josh had come to her in Brian's body. She had summoned him herself. What could it mean but that she loved him and wanted him to come to her? What could it mean but that she had exchanged Brian for Josh in her mind and her affections? That her heart now belonged to someone else?

"Jill? Jill?" Brian was looking for her. He popped his head in the door. "Oh! There you are. You went to bed?"

"I'm really tired," she apologized. "Not used to drinking."

"That's all right. Do you mind if I watch a little TV?"

"Not at all."

"And by the way, thanks. That was great."

"Yes, it was great," she agreed, with a smile that wasn't necessarily meaningful.

It seemed to work. He wandered off to turn off the stereo with its chaste, serene music and turn on some blaring late-night yakfest.

Jill lay there for a while thinking, and then she fell asleep. She dreamed about Josh in many dreams, all of them very strange.

NEWS

S O THEN IT WAS CHRISTMAS, a clear, cold one, and they were driving over to the house where Jill grew up to do the usual Christmas things. Nothing was said about what happened the night before. Brian was more chatty than usual, but it was all about the band and the beautiful sunny winter day and fishing for compliments about the demo Jill had not yet heard.

With four generations on hand, there were four levels of Christmas spirit at the Campbell house. In Peter it was strong as he and his cousins approached the sacred tree with wide eyes. For Jill and Brian, it was still holding on to the spirit and still full of faith in the nostrums but no longer quite so innocent or pure. For Jill's parents, it was another Christmas to look for joy in the children of their children, Jill and her sisters. For Jill's grandmother, it was a time to watch with a tired, quiet smile, watch and wait.

The rest of the week was fairly uneventful. Peter was home from school. Jill worked every day, since it was holiday time and the restaurant was full. But at the end of the week there was some exciting news. Clark Thompson had listened to the demo and liked it. Brian was in seventh heaven. He got plastered on New Year's Eve at Chuck's house (the drummer) and went around kissing all the women, not once but a couple of times, while insisting that he was "going to Memphis like Elvis." Jill watched him with growing levels of alarm and disgust.

It turned out they were serious, however. The whole band actually decided to move to Memphis so they could cut an album with this hot-shot producer, their *Achtung Baby*. And what were they going to live on in the meantime, Jill asked innocently? They already had a plan for that. They were going to get jobs. With six of them splitting the cost, housing would be cheap. And how was she going to pay the mortgage and their bills? He would send money. He swore it.

Jill had mixed feelings about this adventure, to say the least. On one hand, she was excited for them. They all seemed so happy, deliriously happy. They had been dreaming about this for years, and now it all seemed to be coming true. She believed in them. She knew their songs by heart and could imagine them making an album that people would love and want to buy. They had enough good songs for several albums. All they ever needed was an opportunity, and now they finally seemed to have gotten one.

But there were other feelings, too. For almost a year now Jill had been looking forward to the day when she could make a break from Brian and find her own space—but that was not what this was; it was not a real space but a temporal space, and it made it impossible for her to do what she had resolved to do, since she could not bring herself to break up with him just at the point where he was so incandescently happy. She did not want to jeopardize his chances for success in any way.

More than that, there was the little matter of finances. It wasn't like they were rich and could afford to have Brian be away for an indefinite period of time. They were getting by, they weren't doing badly with their various sources of income, living frugally, but could she bank on him getting a decent job where he was going and being able to handle his own expenses and also help with theirs? What reason did he have to think there was any shortage of carpenters in Memphis? Or that anyone would want to hire him?

Then there was just the basic upkeep of the property, especially in winter. Brian did all of the plowing and shoveling and most of the stove wood. These chores, it seemed, were now to fall on her, and Peter, in addition to everything else she was doing. She knew she would have to take more hours at the restaurant to pay their bills. When was she going to find the time to do everything?

One other thing, and this surprised her. Now that he was leaving, she did not know if she wanted him go. It wasn't just the finances or added work; it was something else. She thought she wanted to separate—this was the premise she had been working with for some time—but when she was faced with the reality she was not so sure. It was harder than she thought it would be.

Fourteen years together is a long time. She had a lot invested in the relationship. The thought of giving it up was a little intimidating.

Besides, *she* wanted to be the one to separate. She wanted to make her point and he had come along and stolen her thunder. To go to Memphis and leave her behind was tantamount to saying she didn't mean very much to him anymore. He seemed very glad to part, happy to leave her to her own devices; and she couldn't help resenting him for this, even though she had been planning to do the very same thing herself—or perhaps because of it.

But then again there was Josh, even though she felt a little ashamed at the happiness this thought brought her. She had not seen him for a couple of weeks but he was never far from her mind. She found herself wondering if there was someone new in her life and if Josh was that someone. She did not really want to think this way, but Brian was going away, and he was happy to be going. His happiness was hard on her. She could not help it; she thought of Josh.

Besides, Brian's imminent departure was just an outward sign of something he had done many years ago, as far as Jill was concerned. He had departed from the relationship and married himself to the band and his obsession. Going to Memphis simply meant his separation from her would now take an outward form. Everyone would see the reality that had been there all along.

She was worried about Peter and his reaction to the change in his life. She loved him so much, he was her everything; how did he feel about his dad leaving them and moving a thousand miles away? It was hard to tell. He did not react very much. Boys were so different from girls. Jill wanted him to pour out his heart—she wanted to pour out her own—but Peter was not like that. He was quiet, and this was unsettling.

It had to be difficult for him. Brian was not often present, but when he was they had a good relationship. Peter loved to spend time with him at the studio or the woodworking shop in the barn. He liked splitting and stacking wood with him. Brian was the one who had taught him to skate and ski. In the summer they often went fishing together. Besides, Brian was his father. Jill did not discount it one bit.

And what if she really was interested in Josh? How would she ever explain it to Peter? She could not picture herself doing it. There was a whole history behind her desire to separate from

Brian, but that wouldn't be what Peter saw. He knew nothing about the big chill between them, which she had been so careful to conceal. No, to him it would just seem like she could not wait for his father to go so she could take up with someone else.

On top of that, Josh was so strange, with his pale skin and Delphic pronouncements, so snobbish and lacking in outward warmth or gregariousness. How would Peter feel about him? She was able to overlook his eccentricities because he loved art and so did she; and also, frankly, because he showed an interest in her paintings. But Peter had no such motive to like him. She could not imagine how he would react to the idea of her seeing him. It was almost embarrassing to think about it.

The timing was not right. She decided to put Josh out of her mind. Meanwhile Brian was making his preparations to leave. There was a kind of unreality to the whole thing. He was doing a lot of packing and tying up of loose ends around the house, but Jill was busy with her own things and not very aware of it. They still didn't seem to be able to find time to talk about it as a family. Peter was back in school and involved in hockey and Brian had too many things to do.

The departure date sneaked up on Jill. Before she quite realized what was happening she was standing in the driveway on a Sunday afternoon looking at a caravan of vehicles. The Sprinter was packed with band equipment and the rest were packed to the roof. Jill, Brian and Peter were standing near the Bronco, and Brian was giving her a long hug she didn't feel; and then he hugged Peter, who didn't seem to know what to do with himself. A tear came into her eyes when she looked at them.

Then they were gone. They pulled out of the driveway with honking horns like a flock of migrating geese, and suddenly it was very still on their side of the mountain, eerily still, as it often is in winter when the wind is not blowing. Jill watched Peter all day but could not read him. Whatever he was feeling—if he was feeling anything at all—he was hiding it well. She decided to force the issue at dinner.

"So how are you doing?" she said, with more confidence than she felt.

"Fine," was the inevitable reply, not necessarily snippy, but in a way that indicated a desire not to be drawn into another one of his mother's emotional maelstroms.

"I mean about your dad. Are you okay?" At the word "dad" she felt hot tears rush into her eyes but managed to restrain them.

"Sure. I mean, he has to do this. It's their big chance."

So mature, she said to herself proudly. But what exactly did he mean? "Has to do it in the sense of getting it out of his system?"

"What?" he said, looking at her as if she were crazy. "No—for the band. This could be their big break."

She caught herself. "I hope so. For your father's sake, I really do hope so. Not for my sake, by the way. I hope you realize that. I'm perfectly happy with the way we are. I mean from a material point of view. I don't need a lot of money or things or 'success' to be happy. That's not important to me. In my opinion we're doing just fine as a family and don't have any reason to be envious of anyone else. But your father has worked so hard for this. It would be great if they got a record deal, just great."

Somewhere in the middle of this commentary Jill got lost. She started out with every intention of agreeing with Peter and showing her support for Brian, wound up veering off onto a tangent about the American Dream and its illusions, and managed to botch both.

"I don't know what you're talking about. Are you trying to jinx them?"

She had to laugh. "Not at all. I'm sure they'll do great. They've worked hard, and the new song is fantastic."

This seemed to satisfy him. It sounded like he was reconciled to the change. He didn't mind his father being away if it meant something positive for the band. Interesting, he did not say he would miss him. Of course he wouldn't; Brian was never there. But then Jill felt guilty for having such thoughts. She was focusing on herself and her own problems when something more important was at stake—Peter's relationship with his father. She did not know if Peter saw his absences the way she did. Maybe they just seemed natural to him, since he had never known anything else.

She realized she *wanted* him not to miss Brian. She wanted him to be happy without Brian in order to justify the separation she was contemplating. But this was not fair to either one of them. She knew Brian loved Peter, whatever reservations she might have had about his way of showing it; she knew how important it was for a boy to have a father in his life.

Would she be willing to stay with Brian when he came back— for Peter's sake? That is, if it became clear that Peter wanted them to stay together? This was a hard question. She had been staying with Brian for Peter's sake for many years and was not sure how much longer she could go on, not without some changes. On the other hand she couldn't quite picture herself telling Peter they were separating. It would be even harder than telling Brian himself.

These thoughts occupied her until she went to bed; then, when she was all alone in her room, with no Brian snoring beside her, she thought of Josh. She tried to stop herself but couldn't. She tried to interpose Peter and his face between herself and Josh, but that didn't work either. She was there alone in her bed and Josh was insisting on filling her mind. Where, to tell the truth, he had been coming for some time.

He had a right to, didn't he? He was supportive of her. He was her champion. Jill craved what she was getting from Josh, after suffering through so many years of neglect. She had plenty of reasons for locking him out, but there was one overriding reason for letting him in: he made her feel like she wasn't crazy. He made her feel like her work and her passion and her dreams had not all been for nothing.

She went upstairs the next day, when the bare trees were tapping on the windows, up to her studio and into the closet to have a look at the painting she had made. She understood right away why Brian found it shocking, seeing it now through his eyes. It was sensuous in an eerie way, like a hothouse plant, like an orchid. Actually it was kind of unnerving to look at. It had a raw quality not seen in any of her other work. She wondered where it came from. She didn't remember putting it there.

Jill left the painting in its safe place. She went out and sat in the studio in her favorite chair, staring at the snow-covered mountains and wondering where she was going with her life—perhaps not in such concrete terms—just wondering. Then she had an inspiration. She fetched a canvas from the closet and started mixing some paints. She was going to paint Josh again, as a trial, to find out where her head was at; to try to come to terms with her interest or attraction or whatever it was.

She had an inspiration to paint him at the restaurant, sitting in his booth, since it was the scene of two happy interactions, and also because she liked the possibilities. The restaurant was homey in a pleasant way, with its soft beige décor and checkered tablecloths. She wanted to paint Josh in a humble country milieu.

Maybe she wanted to normalize him. She liked the pale morning light streaming in through the windows, and she wanted to capture the softness in hard winter, which was expressive to her.

She was excited about this project and did not stop to do any sketches, work out any anatomy puzzles, which can be especially perplexing for a sitting figure. She dove right in with the memory of Josh still fresh in her mind. She really wanted to paint his eyes; what was it about those eyes, what were they trying to tell her? They seemed like kind eyes, but there was no point in fooling herself, they also seemed like sad eyes. The sadness and the kindness—they were somehow mixed together, no?

This was what she wanted to paint; she wanted to capture his soul. It was now the second painting of Josh, and she wondered about that. Of course she wondered! She was already in one relationship with a man who didn't seem to have his feet very firmly planted on the ground. Could she afford another? Oh, yes; she was very much aware that Josh did not seem grounded in the normal way. He did not seem connected to anything. It was not much to build a relationship on.

But was she building a relationship? Was that what she was doing? As far as she could tell, she was just painting in her usual compulsive manner—painting the thing that wanted to come out of her head and onto the canvas. She did not stop. Her misgivings did not slow her down. She worked obsessively, just like the last time. Again it seemed like the picture was painting itself.

Jill worked in furious batches. She would paint all day, after work, as much as she possibly could. After she was sure Peter's homework was done she would upstairs and plunge back into her canvas. She couldn't wait to get back to it. She would start painting, and then she would look up and it was midnight—what happened to the time?

The emergent painting was starting to look quite good. She captured the country mood and sensibility that she wanted to convey, with him in it, her point of contrast, her tension. She labored over the face and eyes lovingly and was pleased with the results. She was surprised at how he looked back at her from the canvas. Sometimes she would talk out loud to him. Sometimes she almost imagined him talking back.

She did not idealize the restaurant. She wanted the happiness to emerge from the hominess. It was the first time she had tried to paint with such a pale palette. She invented a new feel for the painting, working in the way she felt about the nice people she worked for as well as her ambivalence about—well, about everything. She wanted the painting to show her happiness without doing too much violence to how the place actually looked if you were in there on a cold December morning.

Because that was the last time she had seen Josh—back in December. It was almost a month now and she was wondering if she would ever see him again. She finished the painting but did not put it away. She did not feel ashamed of it. She left it right out on the easel in plain view. She had done a good job—it was a work of art. There was no Brian to see it, or anyone else for that matter. Peter never went up to the loft. The painting wouldn't mean anything to him if he did.

The painting did not succeed in resolving her ambivalence, however. It did not achieve its primary goal. The more real she made Josh, the more he stood out from his surroundings. He did not blend in and she wondered if he ever could blend in. These were *her* surroundings, the place where she worked several days a week; her people, her station, her life. The painting was a very good representation of what she had in mind, and Josh came out especially well—but he did not look at home. On the other hand, it was her painting. Maybe she exaggerated him that way?

It was funny that she was thinking so much about Josh just then in the dead of winter, because a few days later he magically appeared in the restaurant parking lot.

"Hi!" he said with an awkward grin, standing by his car.

"Hi yourself," she replied. "I see you still haven't buttoned up that coat of yours."

"Not my style. Do you mind?"

"I think it's kind of silly, but no, I don't mind. You and my son have a lot in common."

"I'll have to meet him some day. I see you survived our last talk."

"Yes, it was very interesting."

"I'm afraid I was a little—forward."

"Oh, I don't know. I wouldn't put it quite that way."

"It's just that I was—you know—surprised. By the painting. It was the last thing I expected."

She smiled. "In that case I have another surprise for you."

"Another painting?"

"Yes, as a matter of fact. Do you want to see it?"

"Would it be all right?"

"Sure. I'm heading home right now. You can come along, if you like."

"I would like that."

Why didn't she come right out and tell him the painting was of him? She almost did, but she wondered what he would think. Two paintings in a row? Two such passionate paintings—because to her the new one was very passionate in its own way—an homage to the possibilities of everyday life—strangely with him in it. Whether or not *he* would see it as being passionate was another matter.

To be honest, she herself did not know why she wanted to paint him. Sometimes she thought of him as her safeguard against painter's block. He was interesting, different. But was this the only reason? Or was she falling in love with him? You can paint one picture of a man and it might mean nothing; but two of the same man? What would he think?

She painted him because she needed a subject to paint. But she couldn't tell him that she loved painting him. She would go into the canvas and make love to him in paint. And who was she kidding? She also loved seeing him. She was glad when she found him hanging around the parking lot. It was all she had been thinking about ever since she finished the painting.

Once again he followed her over the mountain in the gold Mercedes. It was getting to be a habit with them. There were a lot of feelings and emotions in the short ten-minute drive. In one sense it was just like showing her paintings to her professors. On the other hand she seemed to have feelings for him of some kind. Painting two passionate pictures of a man suggests that you are in love with him. Was she in love with him? Did she want to be?

At the same time she was aware that there was an entirely different way of looking at the painting. Josh was not like her. He was a city mouse but she was a country mouse. Country mice are too protected to worry about being stylish; but Jill kind of liked country backwardness. She liked the fact that the girl in the local grocery store had an open face and shy smile and was sweet and deferential. She was fully aware that these things are the product of sheltering. But she liked them.

It wasn't that she didn't like Josh; it was more that she *wasn't* like Josh. She wanted him to like her painting—and to like her— but he did not really fit into her world. No, it was more than that. He made an effort not to fit in. Jill was very much about fitting in and not being too full of herself. She watched her father, a brilliant man, fit in all of his life. He was not being false; he was being his true to his kind self. But Josh was not like her father. Not that he had to be. He just wasn't.

Next thing she knew she was pulling into the driveway with the Mercedes behind her. It was like a dream. She saw herself put the car in park and open the door and step out and close it behind her. Her ears were filled with something that was not an actual sound but was like rushing waters, carrying her along in her little boat. Josh got out of his car too and walked to her, his silly black dress shoes crunching the snow.

They went in. It was an overcast January day, quite dark and gloomy, so she turned on the lights. This made her aware of the darkness and the cold, the lights in the darkness, something being pushed back.

"How about some hot chocolate?" she heard herself saying.

"No, I'm fine. I want to see this great new painting of yours."

"What makes you think it's great?"

"Because you painted it."

"You know, you really don't have to flatter me like that."

"I'm not flattering you. In fact I'm the ultimate truth-teller."

"And why is that?"

"Because I have absolutely nothing to lose."

Jill did not know how to respond to this. She started climbing the stairs with him in tow.

"Something's different about the mountains," he observed.

"Yes—the light. Changing all the time. Every time I walk up these stairs I just thank God for the privilege of living here and having the opportunity to see this."

"I love the way you say that."

"What?"

"You 'thank God.' Not something you hear every day, at least not in the circles I travel in."

"You should get out more," she said over her shoulder.

"You know, you're not as tough as you like people to think."

83

This set her back a bit. She did not think of herself as being "tough" at all. She did not have to try to come up with a witty response, however, because they had reached the top of the stairs and he went straight to the painting like a hummingbird to a red coneflower.

A funny expression came over him as he recognized his own face staring back at him. He gave her a questioning look, almost pained, or even angry.

"I know—don't say it. But it's not really about you."

"It's not? I'm in it."

"I know you are. It's really about how surprised I was to see you in my restaurant—well, not 'my' restaurant—but you know, after the parking lot thing. It's about an unexpected moment of happiness."

"Happiness!" he said with a scornful laugh. "You mean that thing where the serotonin kicks in?"

This was not like the Josh of their last conversation. Something had definitely changed.

"I had something a little nicer in mind," she replied.

"Happiness is not what you think it is, not if I'm involved. I don't belong in your happiness painting. Look at me!"

"It was just an exercise. I wanted to see if I could recreate a feeling that wouldn't seem to go with such a mundane setting."

"I know exactly what you were trying to do. I get it. I could go on and on about this color choice [he pointed], or about this blend and what it means, or what you were thinking when you cast the morning light at this angle. I see exactly what it's about. And it's a fine work of art, a little masterpiece. But you don't know me. You don't know where I come from or anything about me. Believe me, I'm the last person in the world who can make you happy."

"Because you're not happy yourself," she suggested.

"It's probably not a good idea to try to psychoanalyze me. You have no idea what you're dealing with. Believe me, I hardly know myself."

"Then tell me. I'm curious. You're very mysterious, you know."

"I don't know how 'mysterious' I am. I do know there is darkness in the world and women never see it because they insist on infantilizing everyone, including men, whom they do not even begin to understand. 'Oh, he just had a bad childhood. He needs someone like me to come along and heal his wounds.'"

"I wasn't really thinking that about you."

"And yet here I am in your painting. Bad boys do not have to have a bad childhood. And bad things start happening when you think that way. A nice girl gets into a car with some jerk because she doesn't want to believe he's bad. She thinks she knows him better than he knows himself—but that's just it. He doesn't know himself. He is not self-aware. He definitely doesn't care about her the way she cares about him. He doesn't care if she gets hurt."

"I will certainly keep that in mind if you ever offer to drive me anywhere!" Jill said with a laugh, trying to deflect his seriousness.

"I shouldn't be here at all. I don't even know what I'm capable of doing."

"I'm not asking you to 'do' anything. I just wanted to show you my painting."

"The painting in which you have me looking like a bad boy in your nice little restaurant. Only it's not because you see me as a bad boy. It's because you have illusions about me."

"So I take it you don't like the painting."

"No, I love it. All your mastery is on display here. I just don't think the subject is worthy."

"I think there's more to you than you realize, or are letting on. You seem to see yourself as a 'bad boy,' but you're the one who got me to start painting again. And you're also the one, if I recall, who was telling me about a 'rainbow love' the last time you were here."

"Did I say that?" he said, relenting to a chuckle. "Must have been in a flowery mood that day."

"See? That wasn't so hard. You're capable of a little humor."

"Even the devil can laugh."

"So the 'devil' is trying to warn me about getting hurt. Is there a contradiction here?"

Josh looked at her. "No, he cares. It's the only thing he cares about anymore."

Jill was stunned. She did not know how reply.

Josh left soon after. She wanted him to sit on the couch with her and talk like the last time, but he said he was meeting someone. Her heart was full after he left. He seemed to like the painting. He would not have said it if he did not really mean it. The one thing she did feel she knew about him was that he was incapable of being dishonest about painting. He loved it too much.

But speaking of love—what about the rest of the conversation? Josh seemed to be in a very strange mood. He practically came out and called himself a 'bad boy.' He did not pretend to be unaware of the darkness she had inadvertently put into the painting and which embarrassed her now as she looked at it more closely. In fact he embraced it. Was he trying to push her away with all of his dark musings?

He was right—men are complicated. Women, less so—at least in the sense that they want lasting relationships; they want love. Men also seem to want love, but their way of going about it is confusing. After all, she did not go to Josh; he came to her. He helped her in the parking lot and then showed up at the restaurant—and this was before he even knew she was a painter. The shortest line between two points was to conclude that he was attracted to her. Otherwise he would not keep coming back.

And yet he seemed conflicted about this attraction. His way of approaching her was equal parts of pushing her away. He had literally run away from her the first time he had seen her paintings, although only after filling her up with his praise. And now this very strange conversation! All brooding and bad boys and dark hints about himself! How was she supposed to interpret an attempt to push her away in order to protect her? "It's the only thing he cares about anymore."

It seemed like he was attracted to her but afraid of his own attraction. She could not make sense of it any other way. He wanted to see her, as shown by the fact that he kept showing up, but he was not sure if he wanted to get too close; not sure, perhaps, if he was ready for a relationship. This was why he depicted himself as a bad boy. He was trying to warn her not to trust him and his apparent interest. He was trying to protect her from getting hurt.

But who was she kidding? She saw him as a bad boy herself. That's exactly the way she made him look in the painting. She loved his interest in her—it rejuvenated her—it made her want to paint—but did she really want to let someone like Josh into her life—her heart? With his dark forebodings and ominous glances? Set aside the perplexing question of whether they really were dark or just a pose; did she want to get involved with such a lugubrious and slightly ridiculous character?

Was there even a path forward for such a thing, with Peter and Brian and all the complications? The timing did not seem right. Her plan of separating from Brian was made impossible by Brian separating himself from her for a putatively worthy cause. She had an obligation to be Penelope, no matter who came to court her. It occurred to her that Penelope might be a good subject for a painting. She could model herself.

But there was one thing overriding all of these considerations. Josh's interest made her happy. It had been a long time since she could remember being happy. Was it wrong to feel that way now?

BLIZZARD

A WEEK WENT BY, and then two, and there was no sign of Josh. None at all. She looked for him in "all the usual places" and didn't see him. It didn't take long for looking to turn into frustration.

In early February she received some interesting news from Tennessee.

"Clark Thompson definitely likes the band," Brian told her over the phone. "Says he really wants to work with us. In fact it looks like we're going to get together with him in a couple of weeks."

"A couple of weeks! What have you been doing all this time?" Jill said with some alarm that she was not able to conceal, although she tried.

"He's not that easy to see. He's a busy guy. And it's not like we haven't been doing anything. We've been practicing. I've been working."

"Fifteen dollars an hour isn't going to get us anywhere. We've got bills to pay."

"I'll get something better. It was the first thing that came along. I've just been so busy with the band, I haven't had time to look."

"So how long are you going to be down there?"

"I don't know. Could be four, five months."

"Five months!"

"I told you, I don't know. That's what Graham's thinking, but none of us has ever done this before. I don't have any idea how long it takes to take to get a bunch of songs recorded and produced. Plus we're not the only band on his schedule."

"I'm sorry. I didn't mean to react like that. I'm just worried about the finances."

"Well, I am too. I know I'm putting you in a bad spot. This is just something I feel like I have to do."

Jill could not bring herself to give him the response she knew he wanted. She had barely managed to scrape together the February mortgage payment. There was a large electric bill that had gone unpaid. She was working more hours at the restaurant—and seeing Peter less. Brian was sending her money every week, but a couple hundred dollars doesn't go very far.

Also there was another large winter storm headed their way, supposedly a potential blizzard. Jill had been doing the plowing, but she didn't like to do it. The old pick-up truck with its exhaust fumes scared her. And it didn't help her with the walkways. Those she had to do by hand—she was not mechanically inclined and couldn't figure out the cranky old snowblower. There had been two storms since Brian left, smallish ones, and even they had worn her out. Peter came out and bravely helped, but he did not have the longest attention span. Most of the hard work had fallen on her.

And now they were talking about the biggest storm of the season. Jill was dreading it. She did not know how she was going to cope. She saw that it was snowing when she went to bed and she broke down and cried. How was she ever going to get to work? She needed to work, she needed the money. She lay in bed listening to the wind pick up and the sound of the snow flying against the windows. It made her feel helpless.

Something startled her awake in the morning, before the alarm went off, while it was still dark outside with the first hint of dawn. It sounded like metallic scraping sounds. Someone was shoveling. Who could it be? Her father? This thought upset her. She didn't want him helping her with his high blood pressure and heart problems. She didn't even want him shoveling his own snow.

Jill jumped out of bed and threw on some clothes. Winter dressing seemed to take forever, snapping on the boots and everything else that needed to be put on in order to stay warm and protected when the wind chill was down below zero. She hurried to the door and opened it. The storm seemed mostly spent, with just a few flakes lingering here and there, but the damage had definitely been done. Looked like at least twenty inches of fresh powder.

She grabbed the shovel and walked out to the edge of the porch and peered into the dim blue light at the figure at the end of the walk. With a jolt she realized it was not her father. It was Josh.

"What are you doing?" she called down at him, half-laughing with—well, hysteria.

"Oh—hi there," he replied with a wave. "Thought maybe you could use some help."

"Don't you have anything better to do?"

"No, as a matter of fact. I know you're here by yourself."

"You should go home. You look cold."

"Don't worry about me. I like the cold."

"It looks like you've made a pretty good start. Why don't you stop now and let me take over?"

"I've got a better idea. I'll shovel from here, and you shovel from there, and we'll meet in the middle."

Jill smiled at the metaphor. Was it a metaphor? In any case she felt she had protested adequately. She didn't want to take advantage of his good nature, and snow shoveling was clearly not his thing, but a huge burden had been lifted from her shoulders just by having him there. She felt like she could almost love the snow again. She tasted the flakes falling on her lips and they were good.

They shoveled to each other, just as he said. She had to adjust her path a couple of times to make sure they would come together—he didn't seem to be paying attention—and then she couldn't help herself. She gave him a big hug. He had to be cold; he was not dressed for winter work. He felt cold.

"Okay, this is not good," she said. "You need to go inside and warm up."

"But we still have to do all this," he said, gesturing to the driveway.

"No, I have the plow for that." She pointed at the (t)rusty old Chevy parked near the shed. "It will only take me a couple of minutes. You go inside. I'll be right in."

"I'll help you clean it off."

"But you're freezing!"

"I'm fine. I came to help."

Josh started off in the direction of the truck, stepping through the almost knee-deep snow in his black leather shoes. Jill shrugged and followed him. They knocked snow off the truck until she was able to pull the door open and climb in. She was relieved when "Nellie" turned over; good thing they had replaced the battery that fall, because it was bone-cold.

"You can't really help me with this," she said firmly. "Please go inside and get warmed up before you freeze to death."

"Okay," he replied with a sheepish smile and started off in the direction of the house.

Jill turned the defroster on full-blast and started backing up to her usual starting spot, the spot where Brian always started, which she unconsciously copied. She turned to get herself into position and put the truck in gear and the plow down. She looked over toward the house. There was no sign of Josh. He must already be inside. She hoped Peter wouldn't wake up and find this strange man sitting in the living room, but there was nothing she could do about that. Actually maybe it was a good thing. A test.

The plowing took a few more shots than usual because of the large volume of snow, but twenty minutes later Jill was done and had parked the truck in its usual place and was scurrying to the house. She was looking forward to seeing Josh and thanking him. She was happy as she threw open the door—but he was not there. She went up into the loft—no sign of him. She could not see his car on the road. He must have gone straight home. Why didn't he stop to say goodbye?

School was cancelled for Peter, of course. Jill made him pancakes and put them in the toaster oven for when he woke up. Then she went to work, a little frazzled and a little late. She and the owner were the only ones who made it in. There were a few customers, mostly from the town crew, but it made her feel good that there was someone there to greet them and make them breakfast. She had a lot to do, wearing several hats, some of which she was not used to wearing.

She was thinking about Josh the whole time. There were so many emotions for her to process. First and foremost was her deep gratitude to him for coming. Not that Josh's contribution was remarkable; she cleared twice as much snow while they were shoveling together. And he could certainly have been better prepared. Josh did not seem to know about snowstorms or how to dress for them. He had his usual outfit on, although at least this time the overcoat was buttoned. He was wearing driving gloves, which don't help very much when the temperature is fifteen degrees.

The main thing he brought her, however, was moral support, which she very much needed. From the moment she saw him she felt energized. Even the old plow did not seem so daunting. It was like the effect he had on her painting. He made her feel she could do anything. She knew why. It was his interest in her. "I knew you were here by yourself." He was concerned about her. He wanted to come to her, under very forbidding conditions, and yoke himself to her burden. This indicated a tender regard.

But then something not quite so edifying occurred to Jill. How did he know she was alone? She had not said anything to him about Brian being away. She was tempted to say something the last time he was at the house but had not found the right opportunity, with all of his dark brooding. It was very strange that he knew. He might have heard it in town, but from whom? Someone at the restaurant? It seemed unlikely. None of her friends would have told him; at least not without saying something to her.

This led to a terrifying thought. Was he spying on her? She thought about the whole business with the keys in the parking lot. He had materialized out of nowhere, almost as if waiting for an opportunity. Then there was the fact that he kept showing up at the restaurant when she just happened to be working there—three times now. It was almost as if he knew her schedule. But how? Was he watching her?

She knew almost nothing about Josh. He kept talking about how 'dark' he was. Maybe it wasn't just talk; maybe it was something more. She thought about Peter being home alone and became frightened. She grabbed her cell phone and punched in the speed dial—no answer. She called again. And then again. Finally he answered—he was all right. His sleepy voice told her why it took him so long to get to the phone. He still hadn't gotten out of bed.

Now Jill tried to laugh herself out of her apprehensions. She could not imagine Josh as a stalker. He was not the type. For one thing he was far too full of himself and concerned about his image to risk being caught stalking, even if he were so inclined, which she very much doubted. It was not stylish to stalk. But it was more than that. Josh was kind, in spite of his Gothic pretensions. Encouraging her was kind. Coming to shovel was kindness of the highest order.

Still—how did he know she was alone? It was strange. She tried not to think about it. Alone, alone—yes, she was alone up there on the mountain with no neighbor within a half a mile. Peter was with her but she was his protector, not the other way around, and she did not see herself as much of a protector. Josh's surprise appearance made her feel exposed. She never missed Brian more than at that moment.

Josh was thinking about Jill as well. After shoveling he found himself in his car, driving back down the snowy mountain. The last thing he could remember was helping her clean off the truck—and then he was driving. Had he blacked out again? Was this dreamscape existence never going to end? He came and he went and did not know why. It frustrated him. It make him mad.

True, pieces of his life seemed to be coming back to him now. He remembered that his father was a doctor and his mother a professor. He was their only son and a bit of a disappointment, he was afraid. Two type-A parents naturally want their children to be as driven as themselves. They expected him to have all A's, but he was not interested in school. They wanted him to excel in soccer, but he didn't like sports. They wanted him to play a classical instrument, but he never could get the hang of the oboe, even though they bought him an expensive one, even though they paid for four years of lessons.

The one thing he did like was fine art. He was introduced to it in college in one of those freshman humanities courses and became obsessed. For the first time in his life he felt motivated to rise out of the slough of academic mediocrity and began to be a bit of a star. He was on fire for art and art history and was getting the perfect grades his parents always wanted. But still they did not seem very happy, or at least his mother wasn't. Art history! What kind of a major was that? What kind of job could he find coming out of college with a BFA?

For a while he justified their concerns handsomely. He could not find any jobs related to his major or talents. Then he ran into a guy named Max Swanderland at a party in Camden, where his parents had their summer home. Max was a couple of years older than Josh. He was intrigued by his background and asked him to come work for him on the spot. Josh demurred, but he wooed him by taking him to the waterfront mansion he had recently purchased and giving him a ride in his Ferrari.

Max was unremarkable in every way except for having an almost fiendish talent for business, and the hub of his many businesses was the Web. It was strange for Josh to be taken under the wing of someone who was only a couple of years older than himself and apparently completely crazed. Max was quite the partier. Every time Josh saw him he seemed either drunk or hung over or some combination of both. He claimed never to eat anything but fast food; never cleaned up after himself or bathed or shaved or brushed his teeth, as far as Josh could tell; always wore the same jeans and a few washed-out t-shirts—and yet he was Josh's mentor and boss.

Then again, the money was good. You had to perform for Max. You had to put out fast—he had no patience whatsoever—but if you did you were rewarded. Josh had no problem putting out. He had a good work ethic. He knew how to use Photoshop in a college-student way, but now he threw himself into it with abandon. He was surprised to find he had a natural knack for design, fortified by his extensive knowledge of art. He couldn't draw, but he knew how to put things together in a dynamic way.

The job was perfect because he could work at home. He rarely had to go to Camden; everything was done online. Money started coming in, but he did not save it. He used it to do what he had always wanted to do—travel and see the world's great museums. His parents had mixed feelings about this. They were glad to see him gainfully employed at last, even if it was only as a Web designer for a company they had never heard of. On the other hand they couldn't help wishing that he did not seem quite so determined to squander it all. Only now did he realize how self-indulgent he had been. He felt ashamed.

But the thing he was most ashamed of was Carol, the poor girl he had killed with his recklessness. He was sure he had killed her. He had not seen her since the accident. He wanted to go to her parents and tell them he was sorry, at least give them the satisfaction of seeing the misery of the boy who had taken their daughter's life, but how? He had never been to their house, not that he could remember. In his present state he couldn't even get himself to conjure up Carol's last name.

He was part of the privileged class that gets away with murder. Only he was not like that, not in his own mind. He was not cold and heartless. He became ill in a physical way every time he thought of Carol. He wanted to jump into the grave and protest his innocence—but he knew he was the one who had killed her. There was no way of getting around it.

Would the horrible memory ever go away? It haunted him and tortured him every conscious moment. Maybe it was a good thing those conscious moments were few and far between, because otherwise he was not sure if he could bear it. Every time he thought of Carol it was like a pounding that came muscling its way into his head. Carol was magnified until he merged with her and could taste her blood on his lips.

There is shame, and there is guilt, and there is humiliation and mortification—but nothing compared with the way he felt when he thought about Carol. All right; so he had not led the perfect life; he had not been the perfect son who does everything just right and makes his parents happy. But a murderer? There was nowhere he could go in his body or mind to escape from the horror of his blood-guilt.

He may have been a bad boy in some ways but he did not want to be one. He was not a bad boy in his heart. He was considerate. He was helpful. He could be kind and very generous, when the spirit moved him. He believed in all the right causes. Sure, he had done some things in his life that he was not proud of—but was that all he had ever done? Why couldn't he remember anything else? Why was it only the bad things that kept coming back to him over and over again and torturing him?

He would do anything, give anything, if only he could have the moment in the car back again, if only he could have a second chance to think of Carol and her safety and not insist on acting like a jerk. It was her feelings for him that made him act that way, her love that he repaid with violence. He went back to the car in his mind and tried to have a second chance, but every time he did he saw the concrete wall coming at him in the windshield. There was no escape. What had been done could not be undone.

This was why he was terrified of Jill. Not of Jill per se, but of what kind of damage he might do. Jill was a second Carol. She had come into his life—somehow—he did not know how—and was a great gift. But something was wrong with him. The accident had changed him, and he did not know exactly how. He could not trust himself when he was with her because he did not know what he might do. He did not seem to know his own mind.

Was Jill real? He had to feel she was. Everything he knew told him she was real—and yet nothing seemed real to him anymore. But what if Jill was real, and what if she was in danger because of him, just like Carol had been in danger and not known it? The thought was terrifying. It was why he reacted the way he did to the restaurant painting. He wanted her to know that she had not made him dark enough. In his own mind he was a black hole; how could she ever begin to understand?

But this was not all he felt about Jill. His love for her was sincere. He did not love her in the sense that young men love women, or even foolish old men. He was way beyond that now. The concrete mass had knocked it out of him. He felt nothing in his loins for Jill; in fact he felt nothing in his loins at all.

No, he loved her as a person, in the same way he should have loved Carol. He liked being with her, in spite of the pain he sometimes felt. He thought about her talking about God while he was standing on her staircase and feeling captivated by the mountain scenery. A warm feeling came over him again as he did. He kept thinking about it because he wanted that warm feeling. So cold out, he wanted it to be warm.

Jill "thanked God" for the light in the mountains. She meant it quite literally. This was not just an empty expression for her; he could tell from the inflection. The play of light in the mountains was literally the handiwork of God to her mind. In the past Josh had always thought of photons when he saw light, if he thought of anything at all, being a sensible and scientifically-minded young man. But Jill was not sensible. To her the light in the mountains was the work of a great Artist.

He who had never consciously thought of "thanking God" for beautiful light was beginning to see things from Jill's point of view. After all, she was a great artist herself. Indeed, he was in awe of her. He compared her to the greatest painters he knew and saw very little difference in the most important things. He thought of the striking use of light in the painting of Jesus and the blind man, especially the shadow on his face. What did it mean? What was she trying to say? It was more than just an aesthetic effect. Jill was not someone who would do anything just for the effect.

He had not been able to get this painting out of his mind. He had made a mess of things at the time, asking her if she was "religious," but now her religious feeling was beginning to rub off on him. It was not just the use of light that brought him back to the painting. It was the healing. Josh was the man with the mud on his eyes, the man with the look of terror on his face. Mud and thick darkness were all he could see through his heavy eyes. Someone was touching him but he did not know who.

Was it God or the devil? He wished he could open his eyes and see.

ANNUNCIATION

J ILL CAME HOME FROM WORK and found a quiet Peter waiting for her. Quieter than usual, she could sense it. She went out and did some more things in the snow, the things you don't do when you're in a hurry to get to work, like raking the flat roof and shoveling to the bird feeder. He came out and helped her. He was not a particularly strong boy, but his heart was in the right place. She looked at him and loved him.

They came in and she made hot chocolate for them and they sat down in the kitchen and looked at the last few stray flakes that were still coming down under a steel-gray sky.

"Who was that guy?" he said at last.

"Guy?" she replied with a deep blush, because she knew exactly what he meant.

"Yeah, helping you shovel."

"Oh—that's just someone from town. He knew your father was away, so I guess he decided I needed some help."

"It was strange. I was thinking of Dad. At first I thought it was Dad. I guess that was pretty stupid."

"It's not stupid at all. You're used to seeing him do all the shoveling."

"But then I saw that guy. It was strange."

"Well, you notice he didn't stay around very long. I don't even know why he came. Maybe he was just trying to put in an appearance—give me moral support—or trying to make himself seem—" she didn't know where she was going so she stopped.

"I miss him."

"Your Dad?"

"Yeah. Any idea when he's coming home?"

"He doesn't know himself, at this point. Maybe a few months."

"Months! The snow will be all gone by then."

Jill did not know what to say. She thought about this little conversation all afternoon. At first she felt badly for Peter. She could not be his mother and his father too. He was stuck with her all winter cooped up on the side of the mountain. She couldn't take him skiing, which apparently was what he wanted to do. She herself did not ski—but it was more than that. They could not afford it. They simply did not have the money for a weekend lift ticket.

Then she couldn't help herself, she became angry with Brian, still chasing his pipe dream and leaving them to fend for themselves. Did he care about Peter? Did he understand how important he was to him? She wished he could see the look he just had on his face. Would it make any difference to him? Did he care enough about them to be concerned about the impact of his absence? It was frustrating to Jill. She could not make him care. She could not take away Peter's pain.

Something else occurred to her, too. Unlike Peter, she did not miss Brian. She wanted to say "I miss him, too"—for Peter's sake; to reassure him that everything was all right between them, but could not get the words to come out of her mouth. She missed Brian when she felt afraid and alone. She missed him when it was going to snow. She missed him when there were bills to pay and not enough money. She missed him when she saw how much Peter missed him.

But she did not miss him the way Peter did. In fact she was happy he was gone. There had been so many gratuitous hurts and so much repressed friction over the past couple of years that having him out of the house was like being on vacation. It was not that they fought, at least not openly; they almost never did. It was more like silent grinding, day after day.

The main cause of the tension, from her point of view, was his stubborn unwillingness to grow up. Everything was on hold for the sake of the band. It was impossible to love him or to have anything like a close relationship with him because he was not present even when he was there. He was holding them at arm's length—her and Peter. He was not really giving himself to them. It was almost like he was trying to make up his mind if he wanted to. And this hurt.

No, Jill did not miss Brian. It was the first time in years that she felt she could breathe, the first time that she was not cleaning up after him and accommodating herself to his schedule and biting her lip when he said things she didn't agree with. Unlike Peter, she was not worried about how long he would be away. She was more worried about when he was coming back—what she would say to him—how she would tell him that she was moving on.

She made dinner and played a couple of games of Scrabble with Peter. When he turned on the TV—*Dr. Who*—she stole up to the loft to look at her painting. She stood in front of it for a long time and just looked. Josh was wrong. It wasn't about him. It was about a moment that made her happy, one of the few truly happy moments she'd had in recent memory. Was it wrong for her to be happy—even if he was part of the moment? Was her happiness really all about him? Surely part of it was the painting itself; the joy of painting. Surely some of her happiness had to do with the quality of the result.

Or maybe it was about Josh after all. Maybe that was why she was standing there staring at him—not trying to understand him—just staring as she remembered the happiness she felt when she saw him sitting there—although she concealed it at the time. She had been hoping to see him again ever since the night in the parking lot. She couldn't imagine how it could happen—and then it did. There he was, sitting in the booth, completely unexpected. It made her happy.

But she concealed it. Why? Because Josh was right. Happiness of that kind is a great liar. There was no way to know when she was looking at Josh whether she was seeing Josh himself or just the idealized version of him she had in her mind—because she wanted to be happy. The desire for happiness made Josh more desirable than he really was. After all, she knew nothing about him. She had no real sense whatsoever of how compatible they might be.

No, that was not quite true. She did have a sense, or a nagging suspicion, which she was trying to suppress. She could not be unaware of his strangeness. She had painted it right into him and was looking at it now. She was more honest as a painter than as a person. She made him dark and she was ambivalent about this quality. Jill did not like darkness.

But was he really dark? Or was it just a pose? She allowed herself to luxuriate in the events of the morning. It was such a delightful surprise—seeing him standing there in the snow, realizing who it was. She had wanted to laugh and she was smiling now. He was so ridiculous standing there in the snow in his dress overcoat—and so wonderful. She closed her eyes and pictured him with his shovel. The black knight comes to rescue the fair maiden, risking life and limb to reach her through the perilous snow.

Then her mind turned to Peter and his painfully honest words—"Who was that guy?"—and all of the joy promptly drained out of the snow bubble. The thing that had brought her happiness was a source of pain to her son, who saw a stranger in the driveway instead of his father. She had a horrible thought—had he seen the hug? It was brief—barely a hug at all—but had he seen it? What was he thinking if he had? Jill blushed again and again.

Suddenly she saw herself in the loft having romantic thoughts about someone other than Peter's father, and she was ashamed. He was right to be suspicious about "that guy." He was not just somebody from town. She could not be honest with Peter about him and his connection to her—and she wanted to be honest. She wanted to be as pure in heart as he needed his mother to be.

But she was far from it. She felt like she was trapped in some kind of hellish neverland. She was attracted to the man in the painting but did not trust the attraction. She wanted to be happy but did not know if the happiness Josh gave her was real or just wishful thinking. She knew she could not be happy if Peter was in pain. If it came down to choosing between Peter and Josh, she would choose her son. She would sacrifice anything for his sake.

Then she thought about the whole impossible situation with his father. She was happy for Brian and his opportunity, but at the same time she felt terribly frustrated. It was not possible to separate from him when he was not there. He would not even give her that much satisfaction. Instead he was off having fun with his friends. He had put her future into abeyance for over ten years and nothing had changed. She was tired of his selfishness. She was tired of his inability to make a commitment.

She could not break off with him long-distance. It had to be face-to-face, when she was in the thick of his indifference to her, not when he had been gone for over a month. Amazing how quickly the heart can heal. She did not love Brian anymore—or did not think she did—but neither was she really angry with him now that he was out from under foot. She was finding it difficult to summon the sense of hurt and disgust that was needed in order to slice one flesh into two.

But even this was not the end of her perplexity. She looked at the painting again and at Josh. What if she did find the courage to break off with Brian? What if he were safely out of the house and out of her life? Could she picture herself welcoming Josh into her life—her house? The boy she was looking at right now in the painting? Because that was how he seemed to her; more boy than man. She looked at the painting and her heart sank.

Suddenly she felt ashamed of it. For the first time she saw it the way Josh must have seen it. Her foolish heart was right out there in the open for all to see. No, it was not just an exercise, as she claimed; far from it. She would not have painted so passionately if that was all it was. She felt naked looking at it. She grabbed it and took it to the closet and hid it in the back with its companion. She did not want Peter to see it. He might recognize him. There would be more questions.

Jill closed the closet door and came downstairs and sat down on the couch next to her beloved son. Part of her longed to lance the wound, see exactly what sort of infection he had, but she laughed herself out of it. Peter did not seem to be as traumatized by Josh as she imagined him to be. He seemed perfectly happy with his TV show, and it was selfish to subject him to the kind of female-talk she knew he hated—about feelings.

He was laughing out loud at the jokey staging and dialogue. Jill tried to enjoy it as much as he did, but sci-fi was not really her thing. After a while she began to feel safe again. She closed her eyes and allowed her mind to wander—and immediately reverted to the morning scene, to Josh's gloves and shoes and how overmatched he seemed by the snow. She laughed. Peter was laughing too; he did not notice. She could laugh with delight at the thought of Josh.

Later that night, after Peter had gone to bed, she went back upstairs to the closet and looked at the painting again. She stood there with her head in the cobwebs gazing at it—her hand on it, tilting it to the ceiling light so she could see. It was well-made and she took pleasure in it. Did she also enjoy looking at Josh? She could not deny that she found him attractive. Teasing man, smiling back at her slyly from her own painting! Coming to her in the largest snowstorm of the year! What was he up to?

Now she thought of something else. She was glad for the help, glad most of all to see him, but he had come to the house without being invited. It broke precedent, and it made her a little uneasy. She looked at the dark man in the painting, the man who described himself as being dangerous, and realized she did not want him to think he had a license to show up whenever he wanted. She wanted to trust him but did not know if she could. She definitely did not want him coming if Peter was there.

But then a week went by with no sign of Josh, and her shapeless fears were replaced by very different feelings. Jill wanted to see him again. She wanted to thank him for helping her and ask him why he had disappeared. She wanted to talk to him about the painting. She had a question mark in her own mind and she wanted to know if he had the same question. But there was no sign of him. She had no way to get in touch with him. All she could do was wait.

Something more pressing began to weigh on her mind in the dead of winter, however. She had missed a period. She had been working too hard and been too consumed with everything else that was going on to dwell on it. After all, she could not be pregnant, not unless it was an immaculate conception. But then she remembered—Christmas Eve! She had tried to put it out of her mind—Brian lying on top of her with beer on his breath—the itchy carpet underneath—but it came back in a flood of unpleasantness. Was it possible? Could she be pregnant with their second child?

Jill could not believe it. Could she really be so unlucky? They make love once in a year—and she gets pregnant? Just when she was thinking about leaving him? When she had stopped loving him? When she had no money to pay the mortgage and other bills and was already at her wit's end being a single mother and working and doing everything else that needed to be done? Having another child with the man to whom she still was not married?

No, she was doubly unlucky—because it was entirely her fault. Her use of the pill had become variable over the past year. Brian had lost interest in her, so why bother? She didn't like taking it anyway. She knew about the health risks. It was not so much a conscious decision as a lapse in commitment to the demanding regimen. She had not taken any at all during the holiday season.

There were so many things on her mind, so many other things she had to do. And now it looked like she was going to pay.

Jill stopped at the pharmacy on the way home from work and bought a pregnancy testing kit. She was not surprised when the results confirmed what she already knew in her heart. She was alone in her little log cabin on the mountain—Peter was still at school—so she sat down on the couch and cried. She cried and cried and cried in the listless February light until she felt kind of listless herself—but the problem did not go away. Crying was not going to solve anything.

Nothing was right about this pregnancy. It wasn't that she didn't want more children. She wanted a whole house full. But she was not married. Brian refused to make the commitment that justified having more children. Also they could not afford it. He was making less than half of what he used to make, and most of what he made was being used to cover his expenses in Memphis. She barely made the February mortgage payment and had no idea how she was going to handle March. They had no health insurance. They didn't think they needed it. They needed it now.

But it was more than the financial and logistical considerations. It was deeply personal for Jill. She did not love Brian anymore. It can be a joyful thing when two people love each other and they find out that a baby is coming. In fact it can be the most joyful message in all existence, as when Sarah laughed. But Jill had been thinking about leaving Brian. She was so frustrated with him over his latest adventure that she was having difficulty even keeping a civil tongue in her mouth.

What kind of life was the baby likely to have with two parents who did not love each other? What kind of life were *they* going to have stuck in an unhappy bond? Brian had been very open about this in the past. Any discussion of having more children was to be put on hold until they knew what they were doing with the band. Jill could not picture herself calling him to deliver the news. She knew he would not be happy. She did not know if she could pretend to be happy herself, or even if she should.

It was her fault. That was how Brian would see it. He wouldn't consider the fact that he had made an unwanted advance on Christmas Eve under the influence of alcohol. None of that would mean anything to him. No, all he would see was negligence on her part. He did not have time for this now. He was trying to make a record. It was his big break, finally, and she had to go and get pregnant? Hadn't they talked about this? Was he not clear about what he wanted? Jill could almost hear him saying these things, the angry tone of his voice.

Peter came home from school and Jill went into a fog. There she was, pregnant, alone on the mountain with her son. She did not know how to tell him about the momentous change in his life. She did not know how she felt about the pregnancy and therefore did not know what to say to her son. She decided not to say anything at all—not right now—there was plenty of time. But concealment made her feel self-conscious. It was strange to hide the news from Peter. So many things she was hiding from him now.

Jill was careful to make everything normal for him. She stuck to their normal after-school routine. She made him his favorite dinner—tacos—and then she made him chocolate chip cookies. On the surface it was very much like any other Wednesday night. After dinner they played a game of Boggle. She made sure he settled down and did his homework before turning on the TV. But she did this as two people. On the outside she made herself seem perfectly calm; on the inside she was a complete mess.

It was a tremendous relief to her when Peter finally said good night and headed off to bed. It meant she did not have to pretend anymore. But now she had to keep herself from crying. The deep breaths came; she put her face into the cool couch. She did not want him to hear her crying.

Jill went to bed as well, after doing a little more straightening up in the kitchen, but she did not sleep. It was almost full moon and she had trouble sleeping anyway when the moon was full and shining on the snow, but that night her heart was full. She could not hide the irony from herself. The baby that she had wanted so much was an unwanted baby. She did not see how it could change from unwanted to wanted. The timing was terrible. The situation was impossible. It wasn't just her feelings about Brian that were troubling her—what about Josh?

She still did not know her own heart when it came to Josh, but the baby made the whole thing seem impossible. She could not imagine him taking one child under his wing who was not his own, never mind two. He did not strike her as the nurturing type. And getting pregnant now! It would look like she did not have feelings for him. Did she have any feelings? She was not sure. But she was not ready to ruin things between them, not just yet. She wanted the beautiful dream to go on and the unexpected encounters and the thrilling conversations.

These thoughts kept her awake most of the night. She dragged herself out of bed the next morning and managed to get Peter off to school and herself off to work, but it was the most miserable day she could ever remember having. She was overtired. She kept making stupid mistakes. People were not happy with her and she was not happy with herself. They could not see the turmoil that was consuming her. They did not know that she needed them to be understanding, and she could not tell them.

At the end of her shift she ran out of the restaurant and did not even realize that she had left her apron on under her coat until she got into the Subaru. She sat there for a few moments in the cold with her hands on the cold steering wheel wondering if she had the energy or the will to drive home. Then she decided to stop in and see her mother. She needed to talk to someone about the new development in her life. She could not go on being the only one who knew.

She drove over to the family home and found her mother in the kitchen.

"Are you all right?" she said. "You don't look well."

"I didn't get any sleep last night. Too much on my mind."

"You want to talk about it?"

"There's not a lot to say. I'm—pregnant."

Betty put down the pie dough she had in her hands and looked at her. "That's wonderful, honey. Isn't it?"

"I don't know. I want it to be wonderful. It's just not the best timing right now."

"Because of this stupid band thing. There—I said it. I'm sorry, but this is ridiculous. Is he ever going to grow up?"

"That's not really it. To tell you the truth, I've been thinking about—going off on my own. With Peter, I mean." Jill surprised herself by bursting into tears.

Her mother came and put her arms around her. "I knew it. I knew something was wrong. Although you always try to put a good face on things."

"You knew?"

"Of course! I'm not blind."

"He just doesn't seem interested in me anymore."

"No, all he cares about is that stupid band."

"They're not stupid. They're good. And I don't blame him. I have dreams too. I just—I don't know. Am I being selfish?"

"You're the least selfish person I know. He's the one who's being selfish. He won't marry you. He spends half his time fooling around. I don't know how you put up with it this long."

"He's not a bad person. I have my own faults. It's just not a great time to be having another baby. If he showed me some affection it would be different. But he doesn't."

"You're wondering if he's even going to want it."

"Well—it's sort of my fault. I forgot to take precautions. He's not going to be happy about that."

Betty wiped the hot tears from her face. "Don't worry. If you need a place to stay, you just come here. You know we would love to have you."

"Oh, sure. That's just what you need—a new baby in the house."

"It will do us some good," she said with a laugh. "Things have been getting pretty stale around here since you kids moved out. Your father will have to stop walking around in his underpants."

Jill left this conversation feeling lighter. It was good to be able to share her momentous news. She smiled when she thought of her mother's highly uncharacteristic outburst against Brian. She had never heard her use such strong language in her life. Jill surprised herself by wanting to defend him. It made her realize she must still have some feelings for Brian. She just did not love him anymore.

The other change came from the open arms. Moving back home was not ideal, but at least it made motherhood seem less impossible. Besides, it was temporary. If it came to that, it would only be until they managed to sell the log cabin and settle their debts.

CONTRETEMPS

B UT DID SHE REALLY WANT BRIAN'S BABY? She wanted a baby—she could convince herself to be grateful about that—but Brian's? Would she think of him every time she looked at it? Would she be able to resist the temptation to transfer the frustration she felt with him to the child they shared together? A baby, yes, but Brian's baby? The way she felt about Brian?

There were other concerns, too. What about her job? She absolutely needed it in order to make ends meet, but how was she going to work and also take care of a new baby? It seemed overwhelming. She did not want to have to resort to daycare. For one thing, there was no way she could afford it. But it was more than that. She wanted to raise the baby herself and not entrust it to the kindness of strangers. Her mother's offer was incredibly generous—and just then, rather tempting. But she could not expect her to take care of her baby.

She was worried about how Brian was going to react—and how she was going to react to his reaction. The most practical solution was for him to come home and take care of them. But was she ready to accept this solution? Did she want to make that kind of long-term commitment to staying with Brian? What if he came home annoyed and full of resentment? Was she ready to spend twenty years with a man who was mad at her for forgetting to take the pill?

And there was something else. She couldn't help thinking about Josh. He seemed like he was in love with her. He made it sound like it was love that attracted him to her. How would he react if he knew there was a baby on the way? Brian's baby? How would any man react? Would he still want to shovel her snow and have teasing conversations? Would he still want to look at her paintings and shower her with praise? He was the only one who praised them.

Jill was all mixed up. She was frightened, she was upset, she was stressed out. She got it in her head that she needed to see Josh again, if for no other reason than to—what? She did not know what, exactly. Her hormones were raging and she wanted to see him the same way she wanted pickles and peanut butter.

Unfortunately she had no way of contacting him. She did not know his number or where he lived. A week went by, then two. Snow and ice were melting and the crocuses were poking up their sleepy heads through the frozen tundra and the birds were returning and making their nests. Spring was lumbering back to Vermont, the season of love—but there was no sign of Josh.

Then Jill had a funny thought. It seemed like he always showed up when there was a new painting for him to see. She knew this did not make any sense—there was no way for him to know when she was done with a painting—but it had happened with both paintings of him. Feeling whimsical, she decided to paint something and see if she could draw him again. At the very least it was a way to take her mind off things.

But what to paint? Jill wracked her brain and could not come up with a single idea that seemed enticing. Then she had a hilarious inspiration. She thought of Brian's comment about Count Dracula. She would paint Josh as a vampire. He was always talking about how "dark" he was. Why not? It would be fun.

She went up into her loft on a relatively mild sunny day in March. Now Jill was not into vampires. She thought the whole thing was silly. But this only made it seem more entertaining. She liked the idea of teasing Josh about his dark persona. It seemed to her that he could do with a little teasing.

She laughed out loud as she started to work. It was almost if the brush could not wait to get to the canvas. Even she was surprised at how easy it was to paint him as Dracula. The vampire theme fit Josh better than she anticipated. He was dark-haired. He was handsome. He was pale. He had his white lock. She felt a little flush when she looked at him.

A week later she was done with the painting and she was still laughing. She stepped back and put her hand over her mouth and just laughed. It was erotic in the old-fashioned sense. Josh had on several more layers of clothes than anybody wore these days and still managed to ooze sexuality. Of course part of the joke was that he did not ooze any such thing in real life.

She wondered if he would get it. She felt confident about it as a painting per se—but what would he think of her little joke? Could he laugh at himself? She wanted him to be able to laugh. She did not want him to take himself as seriously as he seemed.

She started looking for him at work again. She laughed at herself even as she did—the idea that her painting would somehow make him appear was ridiculous—but she kept looking anyway. Something told her he would come.

Eventually he did—although not to the restaurant. She came home from work one day and was startled to see his gold Mercedes parked in her driveway. Jill shook her head. This was not what she wanted. She still was not comfortable with the idea of him coming to the house without an invitation.

Josh hopped out of the car with a sort of half smile. "Hi, there!"

"Hi," she replied, gathering up the grocery bags and not looking at him.

"Are you surprised to see me?"

"I'm surprised to see you *here*. But I've been expecting you."

"Really? Why?"

"I have a new painting," she said, looking at him.

"So—you think that's all I care about."

"Well—do you want to see it or not?"

"Might as well, as long as I'm here."

She couldn't wait for him to see it, in spite of her prickly greeting. There was nothing in the world she wanted more. She went straight upstairs, and he went up behind her.

She stopped in front of the canvas. "What do you think?" she said, forcing herself to seem casual.

Josh had a little smile on his face, but the more he looked the more his smile drooped. Then he started acting strangely. He staggered. He fell backwards in a loud clatter, knocking over the paint stand.

"Are you all right?" Jill said, not sure what to make of this behavior.

Josh did not reply. He stumbled to his feet again and half ran, half fell down the spiral staircase and out the door without saying a word.

Jill's first reaction was to laugh. It was so over the top that she thought it had to be a Harpo Marx impersonation. But then she looked down through the windows and saw him get into the Mercedes and speed away. If this was slapstick, he was carrying it a bit far. Still, she stood there for a few minutes, watching. She was sure he would come back and be his calm, collected self. After all, it was a very good painting. She stood there waiting for him to come back but he did not. There were no cars on the road. She was very much alone.

She sat down in her rocking chair in a daze. What had just happened? It was the strangest thing she had ever seen in her life, even stranger because it was Josh, the one who was always so cool, calm and collected; the one who always seemed in command of himself and the situation. The frantic person who knocked over her paint stand and practically fell down the stairs did not seem like Josh at all.

She did not know what to make of it. She had been looking forward to this moment, to showing him the new painting, to him seeing himself in this dashing and hilarious new persona, and now everything seemed broken. In the case of her paint stand—literally. The top had broken off from the legs.

She sat there in shock for maybe half an hour, unable to move, wondering what could have upset him so—if he really was upset— if it wasn't some crazy game of his—which she was half-inclined to suspect. Was it because she had painted him as a vampire? She knew it was provocative. She wanted it to be. But the reaction seemed wildly out of proportion to the offense.

The painting seemed to strike him like a physical blow, but why? It didn't make sense. He had to be acting—deliberately trying to make a scene or a show for some reason. The only problem was she did not know what this reason could possibly be. She was just trying to be funny. Maybe he didn't have a sense of humor after all.

She knew she had to compose herself. Peter would be coming home soon and she didn't want him finding a mess in the loft and asking difficult questions. She had to get her paints and brushes cleaned up as if nothing had happened. Unfortunately this was impossible. The top of the paint stand refused to cooperate. It would not sit on the legs by itself. The naughty paints and brushes would have to go into time-out on her drafting table.

She clambered downstairs, her feet heavy and clumsy, and straightened up the living room and turned on the lights in anticipation of Peter's arrival. She went into the kitchen and put together a meat loaf and oiled some baking potatoes for dinner—but this was all just busywork. This was doing things in order to avoid having to come to terms with the disaster that had just occurred in her life.

The thing was she had poured herself into the painting. She had not done a half-hearted job. She did not think a half-hearted job would draw Josh—there she went again—or impress him if it did. She wanted to make a great painting for him. This was why his reaction hurt. He rejected her masterpiece. When she looked at it she saw all the love and all the art and good humor that went into it—but this was not what he saw. Something about the painting had driven him away. It was the first time he had rejected her work, and it hurt, like a white space in her mind.

But then she thought about how ridiculous his reaction was. It was not a reaction but an overreaction. This made her realize something. Josh was not someone she could ever love. He made a fool of himself in her eyes. She realized it was not Josh she was in love with but the support he had given her. Josh could not take Brian's place. Wherever she was headed with Brian—whether she could live with him or had to move on—in either case she could not be in love with Josh.

A great calm descended on her. For the first time she thought she saw Josh as he actually was—not just as a figment of her imagination. His pratfall took away the mystique and made him seem foolish and insubstantial. She acknowledged to herself that she'd always had reservations about Josh. She had always known she could not love him, even while she was inclined to wonder.

The spirit of indignation rose within her. She wanted to go back upstairs and look at the painting again and reassure herself that it was good, that she was not misreading his reaction or misjudging him. But as she reached the top of the stairs she noticed a small scrap of paper on the floor. She didn't remember seeing it there before. Curious, she picked it up and looked at it.

There was just one word: "bezalel." She was not familiar with it. Where did the scrap of paper come from? Did he drop it there, and if so what did it mean? Now she forgot all about the painting. She was curious about this scrap of paper. She carried it downstairs in both hands and sat on the couch and stared at it. Could it possibly be something of Brian's? It sounded like a tool of some kind. But it wasn't Brian's handwriting. And why would it suddenly show up now?

"Bezalel." She tried to pronounce the word but was not sure how it was supposed to sound. She continued to stare at it for a long time. She was transfixed by it. She knew why she was so fascinated. She thought it came from Josh. Was it why he had come—to deliver this cryptic little piece of paper?

He seemed surprised to find she had a new painting. She didn't really believe the painting had the power to draw him anyway. It was fantasy, like an adolescent girl lying in her bed at night and trying to draw some boy by casting out her thoughts to the universe. But it made perfect sense for Josh to come to deliver a message, the one she was holding in her hands. It would even explain why he was so bold as to come directly to the house.

Peter interrupted this reverie by arriving home from school. She pushed the scrap of paper into her jeans pocket and jumped up to greet him, trying to hide her confusion. He threw his heavy backpack on the couch and plopped down in exhaustion. Jill sat down again and chatted with him before going to the kitchen to finish dinner.

A little while later he appeared in the pass-through with the scrap in his hand. It must have fallen out of her pocket.

"What's this?" he said, with a surprised look on his face.

"Oh, that!" Jill said blushing. "I don't know. Found it on the floor upstairs."

"You didn't write this?"

"No. Why?"

"That's really weird. We just read about this guy in Sunday School."

"What 'guy'?"

"Bezalel. Oh my gosh—you don't even know who he is, do you?"

"Should I?"

"Yah! He's an artist. He worked on that tabernacle they were building, or whatever it was."

"Okay, hold on—you have to help me. What tabernacle are you talking about?"

"You know—Moses and all that. He was the guy who was in charge of it."

Jill just looked at him. Peter shrugged and left the paper on the counter. When she was sure he wasn't looking she picked it up and looked for some place to hide it. She didn't want it lying around because it made her think of Josh, and she didn't want Peter looking at something that made her think of Josh. She pulled her Bible down from the shelf, the one her parents had given her when she was confirmed, and gently placed the scrap of paper in it like a flower to be pressed.

What did it mean? It had to have come from Josh. He was the only one who had been up in the loft, except for herself. But according to Peter the name on the paper was from the Bible. This surprised her. Could it really come from Josh? It was a mystery.

NOTHINGNESS

AND WHAT ABOUT JOSH? Why did he throw himself down the stairs and out of the house?

It was that painting. It shattered him. He did not know there was a new painting. That was not why he had gone there. He was happy to hear the good news, of course—happy to see Jill laughing and enjoying herself—until he saw what she was laughing about. She made him a vampire! She put him in the type of formal attire the Count had worn in the old movies. A rapacious gold-capped tooth was faintly visible. The pale complexion was from life as he now knew it but horrifying in context.

She was laughing like it was all a big joke. Why? Because she found him out? Because she knew his terrible secret? But how could she know? He himself did not know what he was. Sometimes he thought he might be suffering from a bad concussion from the crash. Other times he thought he must be dreaming. His dreamlike encounters with Jill were the only reality that seemed to break through the gauze of damaged tissue.

There were times, however, when he had other ideas about himself. And they were horrible. They were the worst thoughts you could possibly have about yourself in the worst moments of your life, the kind of thoughts that make you wish you could die or had never been born. Josh used to have thoughts like this occasionally but now it seemed like he had them all the time. He would be standing up in Jill's loft looking at her paintings and a terrible thought would come into his head unbidden, sometimes in confused darkness, sometimes breaking into defined ideas or even images.

He was becoming increasingly convinced that there was something very wrong with this connection he had with Jill. He kept showing up where she was without consciously intending to go there or knowing how he got there. That was the way it was in the parking lot and had been ever since. The incidents at the restaurant were particularly unnerving because he would suddenly find himself there waiting for Jill. He did not remember making a decision to go see her. All he knew was that somehow she had become the center and the focus of his life.

But why? What was it that attracted him to her? This was the strange thing, because he did not remember any initial attraction. All he remembered was the parking lot and the snow, which was as bizarre to him as it must have seemed to her. But the attraction was already full-blown by then. Indeed it seemed he had been waiting for her to come out of the restaurant. The question was why. He could not remember having seen her before that night. Why was he there looking for her, and why was he so interested in her? It was as if she were a magnet and he the ragged filings.

Then there was the unhappy day when the attraction became ambiguous. This he also remembered vividly. It was when he saw that painting, the one with the blood spilling out onto the canvas. A great darkness seeped into his mind and his entire being when he saw that painting and it made him turn cold. There was Jill alone with him in the loft and there was the railing too close and he had to get out of there as soon as he could. Terrible thoughts were trying to muscle their way into his head. He knew he could not push them down. He had to run away.

What scared Josh the most was not the possibility that he was dead, or even the incredible idea that he might be some sort of undead creature. Those things were terrifying enough, but what made him want to melt into nothing was the thought that he might do harm to Jill. He did not want to hurt her. He loved her. He wanted to save her. But his will was not his own. He did not will any of these meetings with her, as pleasant as they might have been. In the same way he did not know if he could will her safety.

What if he had become some sort of destroying angel? What if he was there not to support Jill in her painting but for some more horrible reason that he was afraid even to imagine? He did not want to believe it—but neither could he discount it. After all, he was a Bad Boy. He had already destroyed one wonderful young woman. This thought washed over him in a dark tide and filled him with deep sorrow.

To his own mind he was a figure of darkness. Where consciousness should step in with a sense of self there was only darkness; or more accurately, a void. He had lost his sense of feeling. He could stand in the snow and cold and be indifferent. That was all right, but the problem was he could also stand in the sun and be indifferent. Snow and the sun, they were the same to him now. The center of him seemed to have been lost, and he perceived this loss, this absence, as darkness.

In fact the only light in his life—and his only tenuous connection to reality—was Jill. Or maybe not Jill per se so much as this strange love he seemed to feel when he was around her. He had felt it from the very first moment. It was what made him rush to her side and wipe the snow off her car. This love went beyond language. He wanted to describe it as being filled with color or light, but these were just clumsy images. It was so much more than that. Everything dark and painful went away. He stopped being his unknown self in those rare moments, the cipher he had come to hate, and surrendered to peace.

But this was just what terrified him. Had he come to destroy the only thing that gave him peace? When he was with Jill this love would descend in all of its colors but then the dark thoughts would creep in and there was nothing he could do to stop them. He was afraid of hurting this remarkable woman, this wildly gifted painter. It was not just the light that he wanted to sin against in his dark moments but his own love of painting, embodied in her. She claimed he was the reason she started painting again. Was he going to destroy the one good thing he could ever remember doing?

She was vulnerable, all alone up there in her cabin, like some sort of sprite from an ancient fairy tale of life lived in the deep woods and on the borders of existence. Was he her danger, the dark shadow in the woods, the breaker of the spell of happiness? Was this the reason for the strong force that drew him to her? Did he feel love for her or was love a liar? Did he care about her the way he wanted to or did he go to her house because he knew she was vulnerable and alone? Because she was something fine for him to destroy in his callousness, just as he had destroyed Carol?

It made him sick to think such thoughts. It made him want to cry—but he could not. He saw himself as a monster and wanted to cry at this vile defamation of himself but no tears would come. In the past he had gone out of his way not to cry or show vulnerability. He was raised not to cry. He never saw his mother cry, not even when her own mother died. But now he found he wanted to cry. He was distraught over the hateful change in himself. He was not trying to hold back the tears as he had in the past or suppressing sorrowful feelings of loss. His sorrow could not have been greater—but he also could not cry.

Was he a monster then, a man without tears or pity? He did not want to be. His face was cold. He could not cry. He had no business being around someone like Jill, who was not afraid of the things that gave him terror. Jill *should* have been afraid of someone like him, a killer, a monster, a bad boy. But she was trusting. She was like that the first night in the parking lot. She even invited him into her house. He tried to tell her the truth but she laughed it off. He tried to be honest with her but she would not listen.

She would not let him be what he actually was. And yet somehow it seemed she knew what he was. Didn't she? This new painting—did she know? She was laughing when she showed it to him, but the painting annihilated him. It was the worst pain and terror he could ever remember feeling, worse even than the accident. To die is one thing but to be a monster is something else. It did not matter what you called the thing with the dark thoughts—"vampire" or whatever. Josh was that thing now, a misshapen lump looking for some relief from his agony, a fragment, a bad dream.

But this was not how she painted him. She made him seem dashing. She gave him a sense of fun and camp that he himself did not feel. Was it how she saw him? As someone who was fun? If so, she was very much mistaken. There was no fun in him whatsoever. The things she perceived as fun were nothing more than signs of his confusion about who he was and what he was up to. She made him sexy! He laughed at this thought. It was not sex that drew him to her. The elemental feeling that makes fools of men—he did not have it anymore. Sex was the last thing on his mind.

Jill was oblivious to all this. She made him a vampire but she thought she liked the idea of vampires. She had no idea. His life was not fun or sexy. It was a constant state of dread and disintegration. And then there was this weird obsession with blood. It was almost as if the blood that was splattered all over his car on that terrible night was not enough for him. The taste of blood drenched his entire being and was on the tips of his teeth. When he looked at Jill she was partly covered with blood.

He had gone to her house with the best intentions and a scrap of paper in his hand. A word had come to him, a strange word he could not remember ever seeing before, but he must have seen it somewhere because it came to him so clearly, as if etched in his mind like brass. He had to write it down. Then he began to think it had something to do with Jill. Maybe it was because the paper scrap and Jill were the only tangible things in his life. Was he supposed to deliver this word to her—just as it had been delivered to him? Once he got this idea into his head he could not get it out.

It was the reason for the unprompted visit. He went there to share this strange word. He convinced himself that his motives were entirely pure. He did not want to hurt Jill. He wanted to help her. He had been given a word for her and wanted her to see it. He felt instinctively that this word would encourage her somehow, specifically her painting. There was nothing he wanted more than for her to be encouraged in that way. He wanted Jill to paint. It was very painful for him to think about her becoming discouraged and giving up.

Yes, that was why he had gone there. He drove to her house but she was not there. He could not leave. He was on a mission. He sat in the driveway, holding the scrap of paper in his hand, occasionally glancing at it and trying to remember what it meant. Finally she drove in. She seemed startled to see him there. He could sense her uneasiness about this bold step, about him coming uninvited, now for the second time. And he agreed with her. He should not be there. He thought about skulking away.

There was a new painting and she wanted him to see it. He could not turn down such a request. He followed her into the house with his scrap of paper in his hand and up the stairs. She was laughing and he was thinking to himself how delightful the sound of her laughter was. She was ascending the stairs in the sunlight, laughing, and he wanted to laugh himself. But then he saw it—that horrible painting. There was no question it was a great work of art. It was so powerful that he felt dizzy. Then he realized what it was. He realized what she had done. His mind went black.

He was too stunned to react. The next thing he knew he was falling down and tripping over something. He could feel it sticking in his ribs. His body felt clumsy, numb. He glanced up at the painting in a daze. Then he looked at Jill. Why was she still laughing? Did she think it was funny, this terrible affliction of his? A horrible thought came to him—he hated her. He wanted to hurt her. He tumbled down the stairs and flung himself out the door.

He could never see her again. He made up his mind. Through her he had felt a kind of love he had never experienced in his life, and yet he had these terrible thoughts and was not in control of himself and clumsy and afraid of what he might do. The only remedy was to stay away. Forever.

RESTORATION

O N THE FOLLOWING SUNDAY Jill was sitting in church with Peter in the usual pew, in the back on the left, thinking about Josh and his reaction to the painting instead of listening to the children's sermon. Actually she was thinking about Josh—*and* she was thinking about the painting. She had poured herself into it, but what was it? She had made a very dark painting, but she was someone who loved the light. Josh was also dark. His reaction was dark and strange, incomprehensible, rude. What in the world was she thinking?

She was excited to show him the painting. In her fancy she had painted it to summon him—and he had come. This was diverting, but it was not the source of her delight as she led him up the stairs. No, she was laughing because of the excellence of the painting itself. She was not thinking about the fact that it was a painting of Josh as a vampire. She did not take the vampire thing seriously, and she assumed he wouldn't either. He was far too sophisticated for that. No, her delight came from the opportunity to share her work with someone who knew painting.

But now this struck her as a little daft—and vain. She was not about painting per se. *Ars gratis artis* meant absolutely nothing to her when her professors tried to explain it in school. That was not what she saw when she looked at her favorite painters, the short list of four or five, and it was not what drew her to painting. She was not impressed by technical virtuosity. She had a beautiful vision, involving pain and happiness, faith and fidelity. The art was all about finding a way to get this vision out of her head and onto the canvas.

But then why was she painting vampires? She was trying to impress Josh and had been duly punished for her transgression. Josh was not amused. He acted like a child, running out of the house without saying a word. It made her feel very differently about him. His dark mannerisms did not seem so cute or amusing anymore—or, dare we say it, appealing. He was clumsy, knocking things over and slamming the door. The cultured aloofness and detachment were gone. Josh was a very strange young man. His strangeness had always been out in plain view, but now it was no longer possible for her to hide it from herself.

On the other hand, she was grateful for his rudeness. It woke her up from her ridiculous dream, her amorphous fantasy about Josh and herself. The painting unmasked him and his boorishness—but it also unmasked her. She was acting like a fool, doing things she herself hated. She was trying to pretend Josh was not really what he was, as if she had the power to make him into something else. She was grateful for his support, but he was also very self-centered. Indeed, she had painted him as a vampire, the most selfish creature of all, living off the life-blood of others.

Jill glanced over at her son, who at that moment happened to be smiling at something that was being said. This charmed her. He did not do enough smiling. She worried about Peter and his seriousness. His hand was on the pew between them, and she felt an almost overwhelming desire to cover it with her own. She loved him so much—wanted him so much to be happy. There was nothing she wanted more. But she knew she had to keep her hand to herself. She did not want to spoil his moment with smothering.

Now another painful thought came to her. She had not yet told him about the baby. She was afraid to tell him. He was delicate emotionally, and she did not want him to feel marginalized by a new addition to the family circle or think he would be any less loved. For that matter she had not even told Brian. She was afraid to tell him, too—afraid of how he would react and of being blamed. But it was more than that. She had lost respect for Brian, with all the bills and burdens crowding in on her and his continued absence. She did not think she loved him anymore.

Then she found herself listening to some familiar old words— "Cast your cares on the Lord, and he will sustain you; he will never let the righteous be shaken." Jill looked down at the words on the page and shook her head. It was like waking up, seeing them again, or remembering what you looked like. She did not know how righteous she was, with her unconventional lifestyle and recent flirtation with vampires, but she knew about faith. She knew about the righteousness that comes through faith.

Suddenly everything seemed lighter. She felt like she could tell them about the baby. She certainly knew she had to. In the car, on the way home, she stepped into deep waters.

"So I have some news for you," she said, trying to sound more cheerful than she felt.

"You do?"

"I do. You're going to be a brother."

There was a pause. "You guys adopting?"

"No, silly—I'm pregnant! You probably didn't think I had it in me." This didn't come out quite right.

"You're going to have a baby? Really? Does Dad know?"

"Not yet. I haven't had time to tell him."

This response was greeted with silence. Jill couldn't blame him. It was embarrassingly lame. But what was she going to do? Tell him the real reason? That she didn't love his father anymore and was afraid he would blow up when she told him?

"So what do you think? Are you happy?"

"I guess so. I guess I don't know what to think. I'm kind of in shock."

"You always said you wished you had a brother."

"I was thinking of someone to play with, not a baby."

Jill didn't know how to respond. She longed to reassure him that the baby would not change her love for him or their relationship or family life in any degree, but the timing did not seem right—not until she had a chance to talk to his father and ascertain whether this really was the case.

She was determined to put this dreaded call behind her, but Peter was with her all afternoon, and there was nowhere to go in the house without being heard. They usually called Brian together, but she did not want him to be on the phone if his father happened to lose his temper. She also did not want him to hear the kind of accusations that were likely to be coming her way.

Peter often went out to do things in the yard or barn on weekends, but not that day. He was too absorbed in "March

Madness" and it was too cold outside. In the end Jill wound up sneaking out the kitchen door and shutting herself in the Subaru. She sat there for a long time, trying to get the nerve to make the call, rehearsing what she would say. She was afraid he would blame her, but as far as she was concerned it was his fault. He was the one who had pressed himself on her with his unwanted attentions.

Or was it? She did not try to stop him. It wasn't because she loved him; it was because of the painting. She knew it had upset him. He would have been even more upset if he knew what she was thinking when she painted it. She was far from innocent. She was interested in Josh. He gave her more encouragement in the short time she had known him than she had received from Brian in fourteen years. Was she so wrong to paint him? Yes, she was. She knew she was, and she knew it was the reason for the baby in her womb.

She did not love Josh. His bizarre reaction to the new painting had made this clear to her. Her joke of using it to draw him did not seem so funny anymore. She did not want to draw him. She did not want him coming to her house or anywhere near her son. How could she have thought that someone like him could help her navigate the predicament with Brian and the baby? He was not sensible. He shoveled snow in his dress shoes. Had she lost her mind?

Jill prayed for strength—and for forgiveness. She said the reciprocal passage from the most famous prayer over and over to herself until a sense of calm descended over her. Then she touched the familiar number on her phone. He answered right away. He sounded surprisingly chipper.

"How are you! I've been meaning to call you," he said.

"You have?" Jill replied in surprise.

"I know—hard to believe. You know me and phones. But it's so good to hear from you."

This was different!

"So how's it going?"

"It's been crazy. Sixteen or twenty-hour days, between work and the studio. To tell you the truth it's getting kind of old. I didn't realize what a pain this is. Hours and hours of just sitting around dubbing and redubbing. Trying to make everything perfect. Not really my thing."

"But are you happy with the result?"

"I'll be happy when it's over," he said with a laugh. "At this point I just want to come home and have a normal life again. I want to see you and Peter. I miss you guys so much."

"We miss you, too," she managed to say. "It leaves a big hole when you're not here."

"I'm so sorry about that. I don't know how I'm ever going to make it up to you, allowing me to do all this. I really don't know how you put up with me all these years."

"It's your dream. It's what you've always wanted."

"I don't know. I'm not so sure about that anymore."

"What's going on? Are you all right?"

"I was kind of wondering if—things could be different between us. Not 'different,' but—you know. The way they used to be. We kind of seem to have lost our way. I know, it's mostly my fault—the band and everything. But you guys are the most important thing in my life. I just want you to know that. I just want you to know that *I* know that."

Jill took a deep breath. "Actually I have some good news for you."

"Really? What?"

"You're going to be a father again."

"You're kidding! How did that happen?"

"Remember Christmas Eve? It seems Santa was a little more generous than usual."

"Wow. Amazing. All I remember was that strange music you were playing."

"Are you upset?"

"Upset? No. Why would I be?"

"Well, I guess I got a little lax around the holidays. Sorry about that."

"Don't be sorry. I'm not sorry at all. This will be great."

"You really mean that?"

"Of course I do! You don't believe me?"

"Well, it's just that I know you said you wanted to wait."

"For what? We're not getting any younger. I've been thinking a lot about how much I miss sitting on the porch with you and looking at the mountains. I know I haven't been much of a companion, but I want to change. Maybe we could even make a visit to a church one of these days."

"Did you just say what I thought you said?" she replied with a stunned laugh.

"What did you think I said?"

"It sounded like you proposed to me."

"About time, don't you think?"

Jill could not help it. She started to cry. Mothers on rollercoasters of emotion.

"What's the matter?" Brian said.

"I guess I've been waiting a long time to hear that."

"I know. I'm so sorry."

"I thought I wasn't good enough for you."

"Are you crazy? That had absolutely nothing to do with it. In fact if anything the opposite was true. I didn't think I was good enough for you. And now I made you cry."

"It's not that. I'm just—so happy."

"Do you always cry when you're happy?"

"Sometimes."

"I love you, you know."

"I know. I love you too."

Jill could not move when this conversation ended. Too many emotions. Brian's whole demeanor surprised her. Every time she'd called before—and she was the one who had been doing all the calling—he had been terse and uncommunicative. The change was like Gandolf casting out Saruman. For a moment she wondered if he had been drinking. But no, he sounded like the old Brian. The more they talked, the more her fear melted away. She felt relieved—then she felt happy.

He liked the idea of having another baby! Her fears were completely unfounded. She believed him when he said he had a change in perspective about the band and their lives. People can go down a certain path and people can change. She had gone down the vampire path, and she had changed. She remembered that Brian was her first and only love. She remembered the fun they used to have, how much she enjoyed being with him, how much she admired him, both as a musician and as a person.

Brian was a good person, underneath it all. The band had taken over his life in recent years, but even then he was kind; he was gentle and had a good heart. He was good to Peter, which meant everything to her. He was serious, but he could also be funny at times. On the whole, he had the right priorities. It was hard for her to acknowledge this, but it was true. He was gone too much, working his job and playing with the band, but in his mind he was doing it for their sake. He was doing it so they could have a better life, not so that he could catapult himself into stardom.

He didn't smoke or gamble. He drank more than she liked, but he didn't waste any time at the bar after rehearsals, like the rest of the band. They had the inevitable squabbles that bedevil all couples, married or otherwise, but he was respectful of her. She never had any reason to be afraid of him. She was frustrated with him for putting off marriage and putting off life in pursuit of an increasingly unlikely dream. That was one of the main reasons why she was thinking of leaving him—she was frustrated.

But now she had a revelation. She could not think of any man she would trade for Brian. No one else could string the bow. She realized now that she'd had a blank placeholder in her mind all this time—all the time she'd been thinking about leaving him. Where was she going to find someone she loved—and liked—more than Brian? She had been distorting their differences and exaggerating his deficiencies. She allowed herself to begin to resent him, and then there was a snowball effect as resentment turned inward. Years went by and it kept getting worse and worse.

It was the old Brian that Jill heard on the phone, however; the one she'd fallen in love with. It occurred to her that he was not really what she had been making him out to be. In some sense her negative view of him may even have been a self-fulfilling prophecy. He was negligent in her mind; this colored her way of treating him and may have caused him to live down to her expectations. She perceived him to be pushing her away when maybe she was the one who was unconsciously doing the pushing.

Jill repented of all this. She did not want it anymore—the resentment, the unhappiness, the weariness. Brian had proposed to her. The thing she had been longing for all these years had finally come true. It filled her with joy! It meant he loved her and he valued her. "A good wife is more precious than gold." She did not aspire to quite that level of gem-like perfection, but she felt the force of his words. He had come home to her in his mind. He had returned from his journey.

And had she returned from hers? She felt she had. One conversation cannot heal years of hurts and sorrows, of course, but something had changed in her and she felt the change. Her attitude toward Brian was shifting, relenting—toward them and their possibilities. He said he wanted to start over. She believed it was possible to start over. The old scars never fully go away, perhaps, but it is better to move forward with the intention of not making any new ones. This scarred existence was all there was and all there had ever been. Abraham offered his wife to the king. Their existence was scarred.

The scars did not make happiness impossible, however. If happiness is moving forward in a marriage bond based on sacrificial love with the mutual intention of making things better and building each other up—if this is what a happy marriage truly is—and she could not imagine, based on what she now knew, that it could be anything else—then she and Brian had as much of a chance as anyone else to be happy. Two fallen creatures cannot have the joy of becoming one without the cross of sacrifice. Any other way of looking at marriage was a fraud.

It sounded like he was reevaluating things. "I'm not so sure about that anymore." Was he thinking about giving up his dream? Something about his tone suggested it. She hurt for him, but was it for the best? He certainly did not have to be a rock star to make her happy. Quite the contrary; happy rock stars seemed to be in short supply. And music was not his only gift. He was a very good carpenter. His boss even referred to him once as a "master carpenter" within her hearing. She was an artist who knew art, and Brian was an artist too, as far as she was concerned. She was not a snob. She did not value the heartfelt work of the craftsman any less than the paintings in the MFA. In fact she valued it more than many of them, the ones that were based on little more than vanity.

Maybe most of all—he was happy about the baby! This changed everything. She had lived a month of pure dread since finding out she was pregnant. The economic worries were bad enough, but the thing that really scared her was the possibility that Brian would not want it. She could not raise two children on her own. She did not want to—for their sake. His reaction was impossibly sweet. Her burden vanished. He wasn't just accepting; he actually seemed to be happy about it.

This said a great deal to her. For him to be happy about the baby was the strongest indication of a change in his heart and in his mind—even more than the proposal. It was a tacit promise of commitment on his part, not in so many words but to anyone who could read between the lines. He wanted this baby. He was looking forward to having it with her. And that could only mean that his attitudes toward family life were evolving, as well as his ideas about fatherhood and its responsibilities.

These thoughts made Jill happy. She was still sitting in the car in the cold but she was too happy to care. She did not forget to say a prayer of thanks.

BREAKDOWN

THEN JILL HAD A CHILLING THOUGHT sitting out there in the cold. The painting! Now that her perspective had changed, she had very different feelings about it from when she had first shown it to Josh. In fact she was ashamed of it. She hopped out of the car and went directly to the loft, waving at Peter on the couch as she breezed by. She took the painting off the easel a little more forcefully than was necessary and dropped it carelessly in the back of the closet with its ignominious brethren. Those eyes, those lips! She almost couldn't believe what she had done. What had possessed her?

From the high of her conversation with Brian she now found herself in danger of tumbling to a new Sunday afternoon low. There was no way around it—she had been profoundly disloyal to him with Josh and the paintings. It was complicated—she did not know at the time if she was going to stay with Brian—but even so she was stung by what she had done. It would not be accurate to describe her interactions with Josh as flirtatious—Jill was not a flirt—but she had invited him to her house and been alone with him. She had not discouraged his attentions.

What was she going to do when Brian came back? Should she tell him about Josh—tell him the truth about the man in the painting that had caused him so much pain? How could she tell him—*what* would she tell him? She herself did not fully understand what had happened or her own heart. On the other hand she did not want to conceal anything from him. They were supposed to be starting over. The slate needed to be clean, and it could not be clean unless she came clean. Was it better to be honest or kind? She did not see how she could be both.

Thinking about Brian sent her down another rabbit hole. He still had not given her a definitive answer about when he was coming home. The financial picture was starting to get desperate. She had missed the late date for the March mortgage, and the dunning had begun. Winter had been as expensive as it was harsh. They supplemented the woodstove with electric heat on frigid nights, and electricity happened to be high. Her bill for January was over four hundred dollars. It was definitely not in the budget.

There were all the other usual expenses, too, on top of the January tax bill from the town. She did not want to fall into the trap of paying bills with her credit card, but her dilemma now was whether to use this last resort for the mortgage. She had less than half of what was needed. She had never missed a mortgage payment. It was the first time she had even been late. But the bank did not seem inclined to credit her for ten years of good behavior. No, they wanted their money.

And things were about to get worse. Jill had noticed for some time that the Subaru was making a new noise. It had almost two hundred and fifty thousand miles on it, so it made a lot of noises, but this one was disturbing because it seemed to have something to do with the engine. She took it to the town's one repair shop and was given the bad news. It needed a new transmission. The cost was going to be almost as much as the mortgage.

Jill almost broke down and cried right there in the shop with its nondescript gray walls and dirty concrete floor when Bud gave her the bad news. He was very apologetic. He liked Jill and let her take one of his spare vehicles. Jill drove home feeling about as low as she could feel. It didn't help that the old S-10 seemed to want to bounce off the frost-heaved state road.

She could not bring herself to ask her parents for help, not at her age, even though help had been offered. She thought about calling Brian, but what good would it do? He could not help her from a thousand miles away. The old resentment tried to insinuate itself again. Brian had the other car, the one that worked, but she was the one who was working. If he really loved her so much then why couldn't he come home? If he wanted a fresh start then why was he waiting so long? Jill fought these negative feelings but was not entirely successful.

The Subaru wasn't done until the end of the week. They were busy, and there was some problem getting parts. Jill dragged herself through those three days on sheer willpower, wondering where she was going to get the money and hating the rusted old truck. She couldn't drive Brian's pick-up because she had taken it off the insurance when he went to Memphis. She couldn't see putting it back on just so she could be more comfortable.

She became numb. Three days went by and her expression never changed. She wanted to cry, but not in front of Peter. And not at the restaurant, either. She was still numb on Friday when she walked into the shop. Bud handed her the keys and assured her it was "like new." She tried to hand him her credit card but he would not take it.

"Come on, Bud. It's all I've got. I can't pay cash."

"You don't need to pay me anything. It's all taken care of."

"Taken care of? What do you mean?"

"Like I said—paid in full."

"I don't understand. By who?"

"I don't know if I'm at liberty to share that information," he said with a toothy grin.

Jill could not believe what she was hearing. She gave him a skeptical look but he pretended not to notice. She walked to the car in a cloud. Suddenly it didn't look like her fifteen-year-old albatross anymore. It looked like a gift.

But who could possibly have done it? She called her mother.

"So do you guys have something you want to tell me?"

"Not that I know of," Betty said cheerfully. "What did you have in mind?"

"Something very strange just happened. I had an expensive car repair, but when I walked into the shop it had already been paid."

"Well, that's a good thing, right? Someone's looking out for you."

"Are you sure it's not you?"

"Pretty sure! We didn't even know there was a problem."

"Who could it be, then?"

"I don't know. Sounds like you have a secret admirer."

This comment sent Jill's mind reeling. Did her mother know about Josh? No; there was no way she could. But was Josh her benefactor? It did not seem likely—but who else could it have been? It was not anyone at church. She had not told anyone she was in trouble.

It was Josh. It had to be. He seemed like someone who had money, or came from it. But it was so much! She smiled all the way home thinking about it. Josh was baffling. He could be dark and rude—and then this. Maybe he was trying to make amends. Maybe this was his way of apologizing for how he acted when she showed him the new painting.

Now her view of Josh began to change again. She could not forget his boorishness, but neither could she ignore his kindness. He had been kind to her all along, when she thought about it, in his awkward way. He supported her and made her feel good about herself. He had come to help shovel snow. He had not attempted to take advantage of her in any way. In that sense he was always the perfect gentleman.

In fact there were only two occasions when his behavior had been at all disturbing or inappropriate—and both had something to do with her paintings. The first was the very first time he came to the house and suddenly became ill. The other was the recent debacle with the vampire painting. She still did not understand it. Even if he hated the painting there was no reason for such a demonstration. It seemed like he was putting on a big show, but for what? What was it supposed to mean? Jill had no idea.

She had made a painting of him as a vampire. It was jokey but not in any sense mean-spirited. She was not trying to make fun of him. On the contrary—she had made him look quite dashing and beguiling. Was it the vampire theme itself that offended him? She could not imagine why. The painting was actually quite subtle and restrained in that sense. It could almost be mistaken for a straight portrait of an aristocrat. True, it was a little steamy, but Josh did not strike her as being a prude.

Unfortunately she had no way of knowing what offended him because he had not stayed around long enough to tell her. She was still unhappy with him about that—but now it appeared he had paid for the car! He had come to her rescue in spectacular fashion. She wished she could find him and thank him. For a moment she even thought about returning to town and looking for him.

But that night she had a surprising phone call—from Brian. This was the first time Brian had actually called her since he went to Memphis. He was not a lover of phones or phone conversations.

"So did you have any little surprises today?" he said in a playful voice.

"How did you hear about that? Did my mother call you?"

"Your mother, call me? I don't think so. I have my sources."

"You are talking about the car, right?"

"I am. Bud told me all about it."

"Bud! Why were you talking to him?"

"He called me, I guess it was Tuesday. Said you'd been in. Said you looked terrible and wanted me to know what was going on."

"Are you saying you paid for it?"

"Well—sort of," he said with a laugh. "Actually Kyle paid for it."

"Kyle! What are you talking about?" (Kyle was Brian's boss at the cabinet shop.)

"I made a deal with him. I told him I would give him ten hours a week for free until it was paid off."

"Wait—I'm confused. Are you saying you still have a job there?"

"Oh, yeah. He's been calling me regularly. Wants me back. Lots of new business. Tricky customers."

"And you're really going to do that?"

"Of course! I can't wait to get back."

"I can't believe it. I had no idea."

"Are you happy?"

"So happy. You can't even imagine."

"I'm so glad. I love you."

Now Jill's heart was full. She was glad it was Brian and not Josh. It was a gift with no strings attached. There were so many surprising things and so much good news in this short call that she was having a hard time absorbing it all. First, Brian wanted to come home. It was the second time he had made this clear to her—which was a lot for a man of few words. Second, he had a job. Jill had been worried about this. It was not easy to find good jobs in their little part of the world.

But most of all he had done it for her. He had agreed to come back and agreed to take his old job and work extra time to pay off the loan. It was a clever ploy on Kyle's part, but this only made the sacrifice seem more poignant. Brian was indenturing himself for her sake. She did not believe she had ever loved him more.

PARADISE

A WEEK WENT BY and the weather turned wintry again and the March wind blew and blew and there was another snowstorm—and then there was a change; there usually was at the end of March. The days were getting longer and it was no longer bitter cold but a different kind of cold, in-between. The ground was still semi-frozen but at least there was hope and hearts were beginning to thaw.

Jill heard a good sermon on the last Sunday of the month about wiping the slate clean and came home still thinking about it. She knew she had some cleaning to do to make her house ready for Brian's return. "I will remember their sins no more." The words were very striking to her. She had heard them many times in her life, but they are not for the young. At that moment they seemed dipped in stars.

She was thinking about these things as she made tuna sandwiches for Peter and herself at the kitchen counter. She felt an urge to see the beautiful words in context, so she pulled down her Bible. A scrap of paper fell out—"Bezalel." She stood there staring at it for a long time. She remembered Peter saying it was from the Bible. Suddenly Jill was seized with curiosity. She pulled out her phone and Googled. The following verse popped up:

"See, I have chosen Bezalel son of Uri, the son of Hur, of the tribe of Judah, and I have filled him with the Spirit of God, with wisdom, with understanding, with knowledge and with all kinds of skills— to make artistic designs for work in gold, silver and bronze."

Jill was swimming as she read these words. Her body began to shake. She glanced at Peter, who fortunately was absorbed in the TV, then back at the words. They danced around for a moment on her small handheld device and then they came back together. She was unaware that there were artists in the Bible. She knew about the poets and musicians—but not artists. This was the first time she had ever heard of it. There was a warm feeling in her hands.

She finished the sandwiches and gave one to Peter (no tomato) and went straight upstairs. She wanted to paint. The desire was overwhelming. No, not the frivolous nonsense she had been wasting her time on since she met Josh. Something of substance. Specifically, Adam and Eve. The idea had intrigued her for a long time. Happy thoughts about Brian coming home made it the natural choice.

It was not going to be like the Renaissance paintings. They were about the fall and trying to capture the cataclysmic moment—or they were misogynistic. Jill had a very different idea in mind. She wanted to show them in paradise. She wanted to show love as it was intended to be. She loved the part about "this is now bone of my bones and flesh of my flesh." She also loved the statement about them being "naked and not ashamed." Not for prurience— that was not Jill—but for the interruption.

The painting would practically paint itself. She would bring in her besotted love of nature and create a bouquet of sweetness and enchantment. She took out the biggest canvas she had in the closet and put it on the easel and prepped it. Then she picked up her sketch book. Before long she had an outline of what she wanted. The general composition fell into place almost naturally, without straining. She saw the whole thing in her mind.

She was going to show them from the waist up with their arms at their sides and gazing into each other's eyes. Then she would fill the rest of the frame with colorful flora and fauna. The tops of two trees would be visible in the background—the tree of life and the tree of the knowledge of good and evil. There would be blue sky and sun.

She wanted to make the canvas a cornucopia of fruits and flowers and creatures. All of the beauty had already been provided; her plan was to render it in a new light. There would be roses curling over Adam's shoulder at the end of a thornless vine, because she loved roses. There would be a pheasant and a snowy owl. She did not know if they had such birds but she also didn't care. They were going to be in her painting because they were beautiful and they meant something to her.

There would be a lion. There would also be a sheep. Incongruously, there would be a fish peeking out of a bush. (She thought she would put a little humor in the painting.) There would be a squirrel monkey. There would be tiger lilies. There would be a low-growing rhododendron. It would grant the modesty to Adam and Eve that they did not need or desire. All of this would all be painted with a palette of joy. She had a vision of new kind of realism, created just for this special painting.

Jill was so happy she could hardly contain herself. She fetched her tablet and started searching for models. The plants and animals and sky and sun were easy; the principals took a little longer. She could not find anything that satisfied her completely, so she chose several for each with the idea of turning them into a composite. She could do that. She could already see what she was aiming for in her head. She just needed them for the studies and the details.

The studies were not onerous because they were standing facing each other. There were no complex anatomical challenges to be conquered; it was not going to be that kind of painting. Instead the challenge was in making pre-fallen characters and especially faces. It would have to be partly realistic but also partly symbolic. She would have to allow a certain formalism to suggest perfection to the mind that could not quite remember or imagine it. The light would help her.

It was the complete opposite of the experience with the Josh paintings. She was filled with joy instead of daemonic possession. She did not throw herself into the painting; she was holding back and taking her time, planning for something bigger, something exquisite. After a week of hard work she was ready. She started mixing paints. This was going to be crucial. It was the colors, she knew, that were going to carry the emotional and intellectual weight. She could paint a flower very well, but now something more was needed and it was going to come from the colors.

She kept thinking about people who report near-death experiences. The other-world they encounter is said to be filled with color so intense that it seems entirely new, the color of paradise which no eye has seen but the mind can intuit, as in dreams. Jill's plan was to let her colors intimate paradise. All of the things seen in the painting would be perfectly familiar but also entirely new. Once she knew what she wanted, all she had to do was experiment with the mixing until she broke through and met her calibration. It was time-consuming but it did not seem onerous. She was discovering new things and having fun.

Finally she was ready. It was a Saturday in April and the sun was shining and the birds were singing and Peter was at a friend's house and she'd just had another nice phone call from Brian. She was alone in her loft in her cabin in the woods and perfectly free. She made a few tentative brush strokes, just to break the ice. A funny thought occurred to her as she did this—she felt the brush in her hand and she felt like an artist. She was not the student anymore but an artist. It was the first time she'd had this thought. There was nothing boastful in it; quite the opposite. It was simply a sense of confidence and arrival.

With so much prework, the painting went quickly. Within a couple of weeks it was beginning to round into shape. She liked what she was seeing. Her vision of paradise was possible. It was a challenge because she was trying to "make all things new"; but the biggest challenge of all was Adam and Eve. She had an idea of what she wanted, but it took quite a bit of experimenting to get to the point where she began to feel satisfied. She kept discovering new things and then they would lead her on to new discoveries.

The month of April flew by. Jill spent every spare moment in the studio working on the painting. She felt like she was neglecting Peter and was glad for once that he was a teenage boy who did not want to be catered to by his mother. There were robins chirping in the yard when the painting finally came together. Jill was daubing the canvas in a bit of a reverie and suddenly she just stopped and pulled away because it was done. There was nothing left to do.

Now for the first time she really looked at the painting in which she had been so deeply immersed. It was good. It was done at a very high level in terms of technical execution, higher than anything she had ever attempted before. But most of all it had an immediate emotional impact. It was filled with joy and love. They were tangible. She had challenged herself to make something completely new and had succeeded.

She stepped back and saw a glorious rectangular explosion of color framed by the large dormer windows and the blank gray of early spring in Vermont, the perfect contrast of hope and fulfillment, this world and the next. There was a touch of sadness as she pulled off her frock. She was never happier than when she was painting, and she had never pushed herself so hard before.

She wanted to share it with someone! She thought of Peter but did not want to drag him up against his will. If he happened to see the painting and like it that was one thing, but a command performance was not likely to be gratifying to either of them. She thought of Pastor Redmond, but she had never invited him to look at her paintings before. Besides, what would he make of Eve's breasts in their milky-white glory? Would he think she was crazy—or worse?

Then she had a funny thought. She wanted to share it with Josh! He would be able to understand what she had done—the ideal for which she was striving. Also the painting had been inspired by the mysterious word he left behind. She was grateful. She thought he might like to know.

That afternoon she was picking up some groceries in town and was startled to see Josh on the sidewalk. He seemed so out of place that she had to look twice to make sure she wasn't seeing things. At first she drove past him. She was still smarting from his rude behavior and did not want him to think that she had no pride. But did she have any pride? She wanted to turn up her nose—but she also wanted him to see her new painting.

Plus there was a mystery to be solved—the scrap of paper. Josh did not seem like the type to be ferrying words from the Bible. And yet she was almost certain that it had come from him. She wanted to know if that was the case; and if so, why? What was he trying to tell her by leaving such a message? Did he have any idea of the kind of impact it had on her? No—of course he couldn't.

More than anything she wanted him to know that his message was the proximate cause of her new painting. She felt a strong desire to share this news with him. She doubled back and pulled up beside him.

"Are you lost?" she called out jokingly, rolling down her window.

Josh looked up, startled. "I don't know. I've been asking myself that very question."

"I was wondering—how would you like to see a brand-new painting?"

"You have a new one?" he replied, his eyes widening.

"Of course! I painted it just for you. Well, not really. I painted it for myself. I'm selfish that way. But you can see it. Do you want to see it?"

"I was just wondering if you had any new paintings. I was just thinking about it literally right now when you stopped."

"Spooky! So why don't you go find your car and follow me over?"

"My car?" he said, looking around vaguely.

"You know, that shiny gold thing with wheels."

"It's—in the shop. That's why I'm walking."

Jill made a fateful decision. "Okay, come with me then. We'll just take a quick look at the painting and then I'll take you to Bud's. Climb in! I won't bite."

Josh gave her a strange look but got in the car.

"So—how have you been?" Jill said cheerfully after they were on their way.

"Not sure."

"You're not sure how you've been?" she teased. "You're very strange, you know."

"I know."

She waited for him to say something else but he was silent. "Sorry about that last painting. I didn't realize it was going to have that effect on you."

"Oh—that," he said vaguely. "I was just surprised."

"Surprised? You seemed mad."

"No, I wasn't mad. That isn't even close to what I was feeling."

"What, then?"

"More like—oh, never mind. I can't explain it to you. You would never understand."

"I don't know. I think I'm a pretty understanding person."

"If you were, you never would have let me in this car."

Jill was kind of startled by this statement. He seemed annoyed, sulky. And he was right—she never should have let him in the car. It wasn't smart.

"There's a perfectly good reason for that," she said, trying to sound braver than she felt. "'Bezalel.'"

"Bezalel? What's that?"

"Oh, come on. Are you going to pretend you don't know what I'm talking about? That little message you left for me in my loft. It was you who left it, right?"

"Okay, I guess I might have dropped it," he confessed.

"I thought so. I wasn't sure, since it comes from the Bible."

"Is that where it's from?" he said with a little laugh.

"You didn't know?"

"No."

"So—what? You saw it on the Web somewhere?"

"I'll tell you exactly what happened, since you are so understanding and maybe you can explain it to me. I was walking down a street somewhere and it just popped into my head. As far as I know I had never seen the word before in my life. But I could actually see it in my mind, like it was printed there. And I was intrigued. I wanted to remember it. I didn't happen have a piece of paper, so I went into a bank to write it down."

"Ah, that's what that was. A deposit slip. But why did you bring it to me?"

"Because I thought it was for you. Actually that's the real reason I came that day. I didn't know anything about a new painting. I just felt I had to deliver my message."

"So you got this word in your head, and then for some reason you thought it was for me?"

"Yes, that's exactly what happened."

"It doesn't make sense. I mean, if you knew it was from the Bible then I could see why you might connect it with me. But you said you didn't know that."

"Nope. I just knew it was for you." Of course he resisted the temptation to tell her that everything seemed to be for her now. He did not want her to get the wrong idea.

"Huh. That's really strange. Because you were right. It was just what I needed to hear. In fact it was the inspiration for the new painting."

"Inspiration?"

"You really don't know who Bezalel was, do you."

"No, I told you. I don't know anything about it."

"Well, it turns out Bezalel was an artist."

"Okay. And?"

"I don't know. For some reason I was really moved by that. I can't talk to you about these things because you think the whole thing is ridiculous. You're not going to want to hear any religious nonsense from me or any long drawn-out explanations, so I'll just say it made me want to paint."

"You and the Bible again," he said sardonically.

"Hey—don't knock it until you try it."

"You don't know. It's too late for me."

"What? It's never too late. Even if you were lying on your deathbed it would not be too late."

"As I said, it's too late."

Jill did not have a snappy comeback for this. In fact she had no idea what he was talking about. It was all very mysterious. But it always was with Josh. At least she had gotten him to talk a little, made some contact with the old Josh. The apprehension that had started to overtake her went away.

Josh was thinking very different thoughts, however. He was terrified that he was going to hurt Jill. First of all he was still disoriented over what had just happened. He was walking down the street without any idea of how he got there, thinking about Jill and wondering if she had any new paintings—and she suddenly appeared. It was almost like he knew she would be there. And that was the problem. He did not know how he kept finding Jill—but he also did not trust the fact that he did.

He did not trust himself, which made her trust in him very disturbing. She was so cheerful and carefree when she invited him into the car. She was just like Carol that way. She thought he was one thing when in fact he was something else. He was not sure what, exactly, but he knew he was not what Jill thought he was. She had no concept of the sorts of things he thought about or was afraid he might do.

She invited him into her car! He was alone with her and he was afraid to be alone. He tried to warn her before. He tried to tell her to stay away from him but she refused to take the hint. Or was she flirting with the danger? Did she like bad boys? He thought about the vampire painting. He thought about the "bite" joke. Maybe she knew more than she was letting on. Maybe she knew exactly what he was and didn't care.

But no, that was impossible. He was the Destroyer. He killed Carol. The disjointed memories of that terrible night were running though his mind even now. They were never entirely out of it. He thought he was just out having fun in his car with a pretty girl when what he was actually doing was killing her. He was using her love for him to lull her into complacency.

Since that night there was a black space where his identity should have been. It was black and it terrified him. There was nowhere he could go to get away from the blackness—the void of him—except when he was with Jill. He wanted to be with her because he wanted the black void to go away. But was this the same reason he had wanted to be with Carol? To fill the void?

Was this overwhelming compulsion to be with Jill—if that was the word for it—the same as the lust that had drawn him to Carol? Not that there was any thought of sex. For some reason sex seemed to have gone out of his mind completely. In its place was this desire to see her paintings. The only positive thoughts he could remember having were of Jill and her paintings.

But this was why he was so thrown by the vampire painting. What was she up to? Was she actually falling in love with this darkness of his? She did not understand it. She did not know what it was. He was just a thing now. The fun and jouissance of the dashing figure in the painting had nothing to do with him. His body was numb and cold as if it were not his own. As if it were a compilation of scars.

Josh and Jill were both full of anticipation when they reached the log cabin, but it was of a very different kind. She was excited about the painting she had just made but also wondering how he would react to another "religious" painting. Meanwhile he was just plain afraid—of himself. He followed her up the stairs to the loft with the smells he loved so much. There must be something in him worth redeeming if he loved those smells and he loved art. O Lord, please let there be something! He was surprised at these words. He caught himself muttering them.

"Did you say something?" Jill said, turning.

"No—I don't know," Josh replied shaking his head in dismay.

He took the last few stairs and it was like lead. With each successive step he felt his legs get heavier until they were like lead and he wasn't even sure he could get over the last step, he felt a little dizzy and wasn't sure he could make it, but he took a breath and picked up his left leg with a conscious effort and then he was there, he reached the loft, he looked out the windows and he saw the mountains and his spirit lifted a bit. He couldn't be the thing he was afraid of, the monster. No, he was sure he couldn't possibly be that thing. Not with those mountains in front of him. Such beauty!

He meandered along behind her until they came to the new painting. "Here you go!" Jill said cheerfully, but he thought her smile was a little forced, like she was afraid of him. It was hard for him to come to the painting. Not physically—he was standing right in front of it—but hard to bring his mind to it. He lifted his eyes slowly and began to take in the margins of the canvas and saw right away what it was. He didn't have to ask her this time. He gazed at it slowly in abstraction, bringing himself to the painting. Leaving that dark thing behind and bringing himself to the painting.

Very slowly—it seemed like an eternity—he began to comprehend what he was looking at. He was astounded. There had never been another painting like it, not in the whole history of painting. Gazing at it almost in dismay he felt something he had not felt in a very long time. He felt joy. The joy was actually in the painting. He was able to feel it. The feeling of this new love he had been experiencing came back to him. The feeling of happiness he had never known before.

Now all of a sudden he snapped back in his mind and saw the whole painting—he took it in all at once and was overwhelmed. For a moment he stood gazing in mute amazement and awe. And then he started to laugh. He could not help himself, he started to laugh. It was a joyous laugh because something overtook him, took him out of himself and his darkness.

That something was a sudden realization. He was not there to hurt Jill. The thing he feared the most—the terrible thing—that was not why he was there at all. He was there for one reason only, which was to help her. He brought her Bezalel. He himself had done it, and he was convinced it was no accident. He was there for a positive purpose, to encourage her to make paintings like the magnificent one he was looking at right now; to encourage her not to give up or let the world deprive her of her gift. He was almost sure that was why he was there. What else could it be?

"Is something funny?" Jill said, looking rattled by this reaction.

"No—I'm just so happy. I actually can't believe how happy I am right now."

"Happy! Why?"

"Because of this...painting. This incredible work of art. Unbelievable."

"Honest to God, I don't understand you."

"I don't understand myself sometimes. But this I do understand. You are a genius. Thank you so much for painting this and for showing it to me. I can't tell you how happy you've made me."

"Do you even know what it is?"

"Of course! Adam and Eve. I'm not that stupid. But so completely different from Rubens or El Greco."

"No, it's not about the fall. It's about paradise."

"Oh—I see. I didn't notice the little piece of paper before. So it's really about happiness, then. Even more reason for me to be happy. I've never seen anything like it. The colors, the vibrancy, composition—everything. And what you did with *them*. Those faces! It's like you created an entirely new kind of art."

"That was the whole point. But I thought you didn't like my 'religious' paintings," she teased.

"I never said that. I like everything you do—except when you paint me."

"Well, I know you don't like being painted, but before that I hadn't done anything for a long time. I had given up on painting. And then the little message you brought me. That was very special, even if the method of delivery left something to be desired."

"I didn't do anything but admire what should be admired. And to be honest you have done so much more for me—more than you could possibly know. But I do need you to promise me something."

"Uh-oh. This sounds ominous."

"Not at all. I just want you to keep on painting. So much depends on it. I can't even tell you."

"Yes, because I'm making such a big impact on the world."

"You will. There is a renaissance in painting going on right now. Collectors want them; people want them to adorn their homes. You will find your audience eventually. There are lots of people in the world; you just haven't managed to connect with the ones who will love your art. But you will. In any case, and no matter what happens, don't stop. Because that would be a tragedy."

"Now I'm starting to think you're pulling my leg."

"No, I'm serious. Dead serious," Josh said—and then laughed.

"What is wrong with you?"

"What do you mean?"

"I've never seen you laugh so much before. In fact I've never seen you laugh at all."

"That's not true. But I told you—I'm just happy. I had all these questions. But not anymore. Not after seeing this."

"Questions about what?"

"Well—you, for one thing. Whether you were as good as I thought you were. That's one question that has definitely been answered."

Jill stood there looking at him in amazement. She was pleased by his reaction but did not know what to make of it. And what was with the laughter? She wondered if he wasn't just a little—daft.

"Can I make you some lunch?" she said, more out of politeness than volition.

"No, I should go. I don't want anything to spoil this moment. And don't worry about driving me back. I really want to walk."

"Are you sure? It's almost three miles."

"I'm sure. I want to walk on this beautiful spring day."

Once again Josh rushed off. But this time it was so different. Jill was not offended. It seemed like he rushed off because he was happy. She couldn't decide for whom she was happier—him or herself. She of course was delighted by his reaction. She could not have asked for anything more. But she was happy for him, too, because he seemed so happy. It was the first time she had ever seen him happy. Such a stark contrast from the drooping sulky figure who climbed into her car.

There was a lot for her to chew over in the things he said. First of all she took comfort in reassurance. No one can know how lonely the life of the artist is. No one can understand how difficult it is to carry on when the world seems indifferent and you have no objective way to affirm that what you are working so hard to achieve has any real value. Jill may have talked herself into believing it on some days, but there were other days she could be prone to discouragement and even despair.

That was why she had been able to put away her paints. It wasn't just Brian. She did not want to paint anymore because it seemed pointless. She did not want to go on pouring out her soul into the void. She talked herself into thinking she could live without painting. She would be kind and a caring mother and do good for others and "walk humbly with her God." There was certainly no shame in such a life. It was the life that millions were leading.

But Bezalel changed all that. It was the first time she had ever understood that being a painter could be more than just an avocation. It could be a calling. She could be called to be a painter in the same way that he was called to be an artist in brass. If one truly was called, then to ignore the calling was probably dangerous. It was to shrivel up and die.

This changed everything for her, the way she saw herself, the way she viewed her work. It was not sinful or selfish to paint if you were painting to serve, as she was doing—to bring joy to others as she had brought joy to Josh, to make the world a little happier and lighter, if she could. The only thing sinful was painting to glorify oneself or to exploit others. Jill did not believe she was doing either of those things. She certainly did not want to do them.

As for Josh, everything had changed for him, too. It is no exaggeration to say that he was a completely different person when he walked out of Jill's house. He ran off again but this time it was for a different reason. It was not because of the terrible fear he had been nursing. It was not to protect Jill or himself. No, he did it because he was happy. He wanted to be alone so he could enjoy his happiness, revel in it for a moment, feel the fresh spring breezes on his face.

He also wanted to be alone because he could not tell Jill what had just happened to him. It was not something he could share. What was he going to say? That he was worrying he might really be a vampire or some other horrible thing? That he was afraid of this appetite he seemed to have for blood? That seeing her new painting had freed him from these fears? That he was happy because he knew now why he had come to her? Not as a destroyer but because he had a second chance?

These were things that could not be said out loud. He was not sure how he felt about them himself. So he gave her a warm goodbye and walked out into the April brilliance. The birds were singing and the sun was shining and the daffodils were in bloom and he was in brilliance. He had never understood the light the way he understood it now. Even though it was just natural light to him it was pure joy.

Everything seemed so clear to him. His job was to get Jill to make a new painting of something worthy of her talent. Hence the overpowering joy he felt when he saw it. He had a mission to encourage her to paint. The whole Dracula thing—that was nothing more than his overactive imagination. And his guilt. He was guilty, but he had a second chance. He chose helping over hurting, and it made all the difference in the world.

He had broken out of his past. It was holding him back like a membrane but he had broken through. He discovered a generosity of spirit that he did not know he had. When he was with Jill he wanted to pour himself out for her. He had a great love for her. No, not that kind of love; it was something he had never experienced before. That was why he was so afraid of hurting her, so afraid of himself and the clumsy clod he had become. He did not want to hurt the thing he loved.

And the bloodlust, as it seemed to him? His mind opened like a flower and he knew what it was. He could see the whole scene as clear as day. He was lying on a gurney in the ER. It was after the accident. He looked up and saw the IV and bag of blood and he knew he needed that blood. Without the blood he would die. This was the desire that had been haunting him. Not that he was bloodthirsty, but after the accident he needed blood because he had lost so much.

And now he remembered something else. It was Carol in the car with him, and she was covered with blood. This time he actually saw her, as she was the last time he had seen her. And he started to cry. He felt the tears on his cheek and began to beg for forgiveness from the bottom of his heart. The black veil of sorrow started to lift ever so slightly as he walked down the state road surrounded by tall mountains. For the first time he felt forgiveness was something he could actually have. It was not impossible.

Jill said he could have it. Even on his deathbed he could have it, if he really was sorry for what he had done. He was so sorry. No one could be sorrier. Not that he presumed to deserve it! He deserved nothing but punishment. He hated his brutality. He hated himself for taking an innocent life.

Still, every man has a choice to make when forgiveness is offered—whether or not to be grateful.

SPRING

ILL WAS THRILLED BY JOSH'S RESPONSE, but after he left she began to feel a little guilty. She had wanted so much to share the new painting with him, but what about Brian? She brought Josh to her house but had not even told Brian yet. It wasn't right.

That night she went up to the loft and called him.

"I know exactly why you're calling," he said.

"Really? Why?"

"You want to know how much longer this is going to go on. Believe me, I'm right there with you. I can't wait for it to be over."

"You're almost finished, then?"

"As far as I'm concerned we are. I've had it with the whole thing. First of all we have to fight with other bands for the studio time. Then some people in our own band are making it impossible."

"People by the name of 'Leo,' by any chance?"

"He seems to think he's Freddie Mercury. Everything has to be done a thousand times and then do it all over again. At this point I can't tell if it's getting better or worse. All I know is I'm sick of it."

"So when are you coming home?"

"I gave them an ultimatum. Two weeks. Of course that doesn't really make sense since we paid for the house for the whole month. But it doesn't matter. He has to understand this is it for me. I want to come home to you. I want to see my son."

"Well, I have a little surprise for you when you do come home, a new addition to the house. Hopefully you'll like it."

"You mean besides the baby?"

"A different kind of baby. A new painting. I just finished it. Want to see?"

"Sure!"

She snapped it with her phone and sent him the picture.

"Wow! That's—incredible."

"You don't sound too sure."

"No, it's amazing. I'm just kind of surprised."

"Because?"

"I mean, you know. They're—"

"Oh! That," she said laughing. "Yes, they are. It's supposed to be Adam and Eve."

"I get it. Wow. But doesn't—I mean the guy sort of looks like—or is it my imagination?"

Jill looked at the painting and laughed again. "He does look a little like you."

"I don't know. I'm just saying. Was that intentional?"

"Not really. But now that you mention it, I love it. I must have done it without realizing it."

"And why would you do that?"

"Because I'm so in love with you, of course! No, but really. I painted this because I was thinking about us. I was thinking about how we could get things back on track, back to when we first started, as you said. That's how I came up with the idea of painting them in paradise."

"I want that, too, believe me. I can tell you one thing right now—I'm not going to be spending so much time with the band. Not anymore. I've had it."

"I'm not asking you to give up the band. I just want you to come back to us. That's all that matters to me now."

"You think you can give me a second chance?"

"Do you need one?"

"I don't know, I've been pretty negligent. Right now this just feels like five months wasted to me. On the other hand, maybe it's a good thing. It has definitely opened my eyes to what goes on in this industry and what's important. Let's just say there's a reason why they call it the 'industry.'"

"You never were one for being put in a straightjacket. That's what I love about you."

"By the way, I'm still looking at your painting. The more I look at it, the more I like it."

"Thanks! It makes me feel really good to hear you say that."

"I'm glad you're painting again. I love it when you paint."

"I don't know about that. I kind of had the impression you resented it."

"See? That's what I mean about a second chance. You're right. There were times when I managed to work myself up into some state of resentment over stupid things. But it just kind of dawned on me while I've been down here that I was the one who was never home. I was the one who wasn't pitching in and doing his fair share. I was blaming you when I should have been blaming myself."

"I'm not interested in blaming anyone. I just think we need a fresh start. And you know what? Maybe this whole thing will turn out to be a blessing in the end. Maybe we needed to be apart from each other for a little while in order to remember to be thankful for what we have."

"I can't agree that it's been a blessing to be away from you guys, but I do know what you mean. Let's just say I have a very different view of things now, having been down here. I can't wait to get back to the shop and start working on some projects."

Jill felt like melting after this conversation—she was so happy. Not that she thought it was going to be easy. If anything she was a realist. Brian said he wanted to change but she knew it would not be easy for him. He would have to overcome ten years of habit entrenchment. He would have to give himself a new identity, which is a very difficult thing to do. Also she would have to change! It wasn't all about him. He talked about his resentments, but she had her own. She had to learn to give them up as well.

She had been chewing over certain things for years—to the point where it had become pleasurable to her in a perverse way. She knew she had to give up her bitterness if she really wanted a fresh start. Starting with the bed. She would have to stop facing away from him. It was an antagonistic posture, a show of pride, and had been for years. She had lain like that on the edge of the bed facing away because she did not want to face him and give in. It had to stop right now. It was the first thing she had to do.

She had to make a choice about house chores. Either she had to commit to having an open, ongoing dialogue with Brian about sharing them—as he indicated he was willing to do—or she had to commit to taking up the slack without resentment in order to have any hope of domestic happiness. She had to learn to stop resenting the chores and do them as a sacrifice of love. She had to let go of the bitterness she felt when she saw a sink full of their dishes—not so much Peter's, she confessed, as Brian's. She liked the bitterness too much. That was why she had to give it up.

She had to change her mind about his drinking, too. Not her opinion—she could not give up the conviction that it was bad for him and a bad model for Peter—but the unhappy judgment to which she was clinging. True love overcomes judgment. She could not change him by holding on to her umbrage. No one has the power to change others, certainly not by condemning them, unless "change" means killing them. She hoped this was one of the things he had in mind when he talked about a second chance, and she made up her mind to try to talk to him about it; but in the end all she could do was pray.

After all, Brian had finally proposed! They were going to be married, and this changed everything for her and made her whole world light. It was not the kind of proposal that kids do when they get down on their knee as if they were in a movie and clearly have no idea what they're up against. It was a proposal from someone who had been through the relationship wars and still wanted to make a commitment. And somehow this made it even more special. They knew what the vows were really all about and what they were promising to do.

True love is sacrifice; everything else is vanity. The only way to truly love Brian was to take up her cross and give up everything that was selfish and self-centered. It was hard, but the reward was great. It was better to be someone who has sacrificed for love than to be self-seeking and alone. There were more tangible rewards as well. She looked forward to walking in the woods with him like they used to do. She looked forward to winter nights on the sofa holding hands and watching TV. She looked forward to going to places and sharing the things they enjoyed and new discoveries. She hoped he would come to church.

This last thought led to another idea. She thought again about sharing her paintings with Pastor Redmond. She did not know him very well; he had only been there for a couple of years, unlike the previous minister, who was there her entire life. Jill was naturally shy, but she liked Jack, who was kind and generous. She liked his wife Debbie even more. She was warm and funny and outgoing, traits that can be congenial to the introvert mind, just as a tight rosebud opens to the sun.

Sunday came and she went to church with Peter still pondering this idea and trying to get the courage to put it into action. She made up her mind in the reception line. She was nervous and felt awkward when she finally reached him and put her hand into his.

"How would you like to see what I do?" she said. He looked at her blankly and she realized what he was probably thinking. "No— I mean my paintings."

"Oh!" Jack replied, his smile returning from a brief sojourn. "I heard that you were a painter. I would like that very much. Are you having a show?"

"Actually I was kind of wondering if you wanted to come over some time. Debbie too. You've never seen our log cabin. I think you might like the view."

"You know, that's a very good idea. In fact we will be out this afternoon doing our usual Sunday drive to various and sundry places. Should we stop by?"

"That would be great! Do you need directions?"

"GPS," he replied with a smile.

This was a bold step for Jill. She had not invited the "new" pastor to her house yet for a variety of reasons. For one thing, she was skittish about the idea of introducing herself as a painter; skittish about sounding pretentious and possibly setting herself up for a fall. Also she was self-effacing and did not like to toot her own horn. But the main reason had been her uncertain marital status. She did not know how much Jack or Debbie knew about her and Brian and was not eager to answer uncomfortable questions.

Actually this was the main reason why she avoided socializing in general at the church. There were some parishioners whom she had known forever, had grown up with. Most of them knew what the story was, and some did not approve. There were also newcomers who did not know her so well and who had a very unsettling tendency to ask about her family life. Rather than expose herself to possible censure, it seemed easier to stay in her cocoon, her mountain fortress.

Unfortunately this tended to make her terribly lonely. She was no longer maintaining regular contact with her two very close friends from high school. Both had moved away and could not be visited easily. She had not made that many close friends in college—and they too were far away. It was hard for her to make friends, in part perhaps because of her shyness. But another reason it was hard was that her life had been on hold all these years. She was not married to the man she lived with. She owned a house but did not consider herself to be settled.

Everything changed in her psychological landscape, however, when Brian proposed. She did not have to feel embarrassed or inadequate anymore. Now she wanted Jack and Debbie to come to her house. She wanted to share her mountain views with them—and her paintings. She wanted to have house guests and parties and people coming and going all the time. She was an introvert who loved people.

They arrived at two. Jack seemed to have a good rapport with Peter and asked him many questions about school and hockey and the baseball season, which was underway. Jill marveled at the mature, polite answers Peter gave. They must be doing something right as parents. Jack and Debbie both raved about the log cabin and the views. This made her feel good. It wasn't the praise per se; she liked sharing her special spot and special space.

She had made some fresh iced tea, which she shared with them, and then they went up to the loft. At first the two of them just wandered around without saying anything. Jill did not know what to make of it. She did not share her paintings with many people and was not used to the experience. She held her breath.

Debbie was the first to speak. "Did you paint these?" she said, looking at Jill in awe.

"Well—yes, I did. As a matter of fact."

"No—I'm sorry. What am I saying? Of course you painted them."

"Do you like them?"

"Are you kidding? They're fantastic. I had no idea. I knew you painted, but I never imagined it would be anything like this. I'm sorry—that sounds terrible, doesn't it."

"Look at this one," Jack said, pointing to *The Blind Man.* "Biblical paintings, too."

"I just love this. Look at the faces! The expressions. Wow."

"That may be the most remarkable Jesus I've ever seen. Did you have a model?"

Jill smiled, remembering when someone else asked the very same question. "Actually, no. Not for him, although I did for the blind man. No, it was pretty much out of my head."

"So how does that work? You get a picture in your head and start painting?"

"Something like that. You can definitely imagine someone out of whole cloth, like you do in dreams. It's just a little more challenging because you're not looking at a physical face as you paint. In this case I was thinking of the 'man of constant sorrows,' and also 'he had no beauty, that we would admire him.' I had those two ideas in my mind for a long time before I decided to try this painting. I also wanted the idea of the healer. I just imagined the warmth of his touch."

Jack looked at her for a moment. "You, my dear, are a deep thinker. I mean, it's obvious from these paintings, but you have deep themes running through that mind of yours."

Jill shrugged. "That's what makes painting fun, to be honest. Getting the ideas to come out and still making them look natural. I don't know, it's kind of hard to explain why that's so hard."

"No, I think I understand. Debbie, look at this one. *Field of Blood.*"

"That's terrifying!" she said. "How did you do that?"

"That was a completely different kind of challenge. I never tried to show anything like that before—I guess you could say a combination of terror and anguish and sorrow. It's hard to do without being corny. I'm not sure I'm satisfied with the end result."

"Are you kidding? It's amazing. I feel like I'm right there with him."

"Maybe even in his skin," Jack agreed.

"That was sort of the idea. Did you see this one?" Jill said, leading them on. "This is new. Just finished it, as a matter of fact."

"Wow," Jack said. He looked at the piece of paper appended to the bottom. "*Paradise.*"

"Look how real they are!" Debbie said—to her husband, not Jill, almost as if she weren't there.

"I know. I can see that. Almost more than real."

"I love the whole feeling this one gives off. I mean, all of them are great—don't get me wrong—but this one seems special to me."

"Yes, something about the colors and the way you painted them. Not sure what it is exactly, but it really makes you feel the whole paradise idea. You, my dear, have quite a talent."

"I worked very hard on that," Jill said, feeling pleased. "Especially the colors. In fact for a while I thought about calling it 'Colors of Paradise.'"

"But it's about so much more than the colors. It's about the relationship, both the one we can see and the one that's implied."

"Yes, it's about the relationships," Jill agreed. "I'm glad you can see that."

"Now let me ask you something," Debbie said. "Are any of these for sale?"

"What? They're all for sale," Jill said laughing.

Jack and Debbie looked at each other. "Well, you know, it's kind of funny," she said. "We've been looking for a painting for our living room for a long time. I don't suppose we could afford any of these, however. We weren't setting our sights quite this high."

"You'd be surprised. It's not like people are knocking down my door to buy them."

Debbie looked around again and went straight to *Bonhoeffer*, which was the smallest and least imposing of the canvases. "What's this one? Oh! I see. Jack—look. Your favorite."

"Oh my gosh. So it is. That is quite a painting," he said. "I assume this was when he was in prison?"

"Correct. I had an idea about the possible joy of suffering, if that makes any sense. When you think about it he knew where it was all heading and yet he was resisting the greatest evil on earth. There had to be some kind of joy in that. Or at least I like to think there was."

"I think you did a very good job. I can see the question in his face. And I can see myself asking dinner guests what they see," he said with a smitten smile.

"Dare I ask how much this one would be?" Debbie said. "Someone has a birthday coming up, and this would be perfect."

"I don't know. Five hundred?" Jill blurted, thinking about the April mortgage payment which still had not been made.

Debbie stared at her. "You must be joking. It's worth ten times that, at least."

"If you really love it, and that's not too much, I would be happy to have you have it. I have a little mortgage challenge right now and could really use the money."

She didn't mean to say this last part—it just spilled out. They both looked at her.

"I'll write you a check right now."

"Let me get it framed for you first."

"Are you kidding? Then you won't make any money on it. No, we will get it framed. It's the least we can do for the privilege of even owning such a painting."

She wrote the check and gave it to Jill, who folded it and put it in her pocket without looking at it. They thanked her profusely. Debbie's exact words were that it was like "going to the Met." They wrapped the painting together, and then Jack and Debbie were off with their prize, seeming very pleased. Jill was pleased too. It was the first painting she had sold in years.

After they were gone she went back upstairs and sat in her favorite chair and gazed out at the mountains. It had been one of the most elevating interactions she had ever experienced in her life. They were not just complimentary but seemed somewhat amazed. She cherished this thought in spite of herself. She did not want to be vain, but she also could not help cherishing the thought. Only Josh and her mother had been as generous in their praise. And she knew she couldn't trust her mother to be objective.

What she especially liked, and went over and over in her mind, was the depth of their response. They saw many of the things she had worked so hard to put into the paintings. She thought they were there, but not many people had given her any confirmation. "You, my dear, are a deep thinker." It wasn't that Jill wanted the world to see her this way. It was more about the waitress being let out of her box.

Then she pulled the check out of her pocket and looked at it. Something was wrong—she looked at it again. Debbie had made it out for $1,000. And on the comment line she had written this: "Thank you."

MEMORIES

J ILL OF COURSE WAS THRILLED by the reactions she'd had to the new painting, both from the Redmonds and from Josh but most of all from Brian. She still could not believe he said he liked it when she painted. It meant so much to her. It's hard to explain how much it meant. She kept thinking about those words and they went down deep inside her. They were going to get married and there would be no conflict over the painting. She would not abuse the privilege. It meant too much to her.

She walked on this cloud for a couple of days—but fell back to earth in the middle of a rainy, cold week. She still had not been able to make the April mortgage payment. She was closer with the money from the Redmonds but not close enough. Brian was sending her more money from Memphis but it was being used for other expenses. He just wasn't making enough to help her meet the biggest expense of all.

Also she was having trouble with morning sickness. She forgot what it was like to be pregnant—it had been so long—but it seemed harder this time around. Was it because she was older? Was there a problem with the baby? This thought scared her, but the ultrasounds seemed normal. And no, she wasn't just sick in the morning. It could come on any time. It made waitressing more challenging. It put some strain on her relationship with Peter. She felt so alone. When was Brian coming home?

Then jolly May came rolling along, and there was some beautiful spring weather. It got almost mild and stayed that way for several days. Jill tried to focus on the joys of the season and the tender green buds on the trees and think more positively about the burdens she was carrying, not just financial but also all the work that needed to be done in the house and yard with spring coming on and her pregnant.

She was hanging up wash in the sunshine on the first Saturday of the month when a surprise visitor appeared at the end of the driveway. It was Josh in the gold Mercedes. She immediately thought of Peter, although it was still early and he was in bed. Why did Josh have to come now? How would she explain it to her son? What if he said something to his father? He'd already seen her with him once before.

She dropped the shirt she had in her hand and scurried down the driveway to greet him but mostly to stop him from turning in.

"Hi!" he said with uncharacteristic cheerfulness. "Want to go for a ride?"

"Right now?" she said, glancing around.

"Yes! I need to talk to you."

"I don't think that's such a great idea. I mean, Peter is here..."

"Hop in. It will just be a little while. He won't even know."

It seemed better to go along and get the car away from the driveway than to stand there exposed, so she did what he wanted.

"I found a nice trail up the road," Josh said as they motored along at a leisurely pace. "Do you like to hike?"

"I love to. But I can't believe you do."

"Okay, so I'm not exactly a mountain man. But I do love nature. Really, I do."

They found the place he was talking about and parked and of course Jill knew it; it was the Taverner Nature Sanctuary. And he was right, there were lots of wonderful trails. The one he was interested in went along the side of the mountain where there were some cliffs. She had never been on it before; she liked the one that went around the pond. She looked at him walking in front of her and had to shake her head. Same lame outfit, same dress shoes.

But what was it all about? Why did he want to go on a walk in the woods when by his own admission he was not a woodsman? Was he trying to impress her? Then she had a very unpleasant idea. Did he have something else in mind? She certainly hoped not. It was the last thing she wanted just then. She felt her morning sickness and contemplated turning back.

"Look!" Josh said. "Caves."

"Where?"

"Right here!"

"Oh—you mean the hole in the rocks."

"I wonder if there are any bats in there," he said, peering in.

"Ew, I hate bats," Jill said with a shudder.

"Count Dracula," he said like Karloff, raising his arms.

"Don't remind me. I get so embarrassed every time I think about that. I really didn't mean anything by it. I was just having some fun."

"I know. And I was taking myself way too seriously. Anyway, there's a pretty good view up ahead. Let's stop and talk for a while."

"Okay," she said but she didn't really mean it. What were they going to "talk" about? She hoped it wasn't the obvious thing. She did not feel strong enough to fend him off, if that was what he had in mind. The baby inside her was taking up all her energy. Then she realized she hadn't told him about the baby. This made her smile. It was an excellent way to dampen enthusiasm of that kind.

They reached the spot. The view was as promised. Jill forced herself to sit down on a rock and seem calm.

"So listen, I don't know if you realize how important it's been for me to get to know you," he began.

Uh-oh, she thought. Here it comes. "I've enjoyed getting to know you, too."

"You really sort of turned things around for me. I was going in a—not very good direction. You changed all that."

"I didn't really do anything. In fact it seemed like most of the time I just annoyed you."

"Annoyed me! Never. I was going through some things— there's no point in trying to explain it now. I'm so sorry if I ever did anything to upset you. I don't want to hurt anyone, but especially you."

Jill did not like the warmth of this, but after all it was kind. "You didn't hurt me at all. I could see that you seemed to be hurting. I just hope I didn't make it any worse."

"No, you made it better. That's what I'm trying to tell you. You made everything better."

He looked at her but she did not know what to say. Was this the big moment? Was he about to declare his love for her? She did not want him declaring his love. She looked down at her sloping stomach and thought of the baby and of Brian.

"You do realize I'm talking about the painting," he said.

Jill let out her breath. "The painting! Ah."

"Yes, that incredible painting. I still can't get over it. That's the sort of thing you should be painting all the time. You should never waste your energy on anything less. I want you to promise me that you will never stop painting—that you'll keep on growing and making miracles like the one you just made."

"I thought I already promised you that."

"I know. I guess I seem a little obsessive. It's just very important for me."

"Because you love art?"

"Well, partly," he said with a strange smile.

"So that's what you wanted to talk about. My painting."

"There's something else, too. I want you to make me another promise—that you will try to patch up your relationship with your friend."

She blinked. "You mean Brian?"

"Is that his name? Yes, Brian. Peter's father. Your 'significant other,' as you called him."

"What makes you think there's anything to be patched up?"

"He doesn't seem to be around very much. And let's face it, you wouldn't be inviting me to your house or painting pictures of me if everything was right between you two."

"So you brought me out here to talk about me and Brian?"

"Yes, as a matter of fact. I have a good feeling about Brian, a very good feeling. I know—I don't know him. But you'll just have to trust me on this."

"I do too—and I do know him. But I don't understand."

"Look, I know my behavior must seem strange to you. It seems like I keep showing up wherever you are. I come to your house and praise your paintings. One time I even shoveled your snow."

"I remember. That was very sweet of you."

"I know how it must have looked. I realize now I might have given you the wrong impression. I did not mean to give it, believe me. I never thought of you that way, not once."

"Gee, thanks!"

"No—seriously. It was never about that. I mean if things were different—but I'm glad they aren't for that very reason. I did not come to you to make you fall in love with me. That's why those paintings you made caused such a reaction. It wasn't because they weren't good. They were too good."

Jill paused for a moment. "Okay—I will say that some thoughts may have crossed my mind. You happened to show up at a difficult time in my life. But things are very different now. I am not in the place I was when you first met me. I'm a very different person. And yes, Brian will continue to be a very important part of my life. In fact we're getting married."

"Are you! I'm so glad. You don't know how I agonized over this conversation. I really haven't been in control of the things that happened over the last six months of my life or however long it's been. I know that probably doesn't make sense to you. How could it? The thing is, I was led to you. I never sought you out—as far as I knew I was just going about my business and you were there."

"Except when you came to the house—like today."

"Okay—except then. But even then I didn't come to your house, not in the sense you're using the word. Oh! I better stop right now. I really can't say any more about this."

"But what you're really trying to say is you were never attracted to me in that way. And thank you for that. I don't want you to be."

"I'm relieved."

"I am too," she confessed. "I was a little nervous about this talk you wanted to have. I'm glad it's just about my painting and not anything else. I guess I can share some news with you. I'm pregnant."

"You are!" he said, seeming genuinely excited. "That's great. How long?"

"Since Christmas," she said, and blushed at a certain memory.

"Well, I have some news for you too, some news I think you're going to like. I'm going away. I'm going to get out of your head and stop haunting you once and for all."

"I wouldn't say that was something I was specifically hoping for. But thanks for the heads-up."

"You are being kind. And you won't even remember me when I'm gone. It will be like you dreamed me and that's all."

"What are you talking about?" Jill said laughing. "I can't even imagine that ever happening. You're pretty hard to forget."

"No, I'm very forgettable. You'll see. I won't stand in the way between you and Brian."

"Oh! That's what you mean. Well, I would have to agree with you there. I have enjoyed getting to know you, and to be honest you've been very helpful to me. But Brian is the one for me. I never really thought about you seriously that way."

"That is such good news, so good to hear. That was all I had to say."

Jill did not know how to respond. He was trying to be noble and step aside for his perceived rival, but she was being honest. She did not think of him that way—at least not anymore. Oh, she may have briefly entertained some thoughts along those lines, but not seriously. She could not picture herself with someone as strange as Josh, the exotic creature sitting on the rock in the mountains and looking so hopelessly out of place. Never. He was so pale under the bright unforgiving sun!

They walked back to the car in silence. There didn't seem to be anything more to say after such an intense conversation. Besides, Jill did not want to encourage him. She wanted to believe him when he said he had never been interested in her—she also wanted to let sleeping dogs lie. The best thing that could happen now was for him to drive her home and drive off never to be seen again. If this seems a little cold, consider the nesting instinct.

She did pipe up when they got close to the house, however. "Would you mind letting me out here?"

"Really?" he said.

"Yes. I don't want Peter to see us and get the wrong idea."

"You're right. Absolutely not." He pulled over and Jill hopped out of the car.

"Goodbye!" she said, mustering a particularly bright smile. "Thanks for everything!"

"Goodbye. So glad to have known you. Good luck!" He paused. "God bless you!"

He drove off. She shook her head. So serious! If he only knew how she was really feeling. Why do men always assume women are in love with them? What is it about the XY set? He presumed too much. Still, there was something touching about the gesture, about the desire he expressed to be forgotten, to get himself out of the way for her and Brian. She could not really laugh at him for that. It seemed sincere. It made her feel he had her best interests at heart—even he knew he wasn't good for her!

Then again he had been kind of good for her. Hadn't he? He had saved her from the pit of despair, as far as her painting went. He made her feel validated. He made her feel she was not crazy— she really was a good painter. Of course they could both be crazy, but that was another story. He had given her the encouragement she needed at a crucial juncture in her life. She would never forget him. Never. How could she forget someone like Josh?

She walked back to the clothesline to finish hanging up the wash. The shirt was hanging out of the basket where she had dropped it, the nice one she got for Peter at Christmas. She picked it up and started pinning it to the line with the May breezes blowing in her hair, blowing away all the heaviness of being, in the sunlight, and then she couldn't help wondering—why had she left it like that? She had gone down to the driveway for something, but what? She could not remember now. She could not remember why she went to the driveway at all.

Was she getting forgetful? At thirty-three? Her mother always joked about going into a room and forgetting why you went there, but it didn't normally happen to Jill. She finished hanging up the wash and went inside and made some breakfast for Peter and rousted him out of his cave, as she liked to call it. The word *cave* made her pause. What was it? She couldn't remember. He ate his pancakes and she talked him into going outside and throwing a Frisbee around for a while. She loved him so much. She was happy they could still have a good time together, even though he was a teenage boy.

The fresh air felt good and the sun was shining and the day was resplendent. She drank it in after a long winter and iffy spring. They went in and Jill made him some hot chocolate and tea for herself. She sat down on the couch to relax for a moment before she began the cleaning that needed to be done. She thought about Brian coming home—maybe next week! That would be so nice for Peter. And for her. She thought about the wedding. Where should they have the reception? Right there at home? There were so many plans to be made.

Then she thought about the new painting. She was proud of it. She couldn't wait for Brian to see it in person. The phone rang. Guess who? So glad to hear his voice. They had a nice conversation. The joy of talking to each other had returned, just like when they were kids. Most of their conversations back then were over the phone. He told her again that he loved her. He asked about the baby. She told him about the morning sickness, and he said he was sorry.

It was a long conversation, relaxed and happy, and after it was over she just sat there for a while savoring it and the whole glorious day and her Earl Grey, trying to gather up the courage to pull out the vacuum cleaner and tackle the dirty floors and cobwebs. Cobwebs? It reminded her of something. But what? What was she trying to think of, tucked away in the back of her mind? She could not quite remember.

Something about the loft? What was it? Jill was curious. She dragged herself out of her comfy spot in the sun and went upstairs to look around. Nothing jumped out at her. She looked at the new painting and felt a blush of pride. It was very good. She wasn't the only one who thought so. Brian liked it. The Redmonds raved about it. Wasn't there someone else who raved about it? No; she must have dreamed it. No one else had been up there.

She looked around and this time her eyes settled on the closet door. She went over and opened it and pulled the light string and looked around. Nothing seemed out of place or unusual. It was dusty, but who had time to clean it? She walked in, still feeling curious. And then she saw them. In the back corner near the window—three canvases she did not remember putting there.

Jill walked over and pulled one back to look at it. She literally gasped. She was looking at a painting of a vampire. She did not know much about vampires, but clearly that was what it was supposed to be. A pale young man looking sort of—hungry. He seemed familiar. Where had she seen that face before?

Was this her painting? It was her technique, but she could not remember painting it. Only the face seemed familiar. She pulled it out for a better look. It was so unlike anything else she had ever done. Then she looked at the other two. Same guy! Was that the restaurant? It certainly looked like it. She had often thought about painting someone in a booth in the restaurant, a sort of homage to Norman Rockwell and his incredible composition talents, only in her own serious style, but this was not her painting. And yet it certainly looked like one of her paintings. What was going on?

The thing was the paintings looked new. They smelled new. She thought about what had happened to her in the yard when she was hanging out the clothes. Was she losing her memory? Having some sort of stroke? It scared her. Had she made these paintings and then forgotten about them? One thing was certain—she knew why they were in the back of the closet. They were torrid. And who was the man? Someone she had conjured up out of her imagination, no doubt. She definitely did not know anybody like that. Not in their little town, anyway.

Whoever it was, she did not want him hanging around the house. She could not believe she had painted him in the first place. She had not painted in a year—and then these. The more she looked at them the more she remembered painting them. But three paintings of the same man? He seemed so real, looking back at her. She could almost imagine him talking to her. She could hear him talking.

Was she losing her mind? For a moment she wondered. But there was something she knew she had to do. She had to get those paintings out of the house before Brian came home. They had served their purpose. They got her painting again. But now they had to go. She would never be able to explain them.

FIRESALE

I T WAS THE WEEKEND, so she couldn't do anything about the paintings just then; plus Peter was home and would want to know what was going on. But as soon as she came home from work on Monday she carried all three canvases downstairs and tossed them in the back of the Subaru. She didn't even bother wrapping them. To tell the truth she didn't want to touch them.

There was a gallery in Burlington that had sold a landscape of hers in the past. She had deliberately painted it to sell, and sure enough they had taken it—this after turning her down on several much more accomplished paintings, with a slightly condescending tone, as if to say "Oh no dear, we don't put that sort of thing in our gallery."

They were the kind of arts-world people she couldn't stand—snooty for no discernible reason—and worse, successful. What a joke it would be if they took the paintings off her hands, the ones she didn't want and was embarrassed about! She thought they might. Particularly the vampire. There was quite a vampire craze going on among adolescent girls, or so she was given to understand.

She drove a little faster on the highway than she should have and smiled when she found a parking spot right in front of the gallery, as if welcoming her with open arms. She retrieved the three paintings from the hatch and brought them in. Gene Taylor, the owner, was in his office, looking typically self-absorbed in his annoying wire-rimmed glasses.

"Hi, there!" Jill said boldly approaching.

"Well, hello," he replied, looking up—and she could tell he couldn't remember her name.

"I've got some new pictures I think you'll like."

"Really! That's refreshing. Let's see them."

This was not his usual response to her overtures, and she realized it was because she was being forceful. She didn't care about the outcome so she wasn't her usual timid apologetic sorry-to-impose-on-you self. She walked right up to him and leaned the paintings against the side of his desk and then stepped back to give him some space.

"Three! My, you've been busy." He looked at the first one—it was the tamest picture of the Mystery Man. "Hmmm…this is very nice, I must say. Not like the usual stuff you do. I like this."

"Thanks!" Jill said with a—well, you know what kind of grin.

He flipped to the next one, Josh in the restaurant. "Another one. Your technique has really improved here. Love the colors and the shades. And that face! The girls will love it. Bravo." He lingered over it for a while longer, shaking his head in approval and actually smiling. It was the first time she had ever seen him smile.

Jill almost laughed. She held her breath for the next one though. She had put the vampire painting in the back because she was a little embarrassed by it. She didn't know how he would react. She knew how she would react. That was why she put it in the back. He flipped to it and just stood there looking at it for the longest time. His face was expressionless, his lips drawn tight. What was he thinking?

The pause went on and on, and then it started getting downright uncomfortable. "Wow," he said at last. "Absolutely unbelievable."

"What?" she said, caught between amusement and bewilderment.

"Do you even know what you've painted here? This is amazing."

"Really?"

"Really! This is an incredible work of art. It's so strong, has so much presence. And I must say, your timing couldn't be better, with the whole vampire craze and everything."

"That's what I was thinking."

"See? You're learning. I'll tell you what, I think I may have a buyer for this one right now. Someone was in here not too long ago asking if I had anything like this. Sort of amazing that you happened to show up with it, but like they say, timing is everything."

Jill could not believe it. Or in a way she could. She suspected the paintings might be more salable than her serious stuff but she was a little surprised at his reaction, especially to Count Dracula, or whoever he was. She went home on cloud nine. Not only did she manage to get the paintings out of the house without having to take them to the dump, which is what she was afraid she might wind up doing, but it looked like she was going to get a little money for them.

She needed money just then. Boy, did she ever. She was working as many hours as she could while still trying to be a good mother to Peter but still couldn't make ends meet. She had missed one mortgage payment and missed a payment for the credit card she had used to pay the last mortgage payment. Frankly she was starting to feel a little desperate, trying to handle everything by herself. The creditors were calling and she just hated those calls. She was not a slacker. She paid her bills. Where was Brian to help her?

As it turned out, however, Gene was as good as his word. He called at the end of the week.

"Guess what! I sold your painting. Easiest sale I ever made."

"Really? Which one?"

"The vampire, of course. They went crazy for it. I went in thinking $12,000, and I was right. They didn't even bat an eye."

"What!" she said, not even capable of making the obvious joke. "$12,000?"

"I told you it would be a hot commodity. You hit the mother lode."

"I can't believe it. So much money."

"I'm telling you, it's worth it. It's really an incredible painting. The more I look at it the more I love it. I almost hate to part with it. Besides, $12,000 doesn't mean anything to these people. He's an investment banker and she's a little, well, crazy—just between you and me. Anyway, it seems their two daughters are obsessed with this *Twilight* thing, so she was looking for some kind of vampire artwork to hang in the family room. You just happened to make a painting on demand without knowing it."

"Thank you so much. I still can't believe it. I really needed this right now."

"Well, don't forget some of it goes to me. And I'm going to have to have it framed. But they'll be happy. It's a good investment. It could wind up being very valuable—both to them and to us. That's the best part. I sent a picture of your painting to a friend of mine who owns a boutique printing press. He was blown away. And I mean completely. He wants to make prints and start a whole thing. You could wind up in every rec room in America."

Jill had never heard him sound so animated. She realized what it was: the money. "They'll let you do that? The people who bought the painting?"

"Of course! It just increases the value, so it's a win-win proposition. And also for you, by the way. Congratulations. It couldn't have happened to a nicer person."

This was all quite hilarious to Jill. He was like a changed man. At the same time she was ambivalent about the idea of THAT PAINTING being marketed and hung in homes where young children could see it. She was tempted to tell him to forget about the prints. And how was she going to explain all this to Brian, if things really did go the way Gene thought they would?

On the other hand she had a pretty large chunk of money coming her way—large for her, anyway, if not for the kind of people who had bought the painting. There was the $8,000 that was her portion after Gene took his fee for doing his peculiar kind of magic, and there might also be royalties somewhere down the road for the prints.

One thing about Gene—he was not tardy. Jill received her check in the mail at the end of the week. She came home from work, still wearing her waitress uniform, still feeling bedraggled and footsore from a hectic morning of schlepping tables and helping out in the hot kitchen, and pulled the missive out of the mailbox and just stared at it. She could not quite believe it was true.

After a long stressful winter and spring in financial hell Jill had the exquisite pleasure of depositing this kingly sum in the bank and catching up on most of her bills. There wasn't anything left over for the future, but at least she didn't have to be afraid to answer the telephone anymore or go to the mailbox.

And all because of...that fellow, the one with the haunted eyes and the white lock of hair right in the middle of his forehead. She knew she must have made him up. He was quite improbable. A caricature of an aesthete, like Oscar Wilde; a parody of himself. No one like that could ever exist. Could they?

Now it came back to her, painting the paintings. She saw herself doing it. She remembered when each one had been painted. There was no model. She was painting out of her head, as she sometimes did, not often but sometimes. The image of this strange fellow had come to her and intrigued her. Of course she remembered. It was how she started painting again.

She hadn't intended to paint a series. She started with the first one and was so pleased with the results that she kept experimenting. Her favorite was the one in the restaurant, with him sitting in the booth. She really liked the colors, thought it was a reach that had turned out surprisingly well.

The other one, the one that sold for such an outrageous sum— it started out as a joke. She'd done the other studies and she was just getting back into painting again and had a funny inspiration. Why not paint this waifsome stranger as a vampire? It started out in pure fun but she must have gotten herself caught up in it because the result was rather impressive. In purely painterly terms it was impressive.

Gene had taken the other two paintings as well on commission and had already sold one of them. So they were no longer in front of her. But the face was. What was it about that face and where had it come from? It seemed real to her. It was almost as if she knew someone who looked like that.

One thing she knew for sure—this face had inspired her to start painting again. She was embarrassed by him and had hidden him in the closet, but she owed him something. Somehow she started calling him "Joshua" in these little dialogues with herself. Yes, she named the mystery man in the painting. Joshua suited him somehow. After all, he had saved her.

REUNITED

GOOD NEWS! Brian was coming home. He called on a sunny Sunday afternoon and said he would be home in two days. But now the very thing Jill had been longing for started to make her a little nervous. It was one thing to think about him coming home in the abstract, abetted by the glow of the proposal, and quite another to come up against the concrete reality.

She remembered his comments about the band and his frustration with Leo. Apparently things had not gone the way he hoped during the five-month pilgrimage to Mecca. She wanted him to come home for the right reasons, not because he was running away from something else. She wanted him to be excited about coming home, excited about the fresh start they had talked about. This was not necessarily what she heard in his voice.

It was great for her and Peter—but what did it mean for him? She remembered how happy she was when he said he was eager to get back to the shop and start working on his cabinets. This was the change she had been hoping for in recent years as it seemed less and less likely that Spectrum would ever break through and become financially viable. But the same thing that made her happy could wind up being very painful for Brian. He would have to give up the dream he had been nurturing for much of his life.

What if his dream had been broken? She knew how painful it was when she thought she had to give up painting and the sense of purpose that came with it. She lost her colors. Would the same thing happen to Brian? Would he spend the rest of his life washed out from his dream? Could he be happy with cabinet-making and his family and life in a small country town? He said he could; she wanted him to. But it was going to require a difficult adjustment.

Then again, she had to change as well. There had been a lot of disappointments over the years. Brian was disappointed because Spectrum never seemed to take off; she was disappointed because he kept putting off marriage and was never home. The hardest thing was that he seemed disappointed in her. He did not want to hold her anymore. When he did hold her it was almost pro forma, as if he were doing it for the sake of the narrative. Jill wanted the reality and the narrative to be one.

She was happy about him coming home but apprehensive as well. She knew the hard work of mending and healing had just begun. They'd had wonderful phone conversations in recent weeks, but anything can happen over the phone, which provides the illusion of proximity without the territorial challenges. Living together in the same space was an entirely different thing, as she knew from thirteen years of experience.

Had the band imploded? Was he coming home in a funk? He said he was "reevaluating things." What exactly did that mean? She knew what she wanted it to mean. She wanted him to come back to them not just in body but in spirit; she wanted to be a real family. But was it selfish to hope for these things? Was she stealing that fine thing from him—his single-hearted devotion to his muse? She prayed not to be selfish. Can you pray not to be selfish? Anyway, she tried.

She went into a cleaning frenzy. The house and yard were a mess after a long winter. Peter helped, especially outdoors. She watched him as she cleaned the windows—raking up leftovers from the wood pile, mowing the grass, picking up branches that had blown down during winter storms—and felt proud. He wanted to help. He was excited about his father coming home. His excitement was pure.

Would that hers were also pure! But Jill discovered that some things could not be completely cleaned. She tried to wipe away the past and the unhappiness, the hurts and resentments, but there were still some dirty places that kept showing up when they were not wanted and stealing her joy. She could not clean them the same way she was cleaning her house. She tried to clean them but they would not go away.

She started to pray as she stood there in the sunlight wiping the windows—for a change in herself. She prayed for a clean heart. She prayed for a right spirit to be renewed within her. She prayed for health and safety for their little family. She prayed for Brian, for a safe journey. She did not know what else to pray for Brian, exactly, but in the end she wound up praying for his happiness.

It was a rainy Tuesday afternoon when he pulled in the driveway. He came in and dropped his bags and just stood there for a moment, as if he were a stranger in his own home. Jill was in the kitchen making dinner and Peter was sitting at the pass-through doing his algebra.

"You're home!" she exclaimed as a flush of joy came over her.

Peter got up and walked over to his father, who opened his arms and embraced him. "How are you?" Brian said. "You've grown."

Jill ran to them. "How was your trip?" she said, hugging him and giving him a kiss.

"Long! It's so good to be home. Would have gotten here earlier, but the fuel pump went on the Sprinter. That's what they get for running it on empty all the time."

"Well, the poor old Sprinter's more like a walker at this point. I'm just glad you made it."

The chops were sizzling in the frying pan, so she went back to the kitchen to finish up. Brian followed her and pulled a beer out of the refrigerator. This pained her a little. The first thing he did was pull out a beer. She scolded herself and tried to put the thought out of her head.

"Is it okay if I chill for a while before I bring everything in?"

"Of course! You must be exhausted."

"It's just really good to be home," he reiterated.

She wanted to talk to him but couldn't think of what to say. There had been so much excitement and tenderness over the phone that it almost stood between them now. The sheer physicality of being together after such a long absence was daunting. She asked him the usual questions about the trip, and he seemed happy to answer them, perhaps even relieved; but she had the feeling that he was deep in thought the whole time, even while he was speaking; that the answers were all on the surface of wherever his mind was at.

They sat down for supper. Brian bestirred himself to ask Peter about school and sports. Peter was not very communicative, and this also was awkward for Jill. She could tell he felt shy. But he was thrilled to have his Dad home. The look on his face left no doubt about that. He doted on Brian like a lamb waiting to be fed. Oh, please feed him! Jill thought to herself.

Brian was quiet but not necessarily sullen. Sometimes it was hard to tell the difference with men. When the obligatory interrogation was over he seemed content to retreat into himself and focus on his dinner, which he kept saying was "delicious." He did not talk about what happened. Jill hoped he would, but he didn't. And she could not help him. The wall between a man and a woman came in and made it impossible for her to make conversation. She tried a couple of times without much luck and gave up.

That night when they went to bed he kissed her tenderly but there was nothing more. She did not know whether he wanted her to start something. They were out of the habit of love-making, and she did not know how to read his signals. Maybe he was afraid of the baby. It was kind of like having a stranger in her bed after four long months. She lay there waiting, hoping, thinking, not knowing what to think.

She was facing him. She was determined to break her old habits. She wondered if he noticed. It had been literally years since she had gone to bed facing him. She lay there looking at him and realized he had already fallen asleep. Poor guy, wrung out from the trip. She wanted to scoot up close, hold him in her arms, but something held her back. She was afraid. Eventually she fell asleep as well.

She got up at her usual ungodly hour of five the next morning, put on her waitress uniform, made Peter breakfast, and went to work. She was half expecting Brian to come in for breakfast with that warm smile of his and surprise her, but no such luck. She looked at the booth from the painting, the one with that strange man in it—"Joshua." For a moment she could almost see him there. She wanted Brian to come and chase him away. Brian did not come.

Brian was not there when she came home. There was a note— he had gone to work as well. Jill smiled when she saw it. She picked it up and held in her hands. It seemed like a good sign, going back to work the first day he was home. She wanted to believe it was a good sign. She hoped it wasn't just because he owed Kyle for the transmission bill. And no, she wasn't thinking about the money. She was thinking about something else entirely.

They welcomed him back to work with open arms. Kyle was the front man, the salesman, but he needed someone to run the shop while he was talking to customers and keeping all the accounts and accounting straight; someone he could trust to take care of the details and bring jobs to a successful conclusion. It wasn't just craftsmanship that was needed, or passion, or a sense of responsibility and ownership—it was all of these and more. Not an easy combination to find.

Apparently this had not been clear to Kyle until Brian was not there and he wound up doing all these things himself. He had a notion Brian would come back; he never did take the Spectrum thing seriously. After all, how many bands really do make it? That was why he paid for the car repair. It was a bargain, as far as he was concerned. It was a bonus he was giving Brian for all his years of good work—and Brian was paying him back! He wanted to tell him to forget it but that would have defeated the purpose.

Brian did not know any of this, however. He had no idea what Kyle was thinking. He was surprised at the offer to help with the car repair and at the conditions. And then when he came back he was surprised to find himself anointed as the point man. He had been in that role for years, but this was the first time that Kyle formally acknowledged it, even referring to him as his "foreman."

This was all quite amazing to Brian, who had no idea of the high esteem in which he was held. He loved carpentry. He enjoyed the point man role, for all the troubles and headaches it could bring. It was a way for him to prove himself and show what he could do. He did not share any of this with Jill, however, when he came home at his usual hour with sawdust in his hair.

"You didn't wait around very long," she commented after a hug in the kitchen.

"What's the point? I haven't been there in five months. Might as well jump right back in."

There was no bitterness in this. She thought maybe she detected a tone of resignation, but it could also just be irony. Brian had a good sense of humor. It was one of the things that drew her to him. She hadn't seen it in a while—not since he got swept up in rock star fever—was it back again? She hoped it was. It would mean he was returning to himself, to the Brian she fell in love with.

But the signs of such a return were few. A week went by and then another and Brian was still quiet. There were positive changes in their lifestyle. He wasn't going to band rehearsal every night. Maybe one night a week, maybe a weekend gig, if they had one. He was more engaged in household chores. He did the dishes almost every night. He did the mowing, as he always had, and even helped out in the gardens. That is, when she was working in the gardens he would come out to her, kind of shyly, and ask what he could do. She found things for him to do, she was grateful.

Still, he wasn't talking very much. He often said nice things. He would tell her that gardens looked great or compliment her on her cooking. When he saw her new painting in person he was effusive in his praise, which surprised her a bit. He would talk about things that were going on around town or things they needed to do at home—but there was nothing about the trip to Memphis. It concerned her. The silence made her think—Resentment.

He seemed content, but was he putting on a show? Otherwise why the uncomfortable silences? Why the unwillingness to open up? If he had good feelings about being back, then why hide them? But if they were bad feelings—if he was consciously pushing down disappointment—then it was understandable that he would try to hide them. What had happened in Memphis? Something must have happened to cause the change in him and the fact that he wasn't running out every night to rehearse with the band. But what?

One brisk Saturday in June they went for a hike on a local mountain. They reached the top and sat down and pulled out their picnic lunch. Jill felt emboldened.

"So what's going on with the CD? Is it all done?"

"Yeah, we're done," he said with an ironic expression. "It's definitely done, no matter what."

"I'm so happy! You must feel wonderful." She said this but she felt the chill in his voice.

"I don't know how I feel. I'm just glad it's over, to tell you the truth."

"But this is what you were hoping for. This is your big break."

"Yeah, I don't know about that. I mean, we did finish it, twelve songs. But we have to promote it ourselves. So it didn't exactly work out the way we thought it was going to."

"I don't understand. I thought this big-time producer was taking you under his wings."

"That's what I thought, too," he said with a chuckle. "Our buddy Clark."

"So he's not going to hook you up with a record company?"

"To tell you the truth, I'm not even sure if it works like that anymore. The model has changed, with iTunes and everything. Kids don't really buy CDs, at least that's what they tell me. And as far as Clark goes, I have the impression his 'big-time producer' days are pretty much over."

"I don't get it. Everyone said he was the guy."

"I guess he did have some pretty big hits, but it's been a long time. Basically he's a lot of talk and no action. We kept hearing about all these great contacts he had and how he was going to get our name out there—the same thing over and over again. But nothing ever seemed to happen. He would talk and talk and nothing happened. Finally we just couldn't take it anymore."

Jill was surprised. Everything seemed to spill out of him at once.

"So he was just giving you studio space all this time, hoping you could give him a hit and get him back in the game."

"'Giving'? He wasn't giving us anything. We paid for the studio space and his engineering. That was part of the scam."

"Maybe that's just the way it works."

"No, he had it all figured out. He's got a whole bunch of groups coming in there, and I'm sure he's telling them all the same thing. He gets money for his time and space, and meanwhile there's always the outside chance that one of the groups might actually have a hit."

"I'm sorry. I had no idea."

"Neither did we. We never would have gone down there if we did."

"I'm glad you did," she said bravely.

"Really? Why?"

"You needed to do this. You needed to follow your dream."

"I think maybe 'following my dream' was kind of pointless, to be honest. I feel like I've been such a fool all these years, thinking we were going to make it, like ten thousand other bands, all spinning their wheels and getting nowhere."

"You haven't been a fool at all. The band is great. You have tons of fans."

"We should have just left it at that. I don't know, it was almost like we were possessed. We had all these songs we'd written and we just felt like we had to do something with them, even though I did have my doubts about the whole thing. Maybe that's it. You can't have any doubts."

"Honestly, Brian, I'm just glad to have you home. Not that I didn't want you guys to do well. I don't mean that. But that's not what's important to me."

"But the thing is I wanted to make you proud of me. I mean, you have your art and everything."

"Oh my gosh—is that what you were thinking? That's crazy."

"You don't think of me as a failure?"

"Brian, come on. You think I can't love you if you're not a rock star? I'm not that shallow."

"But I wasted so much of your time. I had you waiting all these years for the band to break through, as if that weren't a crazy enough thought as it is. It's embarrassing."

"You should not be embarrassed about anything. I'm proud of you for not being like the other bands, for not having the killer instinct. Because let's face it, that's what it takes most of the time."

"Yeah, I couldn't hack that—so now I'm a carpenter."

"Would you stop? For one thing, you are a great musician. I love you guys. And you're also a very talented carpenter. There's no difference between being a carpenter and an artist, as far as I'm concerned. A great carpenter is an artist. He just makes things people can actually use."

"Really?" he said kind of shyly.

"Come on. You're just as much of an artist as I am. In fact my two favorite guys are carpenters."

He laughed. "Well, I think I finally had my eyes opened, in any case. I mean, it was kind of pathetic, this poor Clark guy. Very sweet guy, by the way. I have nothing against him. But basically he was a guy trying to look hip with his ponytail and a little too old and too fat to do it quite right. And way too much pot. I just looked at him one day sitting there dropping names from like thirty years ago, stoned out of his mind, and I thought, 'My God, is that me in thirty years?' And that really changed things for me. Because I don't want to be like that."

"You are not like that. You're just the opposite of that. You're very well-grounded. It's just that you love the music so much and you were hoping you could make a career of it. And you still can, you know. You have your music degree. You could teach."

"I can't see myself standing up in front of a classroom. That's just not me. I'd rather be out measuring and making things."

"But you would be a great teacher."

"Let's not get crazy here. No, I know who I am. Or at least now I do. I enjoy the carpentry thing, I have to admit it. When you're making something you sort of get lost in it. You know what I mean?"

"I do," she said with a smile. "I know exactly what you mean."

The best thing for Jill in all this was him opening up to her. He hadn't done it in years. She could not even remember the last time. It made her happy because it made her feel he loved her and trusted her and felt he *could* open up to her, even wanted to. It also made her happy because it made her feel safe. He was hers again. Life wasn't on hold anymore. It could begin.

They made love that night and it was almost like tears in the passion for him, and Jill could feel it in him and his tears washed over her too. There was so much to make up for, so many bridges to be mended, coming home. Afterwards they just lay there tenderly, holding each other and listening to the peepers in the marsh across the road.

DISCOVERY

B UT THERE WERE CHALLENGES AHEAD. He was still drinking too much for her taste. The very next night he drank a six-pack of beer and fell asleep on the couch.

Emboldened by their mountaintop conversation, Jill decided to talk to him about it. Most of all she was worried about him and his health. It could not be good for him to be drinking so much. And she was worried about Peter. He was just getting to the age where there would be a lot of temptations and a lot of peer pressure. Jill did not want him thinking there was nothing wrong with heavy drinking. She did not drink herself, in part for this very reason. Why couldn't Brian see it?

The thing that troubled her the most, however, was his state of mind. He said he was happy to be home. He said he was happy to come back to her and Peter and the shop. But if he was so happy, then why did he have to drink? She could not help feeling he must be unhappy, in spite of his comforting assurances. And the more he drank, the more unhappy, to her mind, he seemed.

Another couple of weeks went by and the irises and pansies bloomed and then it was the season of roses—and there was no sign of a let-up in the drinking. It was not every night, but it was far too often for her taste. He tended to become quiet when he drank. It made her feel there was a barrier between them. It made her feel like he was a stranger.

Did he get drunk? Not really. It was more like he got sedated. Was he mean when he was drinking? Not at all. He had never been mean to her or Peter in that way, drinking or sober. It was not that she was afraid of him in the physical sense, or afraid of violent fights. It was that she was afraid *for* him and his state of mind. Was she good enough? Was he happy with her and Peter at home? It seemed to her that if he was he wouldn't be drinking. And this weighed on her mind.

They were starting fresh and remaking their relationship, but in order for it to work it truly needed to be remade. It needed to be set on a firm foundation of open, honest conversations about just this sort of thing, about the concerns they had and things that were bothering them. They were getting married and they needed to be willing to challenge each other to reach higher and do better. Jill had not challenged Brian at all since he got back. It seemed like a good time to try.

She made up her mind to talk to him. She knew it would be difficult. He would not want to be questioned or give up something that apparently brought him pleasure. But Jill refused to believe that the pleasure was real. To her it was false pleasure and a false reality. She believed it was better to live in the real world, not one distorted by intoxicants of any kind. Otherwise the pleasures of the real world—the real pleasures—would be missed. Also the necessary struggles.

Another week went by before an opportunity presented itself for such a conversation. Peter was with them whenever they were home together, which made it difficult; but on Saturday morning Peter went for a bike ride with a friend and Jill made up her mind to bring it up. She became even more determined when Brian emerged from the bedroom looking groggy from the previous evening's grog.

She made him bacon and eggs and they sat down together at the kitchen table. She chatted with him about the day and the weather until he had finished his breakfast. Then she took a deep breath and began.

"Listen, there's something I've been meaning to talk to you about."

"This doesn't sound good."

"It's just that I'm worried about you. How much you're drinking."

"It's not that much."

"I think it is. How much was it last night? There are a lot of empties."

"So you're keeping tabs?"

"No—I told you. I'm worried about you. Why do you feel you have to drink? Is it because of me?"

He got a bemused look on his face. "Yes, it's because of you."

"No, seriously. Is it something I'm doing?"

"No, it's nothing you're doing. Why would you even say that?"

"But are you happy?"

"I'm very happy," he said with a weary smile that was hard to interpret.

"I don't know, you don't act like it. I mean, if you were happy why would you need to drink?"

"It relaxes me."

"You can't relax with me? Am I causing you stress?"

"No, I have a stressful job. It's just good to come home and relax a little."

"But it's not good for Peter," she said, playing her trump card. "He's right at that age. You know what high school is like. He's going to start driving in a couple of years and I don't think we want him having the idea that drinking's okay."

Now Brian looked pained. "So what is it you want me to do? Stop completely?"

"No, not necessarily. Could you just cut back? Maybe just one beer on weeknights and not quite so much on the weekends."

"Kind of hard for me to have just one."

"Don't you think that's a red flag?"

He looked at her. It wasn't an angry look. It was more like resignation. "I'll tell you what—I'll work on it. I should cut down anyway. Putting on too many pounds."

"You know, you can talk to me any time. If something's troubling you, you don't have to drink. We can just sit and talk about it. I would love it if you talked to me more."

"Yes, I know; that's what all you girls want. You want us to talk to you like your girlfriends."

"You could just talk to me the way you talk when you're with other men."

"Actually men don't do nearly as much talking with other men as women think they do."

"Okay, then just talk to me like my husband. Don't you think husbands and wives should talk?"

He was hanging onto his thin smile, but just barely. "You win. I will try to be more talkative in the future."

That was the end of the conversation. He clearly did not want to go on. She knew it had to be painful to be challenged this way, put on the spot, accused. He got up and did the dishes, which was nice, but he was silent, which made it uncomfortable. He usually chatted with her when he did the dishes, made jokes, but there was none of that. She poured him a fresh cup of coffee in his favorite mug, and he said "thanks," but it seemed forced. He tried to make it sound like it wasn't forced but did not quite succeed.

Brian finished the dishes and was on his way out to mow the lawn. Jill stayed in the kitchen—she had a plan to tackle the cabinets, which had not been cleaned in a while. He walked into the great room and to the front door and then stopped and came back to the pass-through. He did not come into the kitchen. He stood in the great room looking through the pass-through sort of at her and sort of not.

"By the way, you're not necessarily all that easy to talk to, if you want to know."

"What do you mean?" she said, her timbre rising.

"Just what I said. You're kind of intimidating."

"Oh, come on. There's nothing intimidating about me."

"Well, there you go. Exhibit A. And I'm not the only who feels that way. Everybody's afraid of you."

"*Afraid* of me? That's ridiculous! Like who?"

"Like everybody I know. Like the band. Like your friends from the restaurant. Why do you think my mother keeps her mouth shut when you're around? She doesn't do that with anybody else."

Jill was too shocked to reply. She just stood there looking at him with her mouth open. Brian gulped down the last of his coffee and put the cup on the counter and went outside. She, however, continued to be frozen to her spot. Her first reaction was to laugh, but it occurred to her that her love of laughing might just be one of the things he was talking about—that it was intimidating to others. She had never thought of this before, but she thought of it now.

She was devastated by this conversation. She went in feeling sorry for Brian and came out feeling sorry for herself. Were people really afraid of her? It embarrassed her terribly even to think such a thing. In her own mind she was humble and kind. She valued humility more than any other trait. And was she now to find out, at age thirty-three, that others did not see humility in her at all? That they were somehow afraid of her? It was a crushing blow.

Jill went very quietly into the bedroom and closed the door and started to cry. She could not remember a time when she felt worse about herself. Was he talking about her art? It was true that she felt her art had some value. She would never say this to anyone, but she felt she was a good painter and something more. It is impossible to do art at a high level if you do not have faith in your ability to do it. You can have all the skill in the world, but faith is the thing that facilitates the necessary hard work and passion. Faith is what enabled Michelangelo to take a hammer and chisel to the huge block of marble that became David.

An artist has to have faith. But there it was again—she was calling herself an "artist." Wasn't this kind of boastful? She had heard so many people describe themselves as "artists" when to her mind they were no such thing. They were trying to allocate a status to themselves they had not earned. Was she just the same? Was she like all the arrogant artists that she herself could not stand? The opposite of what she in her heart so much wanted to be?

She managed to pull herself together and went out and scrubbed the cabinets with a little more vigor than was necessary. She not only took off the grime but some of the last coat of paint. Brian took Peter fishing when he was done with the lawn and Jill used her free afternoon to drop in on her parents. She found her mother working in her perennial garden.

"So wonderful to see you!" Betty said, pulling off her gardening gloves so she could give her a hug. "How are you?"

"I don't know. I think I'm in shock."

"Really? Why?"

"Brian just said the most terrible thing to me. Oh, I don't mean it like that. He didn't mean it to be terrible, but it kind of put me into a tailspin."

"It couldn't have been that bad. What could he possibly say?"

"He said—well—he claims people are afraid of me."

At this her mother stopped and looked at her. The look went on for far too long. She was smiling, but Jill could tell she was struggling for the right words to say.

"You agree with him! You think people are afraid of me."

"I don't know if I would say 'afraid,' exactly. Let's just say respectful."

"But why? I don't understand."

"Because you are beautiful and brilliant, and people find that a little intimidating."

"Intimidating! That's the other word he used. I don't want to be intimidating."

"I know you don't, my dear. You're not even slightly aware of the effect you have on others. You have a little of Mr. Darcy in you. You think everybody in the whole world is laughing at you, including the grocer and the gas station attendant. You are so terrified of being embarrassed that you put up your shield, and sometimes people can interpret it the wrong way."

"Oh my gosh, you have no idea of how that looks from the inside."

"No—I do. I think I have a very good idea. They call it being an 'introvert' these days, but before we got so clinical we would just say you were sensitive. Things that bounce right off other people stick to you like one of these thorns. You are also much more highly attuned to what is going on around you than others typically are. But it's nothing to be ashamed of. Not at all. It's the very thing that makes you such a wonderful artist. Great art requires great sensitivity."

"I don't want to be a great artist. I want to be a good person."

"You are a good person. You are a wonderful person! You can't help being who you are. God made you sensitive. I would not have you be any other way."

"But I don't feel like a good person. Not if I'm scaring everybody. How have you put up with me all these years?"

"Because I love you. Because you are the most wonderful and gifted person I know. I don't hear your little barbs the way others hear them. I have a better idea of where they're coming from."

"Oh, great! Now I have to take you around with me everywhere I go so you can interpret for me."

"You were born with a blessing and a curse. Your sensitivity is bound to cause you some pain, but it is also the quality that makes you so incisive about others and aware of their needs. It's also the quality that makes you so kind and generous. And you are not a hopeless case, believe me. I know other women that people are scared of, and they *are* hopeless cases, because they do not have your tender heart."

"But what about Brian? He made it sound like even he's afraid of me."

"You are very lucky to have Brian. Most men would not be willing to marry a woman who's smarter than they are."

"I'm not smarter! I'm just a waitress."

"My dear, being smart is nothing to be ashamed of."

"But it wasn't like I was a straight-'A' student or got 800s on my SATs. There were a lot of kids who were smarter than I was."

"It's a different kind of intelligence. It's not book intelligence and I don't think you can test for it. I'm tempted to call it moral intelligence, but that's not quite right either. Let's just say you understand people. You see right through them, which can be intimidating. Meanwhile you are so self-conscious and self-critical that you think the exact opposite is true. You think they are seeing through you—which I assure you they are not. You are my little Sphinx."

"Sphinx and minx, apparently. But what am I going to do? I don't want him to be afraid of me."

"First of all, love and cherish him. Brian is a good person. He's not asking for much from you except a little tenderness. Actually I think he's kind of in awe of you, which is not such a bad position to be in, to be honest. And you are not a hopeless case. Your heart is in the right place. Now that you know about it you can be a little more aware of how you come across to people. You can soften some of those edges that you don't even realize you have and blend in the way I know you want to."

SEASONS

J ILL WAS NOT AS CONFIDENT AS HER MOTHER about her ability to change the arc of her existence. The sensitivity and intelligence about which she had been duly warned now folded back upon itself and caused a short-circuit. She did not feel worthy of Brian anymore. She did not know if she could be a good wife, someone he would want to come home to. She did not want him to be afraid of her, but she also could not stop being who she was. She had a sense of what was meant by "softening her edges." Would it be enough?

She could not wait to talk to Brian again. As soon as they got back from fishing she put a beer in his hand and invited him to come outside to give her some landscaping advice. He gave her a funny look as he followed her out the door.

"I thought you didn't want me drinking beer."

"I need to talk to you," she said as they wandered out of earshot. "I don't know if I'm good enough for you."

"What? I never said that. I never even hinted at it."

"But you're afraid of me. You can't love me if you're afraid of me."

"I'm not afraid of you like that. I just know to be careful about certain things."

"That's what I mean! You don't need a scary wife. You need someone you can come home to and be comfortable with. Is that why you drink?"

He sighed. "I knew I never should have said anything. Now you're going to use this against me, too."

"I'm not using it against you! I'm afraid."

"Of what?"

"That you can't really love me."

"That's not true. I love you very much."

"But I don't want to be this way. I don't want to scare anybody."

"I know you don't. You can't help it. It's just the way you are."

"And you can live with that?"

"Again, I told you, you don't scare me. Not really. You're a good person. I trust you. It's just a little hard to talk to you sometimes. But it does occur to me that people can't always help being who they are. Maybe sometimes we need to make allowances for that."

Ouch! Well, she asked for it. "Okay, I guess maybe I was a little hard on you this morning."

"I wouldn't say you were hard. You just cut me down to size. About two inches."

She laughed. "It wasn't that bad. But point taken. Maybe if I were a little less eager to change you, you could take pity on me and accept me with all my faults."

"I never said you had any faults at all. I just said you could be a little intimidating. And as for changing things—well, I guess everybody could use a change in their lives from time to time."

"But do you still want to marry me?"

"Right now I want to strangle you," he said in frustration.

"No, really. Am I good enough for you?"

Brian just shook his head. "I want to marry you. I love you, as I've told you over and over. Are there things we can work on to avoid getting on each other's nerves? Probably. But do I want to spend the rest of my life with you? Definitely."

"My mother said I need to soften my edges."

"I don't know about that. I will just say that, for a guy, sometimes just being together is enough. We don't necessarily have to talk to feel like we love someone. We're also a little more aware of what's going on than the gals give us credit for. I'm here with you. It's a beautiful day. What more could we ask for?"

Jill came to think of this as one of the most important conversations of her life. It gave her tremendous insight into

Brian's mind and his way of thinking. She had lived with him for fourteen years without really knowing him. There had been some talk in recent years about men being simple creatures who needed nothing more than sex and a good meal. This was not true. Men are not simple at all.

It was a very hard day for Jill, but a productive one. They had opened up to each other about things they had never talked about before, things which were essential and important, which was encouraging. It seemed they could talk about difficult things and still wind up loving each other in the end. She learned something about herself that horrified her initially, but she was glad. Better to learn at thirty-three than never to have learned at all!

Brian did cut down on his drinking, and Jill worked on softening her edges. It seemed to her they had never been closer. Summer was icumin in, beautiful summer in Vermont—they loved it so much. They went for hikes in the mountains and took Peter to the movies and worked in the yard together and took the kayaks out on Lake Champaign a couple of times on dreamy summer days. They were having fun being together. Jill remembered to count her blessings.

Yes, there was physical intimacy. Brian was hesitant because of the baby, but Jill encouraged him. They slept facing each other, often in each other's arms. Sometimes she would wake up at night and lie there quietly gazing at him in the moonlight. "Two are better than one." She thought about how lonely she would be without him. She tried to reach for deep wisdom but wondered in the end if it was itself. Maybe some things don't require so much thinking.

She noticed they had become more attuned to the art of consensus. There was a new deference to each other about what color the porch should be or where the gladiolas should go or where they should go for their hike or whether Peter was spending too much time playing video games. In the past they might have wrangled; or in Brian's case, withdrawn. It occurred to her that becoming one flesh meant letting go of singularity. There was a larger identity to be obtained. This too was a mystery.

Then again—what was there to hold on to? What was there to be gained? Soon enough they would be in their graves, and everything that seemed so important to them in their little world would evaporate into the mist. Jill felt herself drifting into a new way of living, a new bond of mutual trust and gentle sacrifice. The bond was the most important thing to her. When she remembered to put it first, everything else seemed to fall into place.

On one of those mountain hikes Brian pulled out a beautiful custom-made engagement ring and presented it to her. The moment she saw it, caught the sunlight gleaming in the diamond, she started to cry. She couldn't help it. A lot of emotions—years of emotions!—making their way out. She was embarrassed about crying, but it was salutary for Brian. It helped him to realize something important, something he needed to know. It may have been the first time he really believed she loved him.

The wedding was set for August. They wanted to have a quiet little wedding. After all, they had already been living together for most of their adult lives—and Jill was very much pregnant. It wound up being about fifty people, mostly on account of their parents. Jill thought she might have to grit her teeth and get through it, in true introvert fashion, but it turned out to be rather touching. Everyone was so happy to see them finally get married. It was the only wedding she'd ever been to where all the guests had a big smile on their faces; even Brian's father, which was remarkable, because he did not smile easily.

Pastor Redmond married them. He was still excited about the painting he had bought from Jill and managed to work both art and carpentry into his homily. Jill's parents insisted on paying for the reception, which Jill did not expect, under the circumstances. Her father was in a hilarious mood. After consuming a little too much Bushmill's in honor of the Campbell clan he pulled out his bagpipes. The sound of ancient airs ringing through the mountains was pleasant and suitably solemn, if a little monotonous.

There was a catered dinner of steak and crab and fresh garden peas on a beautiful summer evening and champagne for all except Jill, who was being careful. All of the arrangements had been very low-key, so there was little or no stress. It was more like a family party. And they were old enough to be calm and appreciate what was going on and the love on display from both sides of the family.

The Redmonds had quite a conversation with Jill's father about the painting they had bought and about how delighted they were to have it and how everyone who came to the house was amazed by it. They also raved about Jill's other paintings. This was very striking to her father, who had a bit of the Old World deference for the pastor and his wife. From that moment on he began to think differently about Jill and her paintings. He mentioned this to Betty after the guests left. Her only comment was "about time."

Peter was the happiest of all. He was quiet, but he beamed, and Jill knew what he was thinking. She felt a little ashamed. They had put him through so much over the years, the uncertainty, the unwillingness or inability to make a commitment. She knew it was hard on him. But now his eyes were dancing. At one point he was walking by and she reached out and took him in her arms. He hugged her back. "I love you," she said. "I love you too," was the tender reply.

Everything changed for Jill and Brian after the Memphis experience. Brian stopped going to rehearsals every night and stopped pushing so hard for gigs. He seemed perfectly happy with that. Some of the band members weren't quite so happy, but he assured her he didn't care what they thought. He was happy just playing to play, just having fun with the music and making a little extra cash on the side. His carpentry was where he was focusing his creative energies now.

He was home more than he had ever been and spending time with Peter and Jill. He seemed to enjoy being home. Jill did not know how much of his pleasure was real and how much might be the result of a conscious effort to be a good husband and father—she had learned that men aren't simple. He was thoughtful and considerate, however, and that was enough for her.

He kept up his new habit of being helpful around the house. This gave Jill more freedom to do the thing she loved so much. She did a portrait of him in his workshop, shaping a piece of wood. It was so good that he was moved to say he was impressed, even though he hated pictures of himself. She did one of him and Peter fishing in the canoe. Then she started working on a painting she had long wanted to do—of Christ kneeling at the seashore, cooking up breakfast for his friends.

Meanwhile she was surprised to find money coming in from the prints of the vampire painting. It was a trickle at first, but it grew into a steady stream. She started quietly paying off the debts that had piled up while Brian was away. She was the one who handled the finances; she didn't bother to tell him where the money was coming from. Art buyers began to pay attention to her. A collector came out and offered her $20,000 on the spot for *Cosette*. She almost fell over. But the money came in handy. They used some of it to make Brian's new CDs.

She felt so grateful for everything, sitting on the porch on a summer evening with her usual cup of tea. She gazed out at the mountains in the summer light, full of density and deep shadows, capricious moods. She watched the light with her perceptive eyes and thought about things and was amazed.

EPILOGUE

J ILL HAD THE BABY IN SEPTEMBER. She was excited about it and so was everybody else, especially Brian. He was the perfect husband during the most difficult part of the pregnancy. She was more thankful than she could say to have him by her side and holding her hand as she pushed for the baby.

She pushed so hard that she seemed to black out for a moment. When she came to again Brian was standing by her side with a comical look on his face.

"What is it?" she said weakly, reaching for his hand.

"His head."

"His head! What about it?"

"Oh, it's fine. He has a full head of hair, this brown fuzz, and what's really weird, a little white lock of hair, right here," he said, gesturing to his forehead.

Jill blinked as she thought of the paintings and…him. "That is strange. Are you sure?"

"Pretty sure. But don't you remember? Just like that painting you did. You know, Count Dracula."

"You remember that painting?"

"Remember it! Of course. It would be kind of hard to forget it. But it's like you prophesied this. It's like you somehow knew what was going to happen."

"I had no idea. Just a coincidence," Jill said, wondering.

"Anyway, looks like we have a John, instead of the little Anna we were hoping for."

"Two boys, that's fine," Jill replied. Then she had an inspiration. "How about 'Joshua'?"

"Joshua? Perfect. We can call him Josh."

THE END

ABOUT THE AUTHOR

Jay Trott is an author of essays and fiction who lives in sunny Connecticut. with his wife Beth. They have four children and love long walks and good company.

Made in the USA
Charleston, SC
15 December 2015